ON THE POLE

HOWARD BROOKS

Copyright © 2010 Howard Brooks
All rights reserved.

ISBN: 1439258473
ISBN-13: 9781439258477
Library of Congress Control Number: 2009909527

Prologue

6:31 a.m., Malabo, Equatorial Guinea

"It is written that God and the Prophet are with us," said Ebrahim, taking Azeem's hand. "In heaven, I will be honored to call you brother."

Azeem stared in the inky blackness of the country he despised. The humid air was difficult to breathe and the infidel natives worshiped spirits in the animals and trees. "I, too, will be honored," he said, wishing he had Ebrahim's calmness and resolve. He often prayed that God would make him more like his friend.

Azeem took a long breath, and then exhaled slowly to calm his nerves. He was glad for the partial darkness. It hid how white his knuckles were on the wheel. That morning, in the deserted mosque, he had promised the Prophet that he would complete his jihad. Revenge focused his thoughts. His mother and father, his sisters, they were all dead, killed by American bombs.

12:31 a.m., Warwick, Rhode Island

"Alexandra, I want to fuck you!" screamed a man at the foot of the stage. He grabbed his crotch with one hand and waved a bill in the other. His buddies good-naturedly pulled him back into his chair. Alexandra smiled down at them as she performed a U-turn at the top of the brass pole and then spiraled down headfirst. The snake like move was a proven crowd pleaser. When her hands touched the floor, she released her ankles and bent backwards in a graceful arc. Her platform soles touched lightly down on the stage of Club Lido II.

"Who's the groom?" she asked as she danced toward the bachelor party. She pulled the waistband of her G-string, wedging it up her labia, rubbing herself till they imagined her wet.

"Dave," screamed his table mates pointing to a very drunk thirty something, having difficulty remaining in his chair.

6:33 a.m., Malabo

"Azeem, it is God's will we will be together in paradise," said Ebrahim, putting his arm around the younger man. Azeem returned Ebrahim's embrace and felt his courage grow.

"God willing, brother, Allahu Akbar." whispered Ebrahim before exiting to his explosive laden van.

Azeem eased into the sparse early morning traffic. The capital city's narrow, dirty streets wound down to the harbor in streams of dust and cars.

Ebrahim drove a short ways, pulled into a narrow alleyway, and stopped. He pulled a laptop computer from under his seat and launched a program named "Trackit." The screen showed those same dirty, narrow streets as a black web. A pulsing green dot moved slowly across the screen. Ebrahim watched Azeem's van move onto a thicker strand, the main thoroughfare.

12:33 a.m., Warwick

"You got to fuck me tonight, Alexandra, because after the wedding, I can only screw Debbie," said the drunken groom, forlorn at the prospect of monogamy. He placed a crumpled ten-dollar bill on the stage.

"Debbie's a very lucky girl, to marry a stud like you," said Alexandra as she danced closer.

"Damn right, she is. My little brother's a terrific guy." Another man bellowed beer breath and crushed the groom in a one-armed hug.

"Are you the best man?" Alexandra stepped on the bill, looming over them.

"This is my brother, Charlie. He's standing up for me tomorrow at Our Lady of the Assumption," said the groom.

"Oh, that's where I go to confession."

"Do you have a lot to confess, Alexandra?" asked Charlie.

"Yes, I'm a wicked girl." Alexandra tucked the bill into her garter and then bent backwards again, bridging to the ground. She kicked up into a handstand, slowly took one hand off the floor, and balanced on the other. Her free hand went to her crotch, pulling the material to one side as she opened her legs. Loud hoots of approval rose from the audience.

Alexandra stepped down, boot by her face like it was easy, and stood up with a toss of her hair. In the span of their held breath, she was in a full split, directly in front of Dave. She leaned forward, moving her shoulders to the music, spinning her large breasts counterclockwise. They were almost brushing the groom's face. A wink and she reversed their direction.

"Can Debbie do that?" she asked.

"No." Dave sounded grave and concerned.

"Bring her here after the wedding. I'll teach her."

6:45 a.m., Malabo

The Americans will learn there is no safe place in this world, thought Ebrahim. Oil companies had invested heavily in Equatorial Guinea. It was a non-Islamic country with a compliant dictator who was willing to overlook oil spills and environmental damage as long as money flowed into his Swiss accounts.

Ebrahim watched the pulsing green dot approach the harbor and turn onto the shore road. A global positioning system in Azeem's van broadcast its location within three meters. Ebrahim's laptop mapped it onto Malabo's streets.

Ebrahim had a master's degree in Computer Science from Carnegie Mellon University. The irony of what he was about to do was not lost on him. It depended on American satellites communicating with a laptop designed in Silicon Valley, executing software developed in North Carolina's Research Triangle.

The residential compound was located on a choice section of the harbor. Every other day, a company plane arrived from Europe with luxury goods to make life comfortable for Westerners. One of those planes had brought both the laptop and the explosives.

Ebrahim zoomed in the map till he could see the outline of the high-walled compound. There were two apartment buildings and an office low rise. There was even a private beach, walled off to keep the locals away.

The green dot was now only a few blocks from their target. Azeem would ram the heavy truck through the gate, drive to the closest apartment building, and set off his bomb.

But if Azeem failed, Ebrahim had an alternative. He picked up a cell phone from the seat beside him. It listed the cell phone hidden in Azeem's van. His call would detonate one hundred and twenty kilograms of military grade C-4 explosive.

12:45 a.m., Warwick

"How are the animals tonight?" Bathsheba asked backstage. Bathsheba was scheduled to go on next. Alexandra hurriedly pulled bills from her garters and stuffed them in a bag.

"Bachelor party, center stage—groom's name is Dave, best man is Charlie."

"They giving up the green?"

"Yeah, but they're almost too shit faced to function," said Alexandra, slipping the G-string down.

"Wonder what the bride's doing?"

"I hope she's getting her brains fucked out." Alexandra picked up a water bottle, opened it, took a drink, and then held the cold plastic against her nipples.

"Alex, you want a big wedding?"

"I suppose."

"Let's get married then."

"You're already spoken for. Remember Carrie?"

"She'd love a ménage a trois. Oh, I almost forgot. Mike said to bring the groom on stage and comp him a lap dance. Go all out."

"Does he want me to blow him, too?" asked Alexandra.

"He wants to attract more bachelor parties. I suggested we bring in the bachelorettes, but he wasn't interested."

"Time to get back to making a living," said Alexandra, hearing the opening notes of her fourth and final song. She glanced in the mirror to check her hair, pushed a few curls into place, gave her nipples a pinch, and then stepped back on stage naked.

6:55 a.m., Malabo

"God and the Prophet are with me," screamed Azeem flooring the accelerator. The gate had opened for a white Mercedes. As the Mercedes drove through, the guards spotted the onrushing van. One frantically pressed the button to close the gate; the other fired a long panicky burst that exploded the windshield.

Azeem ducked behind the dash as the shattered glass peppered his face. Both guards were now firing. The heavy truck slammed into the partially closed gate and flipped over. It slid forward on its side in a shower of sparks. Azeem lost consciousness when a bullet grazed his skull.

Azeem opened his eyes to see a guard pointing his assault rifle through the broken windshield. He frantically attempted to press the detonator only to discover it was no longer in his hand. When he looked again, he saw that the guard was smiling as he pressed the trigger.

12:55 a.m., Warwick

Alexandra placed a chair in the center of the stage. "Come up and join me, Dave." Alexandra offered her hand to the groom.

The DJ boomed over the club's PA system, "Everybody, give it up for Dave. The lucky bastard's getting married tomorrow." Dave panicked at the prospect of being on stage. Alexandra grabbed his wrist. With Charlie and the others pushing, she managed to pull him onto the stage.

"I can touch you, but you can't touch me. Those are the rules," whispered Alexandra as pushed Dave into the chair.

"We're having a party at the Wyndham. Want to come?"

"I love to come," said Alexandra as she gracefully kicked up a leg, landing her black booted instep on the chair back barely touching Dave's shoulder. He startled. She lunged forward, her sex an inch from his face. The crowd applauded enthusiastically. Charlie shouted, "Eat her pussy".

"You smell good," Dave said as she unbuttoned his shirt.

"Like a summer evening," said Alexandra bringing her bare sex to where it almost touched his lips. Her fingers pinched his nipples as she tongue kissed him.

Alexandra bracketed his face between her cupped breasts. "Make like a motorboat, Dave."

7:05 a.m., Malabo

Ebrahim saw that the pulsing green dot inside the compound wasn't moving. He waited for the sound of the explosion. When it didn't come he pressed the phone's call button. There was one ring and then silence. Seconds later, Ebrahim felt the ground rumble. Even kilometers away, he felt the blast roll over still sleeping Malabo.

God has been merciful and just, Ebrahim thought. I will tell Azeem's family he died a martyr. He closed the laptop and started the van. He would drive to a nearby fishing village. Arrangements had been made to smuggle him to Kribi, in Cameroon. From there, he would take a coastal steamer up the coast to Rabat. He would rest a few days, then travel to Canada and cross the United States border.

It was not his choice. He had planned to die with Azeem, but at the last minute, his superiors ordered him to remain alive. They needed his talents in America.

1:05 a.m., Warwick

Alexandra hurried to the dressing room. Her best opportunity to sell trips to the VIP Room was immediately after dancing on stage when the audience had a hard on for her. Dave certainly did. She grabbed a towel to wipe off the groom's drool and her own sweat.

The place was empty except for Tiffany whose interest was commerce. "How's the crowd?"

Alexandra selected a costume off the rack and started to dress. "Decent."

"Good, my rent's due tomorrow. Did you hear Brandy got a hundred dollar tip for a single lap dance with this old dude? And I mean he was like a hundred. Brandy said she had to help him up after the dance."

"Lucky girl, I could use a customer like that." Alexandra sat down to repair her makeup.

"Have you made the house already?" asked Tiffany. Every dancer paid two hundred dollars to the club for a Friday night shift.

"Yeah, I'm good," Alexandra said, as she stood up to hurry back to the bachelor party.

Chapter 1

"Mrs. Kabel wants to see you immediately, Hamo," said Sloan, the security guard manning the reception desk. He said "immediately" as if he were sounding out the syllables for an eighth grade spelling bee. I glanced at my watch, seven forty-five, and quietly thanked my cat, Syllabus, for waking me up early.

Syllabus didn't have a reason to jump on my chest thirty minutes before the alarm was set to go off. He wasn't hungry, and his litter box was clean. He was just being a bastard. We hadn't gotten along since I had him neutered for raping the neighbor's purebred Persian.

Work started at eight sharp. Mrs. Allison Kabel wasn't your typical high tech CEO who believes in flexible hours and Friday afternoon beer and pizza parties.

I placed my right index finger against the reader. A beep and a yellow flash indicated it had read my biometrics and recorded my entry time. A green flash signified I was truly Alexandra Hamilton Thornton—known as Hamo to my co-workers and other names elsewhere. The electric lock clicked open and I stepped into my other world.

I smiled at Sloan as I passed, wondering how long it would be before Mrs. Kabel decided biometric recognition eliminated the need for security guards.

Early or not, I was anxious. Andover Data Systems had fired twenty percent of the staff three months ago. Business hadn't improved, and there were rumors of another layoff. But if I were being laid off, my manager would do the honors. Mrs. Kabel didn't dirty her hands with that sort of unpleasantness.

Maybe I had won employee of the month, and everyone was waiting to take my picture for the company newsletter. I would get temporary custody of a cardboard sign allowing me to park next to Mrs. Kabel. That brought to mind an image of my three-year-old Acura parked beside Mrs. Kabel's new Mercedes.

Executive offices were on the second floor. I took the stairs and then walked past doors with nameplates of increasing rank until at the end there was a small seating area, a desk, and behind it, Marie, Mrs. Kabel's Administrative Assistant.

"Have a seat, Hamilton, Mrs. Kabel will see you in a moment," Marie said. Apparently, "Immediately" did not mean right now.

Marie looked me over then by some mysterious means conveyed her disapproval of my attire. Marie and her boss were relics of a time when management expected the employees to wear business suits with ties.

I don't dress badly compared to Earl Bowers, the programmer in the cubicle next to mine. Earl's tee shirts display the name of country and western bands. His jeans are usually smeared with grease from his hobby of restoring 1965 Mustangs. He doesn't bother with details like personal hygiene; he wasn't impressed by the air freshener I placed in his cube while he was at lunch.

Earl was the programming genius who developed the tools we lesser mortals needed. People as brilliant and productive as Earl can dress—and smell—however they want to.

I was wearing my day job disguise. Its purpose was to make me unrecognizable to anyone who saw me at my night job. My blonde hair was in a ponytail. I wore no makeup. Gold, wire rimmed glasses and plain pearl studs gave me the look of a woman who would rather curl up with a good book than go out on a date. A loose, bulky, knit sweater and dress slacks concealed my figure. I had modeled myself after my high school librarian.

Waiting gave me opportunity to worry. Mrs. Kabel had found out about my stripping. She would terminate me personally, as an example to others. A picture of her showing me the door would be on the front page of the company newsletter.

Actually, I had two jobs that would damn me in the eyes of management. But no one would connect me with my Web business.

I started thinking about what I would say when she confronted me. I'd quit on the spot, call her an old bitch, and walk out. No, that was stupid. I'd deny everything. I needed the income if I was going to pay off my school loans.

The Employee Handbook stated that employees were allowed to have second jobs only with management's prior written approval (that would never be given). Second jobs were an embarrassment to management. They implied (correctly) the company didn't pay a living wage.

Your signed statement that you'd read and understood the rules was in your personnel file. Failure to comply was grounds for dismissal.

Mrs. Kabel would tell Human Resources to classify me as "do not rehire," insuring no other employer would take me. Unemployment would provide a pittance for twenty-six weeks. I would lose my health insurance.

Chapter 2

Money was the reason I started dancing. It was what brought me back after I quit. My sister claims it's my way of thumbing my nose at our vanished father.

Dad taught American History and belonged to the economic determinist school. He believed money is the motivating factor for most if not all human endeavors.

I started nude dancing when I was in college. I was bright enough to get into a good school but too poor to afford it. Colleges advertise that they offer aid to worthy applicants, meaning dirt poor and minority students. When I applied, my parents were still together, disqualifying me for financial aid.

Dad disappeared the summer I graduated high school. He emptied all our bank accounts, including the one containing my first year's tuition. The fact that I had earned part of it didn't deter him for an instant.

Aunt Catherine, Dad's sister, says he is alive and well, but she won't tell Mom where. "He's started a new life and is very happy." I hope she's wrong.

I told my sad tale of departed father and purloined funds to the dean. She offered me loans that I could pay back upon graduating. The loans only covered tuition and books. During my sophomore year, Mom lost her job. I started working for minimum wage as a cashier in the college bookstore for pocket money. Then Gloria appeared in my life.

Gloria was a tall, striking blonde with breasts that had gravitational pull, drawing eyes wherever she went. She was in one of my classes, and we studied together for the final. One night, after two bottles of chardonnay, she confided that she danced nude at a chain of clubs south of Boston.

I hadn't seen her for a while when she showed up in my checkout line at the bookstore.

"You don't look so good. How's it going?" asked Gloria.

"Fair to shitty," I said. My grades were suffering from working long hours and the stress of always being broke.

"You can't make any serious money doing this."

"No shit. The pay sucks, and my supervisor keeps hinting that unless I blow him my job will disappear," I said.

"I know a way you could make money, lots of it," said Gloria.

"Legally?"

It was a fair question. The best paying jobs on campus were selling drugs and fake IDs.

"When you get off, call my cell. We'll meet and talk."

At first, I told her no way; but then she mentioned clearing fifteen hundred a week. When you can't afford diet soda that kind of money makes you reevaluate your principles. But there were other issues.

"I don't have the body for dancing and I've never danced," I said, thinking of my borderline B cup breasts. I was an A throughout high school and had only recently decided I needed a bigger bra. My big breasted sister says that I am dreaming. I'm a skinny five-foot ten and not among the blessed.

"Anybody can learn to dance. You think these puppies are real?" Gloria clutched her boobs.

"I always assumed they were." I didn't want to be rude. Nobody's breasts were naturally that big.

"Feel them," Gloria said, offering me her chest. I glanced around the coffee shop. It wasn't crowded. I reached over and placed one hand on a very firm breast.

"Nine hundred cubic centimeters of saline solution for a thirty-eight double D."

"They're nice," was all I could manage.

"Alex, you've got a great face and body. All you need is augmentation. You'll also need to dye your hair blonde and wax your pussy," said Gloria.

"Didn't they cost a fortune?" I asked.

"Doctor Keller charges fifty-five hundred," said Gloria.

"I don't have that kind of money nor can I dance."

"Dancing is the easy part. I could teach you. The guy who owns the clubs where I dance owes me a favor. Let me talk to him. Maybe he has some ideas."

A week later, I got a text from Gloria, asking to meet.

"I've had a brainstorm. I ran it by Arnie, and he loved it," said Gloria. Arnie Rothstein owned the clubs where Gloria danced.

"I'm interested." I had twenty dollars in my account and seven dollars in my pocket.

"We dance together with you dressed as a high school girl and me as your principal. Did you play soccer or field hockey in high school?" asked Gloria.

"Both. I've still got the uniforms." I had been co-captain of the field hockey team the year we won the state championship.

"Great, we sex up the outfits and pretend you've been sent to my office for punishment. I order you to drop your panty and spank you a little bit. Then we both strip, and dance together with some girl on girl action. Your breasts are small, but that fits with the routine. What do you think?" Gloria looked like she'd discovered the cure for cancer and expected a call from the Nobel Committee.

My answer was based on sheer desperation. "I'm in. Let's make it happen."

Being nude wasn't as difficult as I thought it would be. Gloria took me to the club in the early morning to rehearse our act. For the first hour, I got to wear a bikini. Our audience was the cleaning crew and someone re-stocking the bar.

"Lose your top," said Gloria as she pulled her shirt off. That was the easy part. After another half hour, Gloria announced it was time to get naked. I slipped out of my bikini bottom without a panic attack. "Just pretend there's no one watching until you get used to it," advised Gloria.

Over time I reached the point where I liked having men look at me that way. Today, I could ride naked in the St. Patrick's Day Parade.

There was another self discovery. I am someone who loves to dance and I was good at it. My style is athletic. I do handstands and full splits.

"You're a natural," declared Gloria after I successfully repeated a complicated series of steps on my first try. I also learned to climb a brass pole, touch the ceiling, turn around and spiral down head first.

A week later, I walked onstage wearing my Lynnfield High School field hockey uniform, modified for maximum slut effect. I shortened the skirt till it was an inch below my butt. Instead of black spandex shorts, there was a white G-string. I'd exercised and dieted to tone my abs. Every square inch of flesh had a drugstore tan. My dyed hair was in pigtails, and I was wearing so much makeup I thought my face would crack.

If the girls on my team had dressed that way, field hockey would be America's number one sport. For props, I carried my hockey stick and wore my shin guards—at least for the first two minutes.

In high school, I was the token female computer nerd, the only girl member of the chess and math clubs, and a habitué of the computer lab. Socially, I was so nondescript and pathetic the popular kids didn't pick on me; they didn't even know I existed. Now I was an up-and-coming sex idol.

Gloria was dressed in a black leather miniskirt and jacket. Her boobs were pushed up, spilling out between the lapels. She wore horn-rimmed glasses and looked like every teenage boy's fantasy principal. She coached me to work the men lining the stage. I learned what it took to make them place a bill on the edge of the dance floor.

"They're paying for a few seconds of your undivided attention. The trick is to give them just enough so they want more," was Gloria's sage advice.

While I was growing up my father kept me away from boys. He was the kind of dad who meets you at the door and demands an explanation if you five minutes late. I never dated, let alone got into in a serious relationship.

Gloria said not having the baggage of bad relationships made me trainable. According to her, I had a gift for getting men to give me their hard-earned dollars rather than wasting them on their families.

The first time we danced before an audience, I kept thinking I was going to pass out, wet myself, or throw up. Somehow, I managed to get through it and stay dry. At the end, I scurried around the stage, picking up bills from customers who'd just relived their high school fantasies.

We were a hit. Gloria and I cleared three thousand dollars in the first week, and she handed me half. I felt guilty taking it, since the act was Gloria's idea and she had taught me everything. But I said thank you and pocketed the cash. Having real money in my hands for the first time in months changed something in me. Like Scarlet in *Gone with the Wind*, I swore never to be poor again.

Arnie owned four clubs, so we rotated among them, doing three shows a night on Friday and Saturday. We varied the routine to keep it fresh as long as we could. I'd played soccer, so we added it to our repertoire. Although I was never a cheerleader, I found a cheerleader outfit at Goodwill. Gloria figured we had three to four months before we wore it out.

With Gloria's tutoring and the help of her current boyfriend, I mastered the art of table dancing. I started at one of the Massachusetts clubs where physical contact was illegal. You didn't touch the customer, but if you wanted a good tip, you had to come within a millimeter.

Next was Rhode Island where lap dancing was allowed. Psychologically, it was a huge step. Rubbing your bare ass across a man's crotch till he's hard is the essence of lap dancing. It's as close to prostitution as you can get without going pro. However, it was too much money to pass up. The club took every penny the customer paid for a three-minute dance, but tips amount to a thousand a week.

After three months, Gloria announced she was leaving Boston for Los Angeles. Gloria had decided that a degree in Communications was less lucrative than dancing nude, making porn, and being an escort.

"What should I do?" I asked her. I was losing my mentor and my act. By that time, I was hooked on the money. Going back to being a cashier was not an option.

"Get a boob job and dance. Arnie says you've got what it takes, and he knows. You don't need me," Gloria said.

I made an appointment with Doctor Keller. We decided on a 36D bust. I wasn't as tall as Gloria, and I didn't want to look like a freak. The operation was painless, but for three days after, I felt like a car was parked on my chest.

For the next four years, I danced every chance I got. It would be nice to say on graduation day I had a tidy little nest egg to pay off my college loans; but all I had was a closet full of expensive clothes, especially shoes, some beautiful and costly jewelry, and a highly modified body.

I'd returned a dozen times to Doctor Keller. My nose is straight and thinner, and my lips are fuller. My butt has almost perfect curvature. Fat from my abdomen and hips was melted, sucked out, and stored in a jar. Dr. Keller's associate reduced my inner and outer labia, making them symmetrical. She also trimmed back my clitoral hood.

Money management wise, I was a disaster. I figured that I was going to get a great job after college, and I should enjoy my student days. Actually, I didn't think at all. I bought whatever caught my fancy.

I graduated with a Masters in Computer Science. My concentration was network systems security. I quit dancing after ADS made me a job offer with a starting salary of $52,500. I stayed away for almost a year, focusing on becoming a Certified Information Systems Security Professional.

My college loans totaled $162,600. The monthly payments were mainly interest. When I found myself struggling to pay the minimum on my credit cards, I went back to Arnie and asked for a couple of shifts. My plan was to get totally out of debt, then give up dancing for good.

A year ago, after an incredible run of generous customers, I had a life changing revelation when Bathsheba and I were discussing our windfall.

"Tomorrow, I'm going to Tiffany's, or DeScenza Diamonds," I said.

"I'm going to put this in my safety-deposit box," said Bathsheba, patting her purse.

"You have a safety-deposit box?" I asked surprised. Somehow the idea of nude dancers and safety-deposit boxes did not compute.

"Of course I do. Look, Alexandra, you can't dance past thirty unless you want to wind up in biker bars being raped on the tables. You need to save," she said.

I'd never saved a dime. I was mortified that Bathsheba—high school dropout, lesbian, escort, and occasional cocaine user—had the wisdom to retain her earnings, while overeducated me lived from paycheck to paycheck.

I went to my bank the next day and rented my first safety-deposit box. That was a milestone in my life. I could feel something change in me as I carefully counted the cash before placing it in the box. Then I took it out and counted it again. A week later, I came back and added more money, triggering a complete recount.

Overnight, I went from being an out-of-control consumer to a disciplined saver. I've got three boxes now at three different banks, and I can never resist the urge to count it all when I open a box. I rationalize my odd behavior, telling myself I'm saving for a secure old age and avoiding IRS scrutiny. Tommie says I have a sickness about money and should see a therapist. Maybe she's right, but I don't want to spend the money to find out.

"Miss Thornton, Mrs. Kabel will see you now," said Marie interrupting my train of thought.

Chapter 3

"Hamilton Thornton, this is Bradley Dickerson of the FBI, Major Stewart Caulfield of the Massachusetts State Police, and Ross Hunnicut of Millennium Construction," said Mrs. Kabel, introducing me to the men seated at her conference table.

As we played the shake hands and exchange business cards game, I brightened. I was not going to be fired. An assignment meant that I was still employed. And this looked like an important one.

My boss, John Dryer, was there. I took the empty seat between John and Major Caulfield. Since I sometimes drive the interstate over both the speed and blood alcohol limits, knowing someone in the state police seemed advisable.

The meeting had obviously been in progress for at least the fifteen minutes I kept Marie company. I had been intentionally kept out. Perhaps they argued over whether I was qualified.

"Hamilton, unusual name for a girl," said Bradley, starting the conversation on a sexist note. He wasn't wearing a wedding ring, and he was extremely good looking.

"I go by Hamo," I said. When I started at ADS, I insisted that everyone call me Hamo to disguise my sordid past. I was terrified that if I went by my first name, one of my co-workers would ask if I was the same Alexandra who rode the brass pole at Foxy Lady II.

For some reason, Mrs. Kabel refers to me as me as Hamilton. I sign my name A. H. Thornton. None of it makes any sense, but I'm used to it. My sister, Thomasina Jefferson Thornton, goes by Tommie. She says I am trying to hide from who I really am.

Introductions over, Mrs. Kabel started, "Let me begin by stating that nothing discussed here will leave this room. Notes are not to be taken." She was looking directly at me, as if I were the blabbermouth of the group. I closed my notebook and set down my pen.

"Good. We have an interesting opportunity, Hamilton, and we're counting on you to help us," said Mrs. Kabel.

In current business speak, opportunity means problem. Challenge used to mean problem, but the MBA schools decided to replace it with opportunity because it sounds more positive.

"And you'll be doing your country a service," Bradley added.

"What can I do to help?" I asked, sounding a bit too eager.

"Ross is the Chief Security Officer of Millennium Construction. Why don't you begin, Ross?" Mrs. Kabel said.

Hamo, Millennium Construction is a global concern headquartered in Lowell. Much of our work is international. The company builds roads, bridges, and sophisticated traffic management systems. We also do oil and gas pipelines, warehouses, refineries, manufacturing plants, almost anything industrial. This will give you an overview of what we're all about," said Ross, handing me the company's annual report and some brochures.

It was time to lie. "I've heard of Millennium. What's the opportunity?"

"There have been unsubstantiated reports of a terrorist cell operating within the company. Personally, I think these reports are ludicrous, gossip spread by a competitor."

"How reliable is the source?" I asked, alarm bells going off in my head. Terrorists were dangerous killing machines. I was trained to pursue nerdy accountants, programmers who change a few lines of computer code to deposit the occasional check in their bank account.

"That's classified and not relevant to your assignment," said Bradley. I sensed he was one of those people who had to control the conversation in any meeting.

"Do we know what type of activities are being planned or executed by the terrorist cell?" I asked.

"Not at this time. Our sources are not definitive," Bradley again.

I was doing great until that point; so it was time to say something stupid. "Why not just investigate everyone with an Arab background?"

"Hamo, they can't do that," John Dryer said, embarrassed.

The other men shifted in their seats as they gave each other knowing looks, as though to say, "What else would you expect from a woman? Things haven't been right since they got the vote. I wonder if she gives good head. The dumb ones usually do." Mrs. Kabel gave me a look that said I was not to speak again, unless spoken to.

"The company has many thousand Arab and Arab-American employees. We do not and will not discriminate against them." Ross said huffily.

"Sorry," I replied. I thanked Allah I hadn't said fire all the towel heads.

"Our intelligence points to cyber terrorism in the information technology department," said Bradley.

I stopped myself from asking why, but I did nod.

"A top down investigation by the Bureau has not turned up anything, but that's not unexpected. Terrorists have become increasingly sophisticated in the use of information technology. It's conceivable, but unlikely that a terrorist cell is operating within Millennium," said Bradley.

"Millennium has critical projects underway in the Middle East that would be prime targets. Its corporate policy is to fully cooperate with the authorities," said Ross.

"Projects deemed vital to American interests," added Bradley, determined to get the last word.

I made a stab at redeeming myself. "I will do everything possible to identify any terrorists at Millennium."

"Good. We've come to ADS for assistance in determining whether there is any validity to our intelligence. We need someone with your skill set to join the IT staff at Millennium and work undercover. After discussing our requirements with Mrs. Kabel, she identified you as the best person for the job. She speaks very highly of your abilities," said Bradley.

I tried not to look surprised. Allison Kabel normally passed me in the hall without speaking.

However, during the last six months, I had worked three undercover projects involving fraud and embezzlement. I identified the crooks and gathered the necessary proofs. The companies quietly fired the offending employees. Trials can be very embarrassing for corporate executives. Who knows what an angry ex-employee might reveal on the witness stand.

"Only the VP of IS&T, Saul Ebert, and I will know your true identity," said Ross.

"IS&T," I asked?

"Information Systems and Technology, Millennium is a leader in developing advanced system technology to assist our Engineering and Construction personnel to be more productive," said Ross.

"Given that it is a matter of national security, I'm surprised the FBI isn't providing someone," I said, risking Mrs. Kabel's ire.

"It's a resource issue," said Bradley curtly.

I guessed the FBI thought there was little chance it was true. Hopefully, I was on a cover-your-ass assignment. I wasn't likely to find anything, but just in case I did, nobody at the Bureau would be splattered with shit for inaction.

"And what's your role in this, Major Caulfield?" I asked the uniformed officer who hadn't said a word since the meeting started.

"We're there in case things get rough and you need additional support," said Major Caulfield. "We're your backup."

"But keep in mind that you're only there to gather information. If you observe anything suspicious, you immediately turn it over to me," said Bradley.

"If Bradley is unavailable, you can contact us," said Major Caulfield.

"I'm available twenty-four seven," said Bradley.

This was the first time I'd observed an interagency turf war and it was damn exciting. I resisted the urge to flirt with Major Caulfield to piss off Bradley.

"We're not asking you to do anything dangerous, Hamilton. As soon as you discover anything, you inform John," said Mrs. Kabel with an air of finality.

That sounded responsible, but I suspected for two hundred per hour, she'd send me into Hell to investigate Satan's IS&T Department and keep me there as long as Satan was willing to pay. It was also her way of saying I was to tell ADS first, and she'd make the appropriate decision of who to tell next, based on maximizing revenue.

"All right, when do I start?" I said, sounding more positive than I felt. I wanted to ask, "Suppose the terrorist cell learns of my mission and blows me away…who'll feed my cat?" But I kept a determined look on my face. Lack of zeal would get me added to the layoff list.

Chapter 4

"Personally, I think this is pure bullshit, but that's between us," said Saul Ebert, vice president of the IS&T Department. "Some dickheads at NSA were listening to some towel heads jabber over a cell phone. They hear Millennium's name and go shit crazy. Poor bastards were probably looking for a construction job."

It was Friday afternoon and we were meeting at a Starbucks near Millennium's corporate headquarters in Lowell, Massachusetts. Saul shared Ross Hunnicut's assessment of the probability of a terrorist cell. He just had a less politically correct way of expressing himself.

"I'm sure you're right, Saul, but don't shoot the messenger," I said. I'd dealt with IT executives and they came in two flavors: stressed and stressed out. In that job, if you lasted five years, you set a longevity record. Saul was in his mid forties, balding, with a paunch that made the bottom three buttons of his shirt gape open.

"Millennium sounds like a great place to work. How long have you been there, Saul?" I said.

"Four years last month." Saul sounded resigned to the fact that if terrorists were discovered in his department, he wasn't going to see his fifth anniversary.

"So, how do we handle this?" I asked

"I've given it some thought, and now that I see you're easy on the eyes, I know what to do."

"What's your plan?" I wanted Saul to get on with it. It was Friday. I had to go home and get ready for my night job.

"We're rolling out a new system for managing the company's projects. The CEO himself godfathered this baby so for once we have all the resources we need. There's nothing in the industry with equivalent capability," he said.

"How do I fit in?"

"You'll join the installation and conversion team. Ross says you know DataScript, so that's a plus. Over the next ninety days, we're going to install MillProMan in every one of our subsidiaries. You'll have to travel. This is the documentation," said Saul, handing me a cloth bag with a half dozen binders in it. "Millennium Project Management System" was silk screened on the cover along with "Company Confidential."

"Looks impressive." I took the bag and wondered how I would find the time over the weekend to digest a month's reading.

"Well, learn what you can. I'll fix it so your boss, Max Elkins, doesn't have high expectations," said Saul.

"How will you do that?"

"I'll tell him that a certain senior executive told me to hire you. You and he enjoy a close personal relationship, if you get my meaning. IS&T is fully staffed, so I can't add you to the payroll without a damn good reason."

"And Max will go along with someone being hired for those kinds of reasons." I said.

"He doesn't have a choice. My department has served as the parking lot for his bimbos before," said Saul. It was interesting Millennium tolerated senior management placing their girlfriends on the payroll. If you think about it, it was just another form of executive perk, like season tickets to the Red Sox.

"And what's the name of this executive who I have a relationship with?" If you're supposed to be sucking somebody's cock, it's better to know his name.

"I'd rather not say," said Saul.

"Shouldn't I know, since I'm his girlfriend?"

"You'll know inside a week, probably less," he said.

I would show up Monday at eight thirty, go through employee orientation, and then join the MillProMan installation team. I made a mental note to dress semi-slut. Being a bimbo has its advantages. They'd think I was incapable of understanding anything I overheard.

I left Saul to his misery and headed back to Saugus. After Dad disappeared, Mom sold our home in Lynnfield and moved one town over. On my uncle's advice, Mom used the equity to purchase a duplex. She rented out the other half to help pay her mortgage. The building already had a tenant, so Mom thought she was set. Unfortunately, that only works if the renter actually pays the rent.

Every month, Lenny promised to pay, and every month, he didn't. I ran a credit check. He had the money. I tried to let Mom handle it, but when she told me she was getting behind in the mortgage, I hired Tice, from club security, to solve Mom's collection problem.

Club security moonlight as collectors and repo men. Tice knew exactly what to do. He knocked politely on Lenny's door to ask for the last four months rent. Lenny answered, expecting to tell Mom to piss off. He was more responsive when he saw Tice's massive frame standing in his doorway. Tice made it look easy. Of course, a lot of things are easy for a guy with the body of an NFL lineman, biceps the size of Lenny's head, and a shaved skull covered in Maori tattoos. Lenny's hand shook as he scribbled a check.

"If this check bounces, I will be very unhappy," said Tice.

"It won't bounce. I promise," said Lenny, summoning every ounce of sincerity he had in him.

Tice and I drove to the bank and cashed it. Tice also told Lenny he would be collecting rent in the future. Two days later, Lenny moved out.

Realizing my mother would never be able to handle renters, Tommie and I leased the other half of the duplex. I was twenty-four, living with my twenty-seven-year-old sister. It grated on me, but I decided to put up with it until I paid off my college loans.

I check on Mom when I get home. She and Tommie were in front of the television, eating a salad. Tommie became a vegetarian in her last year of college. Since staying in shape was essential to my dancing, I mostly followed along.

My mom's still a pretty woman. Everyone says I look like her. She and I are both slender and long limbed. Tommie takes after Dad's side of the family. The Thorntons are built like dockworkers.

I filled a plate from Tommie's bowl of greens—she kept it full as obsessively as I counted my safety-deposit funds. When I sat down, I saw that Tommie was wearing a garter belt and hose. I didn't know Tommie even owned a garter belt. Her boss must have been planning a booty call. I fought the urge to get pissed. It was her life.

Tommie is a dental hygienist. Three months ago, she began an affair with the dentist, Harold. My sister's love life was none of my business, but her relationship with Harold was so one-sided; it drove me nuts. Harold was married, fat, self-centered, and demanding. Tommie was in love with him. In her eyes, Harold could do no wrong.

She wouldn't see him outside of work for days, and then he would show up, unannounced, for a quickie. I've seen him arrive, rush her into her bedroom, and be gone in twenty minutes.

Other times, he'd say he was coming over. Tommie would spend hours getting ready; then the motherfucker wouldn't show and didn't call. She would cry herself to sleep, but God help me if I told her she deserved better.

I left Mom's fast, to avoid saying anything. Home, I said hello to Syllabus, who allocated me a tiny fraction of his attention. A friend once told me a cat is like a French whore. They provide the absolute minimum amount of love needed to keep yours.

I got a diet soda from the refrigerator, went to the spare room, punched in the code to open the door, and walked into the world headquarters of Dolly Madison Systems—my Web design and hosting company.

Chapter 5

ADS's first layoff convinced me I needed to do something more long term than computer forensics or stripping. Outsourcing of high tech jobs overseas made it unlikely my skills would guarantee employment over the next forty years. Everyone at ADS knew somebody whose job had been relocated to Mumbai.

Tommie suggested I go to nursing school. But going back to school would put me into more debt, and being around sick people made me ill. Law school also meant more debt, though Mom thought I would make a terrific lawyer. "You think well on your feet, Alex."

By accident, I discovered a job that didn't require additional schooling. One night, two other dancers and I were sitting at a table with three men who worked in the Web group for a Boston financial services company. I listened as the dancers complained about their sites.

"They charge me three hundred a month and the fucking thing was unavailable three days in a row. Some of my regulars left. I lost two thousand bucks, minimum," said Eva, a Latina without a green card who lived with an ICE agent.

"I cancelled my Web site. The damn thing didn't work right. Guys were telling me that they requested dates and I never got back to them. It was losing my e-mails," said Devon.

At that moment, the guys decided it was time for a private dance, and the conversation ended. But it did get me thinking about starting a Web business. After the layoff those remaining were assigned the work of the departed. I was given responsibility for the corporate Web site. There wasn't much to do, since the information didn't change unless Mrs. Kabel fired one of the senior managers. I spent, at most, four hours a month updating it. But it was enough to refresh the skills I learned in college.

I began collecting the business cards dancers hand to customers who ask for an escort date. Most list only a telephone number. A few have an e-mail address, and small fraction a Web address. I visited their sites and concluded most were poorly designed and unreliable. I'd taken a graduate course on how to start your own company. Before reality dawned, computer science students expected to become entrepreneurs and ultimately billionaires a few weeks after graduation. I retrieved my textbook from an unpacked box in the basement and religiously followed every step. Even measures I thought were unnecessary later turned out to be good ideas. The result was Dolly Madison Systems.

DMS currently hosts forty Web sites, each devoted to an individual nude dancer. In the parlance of porn, these are "Hard R" sites, meaning they don't show penile penetration or ejaculation. There is full nudity, but no full-on pussy shots. Technically, I'm in the soft porn business. That leaves me in an uncertain stance with the law. Each of the fifty states has different laws. I read two boring books on pornography laws and came away confused. Last time I looked, there were over ninety thousand hardcore sites featuring everything from anal to zoophilia. So why worry about soft porn?

Every DMS site lists the availability of the dancer as an escort. Since I don't process payments, I'm not technically a pimp, but not every district attorney in the US would agree. As far as I know, no soft porn Web host has ever been prosecuted. But that could change with politics. Ambitious DAs are always trying to capture the political support of the righteous. Crusading against the sleazy world of sex for hire is an easy way to do it.

My mother says that working three jobs is too stressful for me. She complains that I work too hard, that I will never get a husband, and that my money lust is an unhealthy obsession. She's right, but I don't know what to do about it.

Checking DMS is part of my daily routine. I sit at the control console, where a computer named DMS-Master monitors the servers. Every two minutes, it's programmed to perform a dialogue with each server. Their exchange sounds something like this.

08:14 Hello DMS-1, this is DMS-Master, everything OK?
08:14 Yes, DMS-Master, all is well, thanks for asking.
08:14 Hello DMS-2, this is DMS-Master, everything OK?
08:15 Yes, DMS-Master, all is well, thanks for asking.

If any of the six servers fail to respond, DMS-Master is programmed to text my cell phone with a message, "DMS-n is unresponsive." I try to remotely restart the server using my desktop computer at ADS or the laptop I keep in my car. If that doesn't work, and I have to run home, I make up some excuse to tell my boss. These days, it isn't much of a problem. I haven't had an emergency message in over a month.

After I checked the status of my Web servers, I reviewed the counters to see how many hits each site had in the last twenty-four hours. Brandi's site was in the lead; it had been visited over five hundred times. Brandi Doucette was a nineteen-year-old dancer with an incredible body and charisma on stage. People think nude dancing is all about tits and ass, and they couldn't be more wrong. I've seen dancers with fantastic faces and figures fail, while the less favored prosper.

My typical site shows images of the dancer, fully dressed, semi-nude, and nude. I recommend that the dancers update the images regularly to keep their sites fresh. The smart ones include a few shots of themselves in office attire, looking accessible. In today's corporate environment, a male employee can lose his job for looking too long or too closely at a co-worker's chest. But sexual repression incites desire.

Each site lists club dates for devoted fans. Most include a short usually fictitious biography, the dancer's sexual preferences (boys, girls, both), a blog if the dancer had literary ambitions and can spell, and a listing of other services—such as escorting, bachelor parties, or lingerie sales. There is an email page to request a date.

On the first of each month, I debit each dancer's credit card $250—except for Bathsheba, who is still enjoying her one year complementary ride for being my first customer. My largest recurring expense is the two high-speed data lines connecting DMS to the Internet.

I was building two new sites, and there were five on my waiting list. I'd considered leaving my day job to concentrate full time on DMS. There are four hundred thousand women dancing at clubs in this land of opportunity. But having a respectable day job with a good health insurance plan was important to me. And for that matter, America might forsake the sexual revolution and return to the ways of its Puritan ancestors. Owners of sexually explicit sites will be marched through the streets of nearby Salem then branded with a scarlet letter.

Each site also has a link for e-mailing the Webmaster with any problems. My problem was that the address collected so much SPAM that the little finger on my right hand got sore from pressing the delete key. Advertisements for home equity loans, prescription drugs, and ways to enlarge my penis had to be purged. I was working along when I saw it. I went cold. There was a message. The subject line read, "Greetings, Alexandra Hamilton Thornton."

"Stay calm," I whispered. Some clever bastard had figured out I was the Webmaster for DMS. It was supposed to be a secret. I danced as Alexandra Winston, and that was the name on DMS's incorporation papers. Winston was my mother's maiden name. No hint of my real name was anywhere in DMS. All e-mail was addressed to Abigail Adams Systems, another of my corporate identities.

I took a long, deep breath and opened the message. For e-mail, it was damn long.

Chapter 6

I scan most emails, but I read this one through three times, like a math problem.

My dearest Hamo,

This is the first of many messages, and I hope it will lead to a long relationship. I find your nickname, "Hamo," intriguing, but not feminine enough for such a beautiful woman. Still, it somehow suits you. What with working at ADS, dancing nude for Arnold Rothenberg's sleazy establishments, and being Web mistress for porn sites, you don't have much time to just be a girl.

How long since your last date, Hamo? Is that your choice? My answer would be yes. Hamo doesn't want a man to get close to her. He might empty her precious safety-deposit boxes and disappear like Daddy. Maybe I'm wrong, and love of money is your all-consuming passion. By the way, I think you obsess too much over those college loans. You'll get them paid.

My goal is to become the man in your life. At this point, you're terrified and angry I've learned your secrets. You think I'll inform ADS, and Mrs. Kabel will fire you on the spot—

or that you're being stalked by some madman who'll cut your throat.

Perhaps you're thinking of going to the pistol range to practice with your new Sig Sauer Equinox, an excellent weapon. I have one myself. I'd be curious how you rate it against your Glock. The silhouette target you practiced on last Saturday showed good marksmanship from fifteen yards. With better breath control, you could be an amazing marksman. I suggest you practice with your left hand. You never know when the right might be unavailable.

Please do not fear me. I mean only the best for you. Over time, I'll earn your trust and eventually your love. The first step in any relationship is communication. It isn't in your nature to answer a message like this. So, I must compel the start of our dialogue. If you do not reply to my messages, I will inform Cynthia Simmons her husband is having an affair with your sister. I've attached a photo as proof.

Funny how those we love are also our greatest vulnerability. I know you don't want Tommie unhappier than she already is. Please respond by answering the following:

1. What is your favorite flavor of ice cream?
2. Do you feel a spiritual connection to Jim Morrison when you dance to "Riders on the Storm"?
3. If one of the dancers at the club were to have an accident, who would you want it to be?

I should mention the nail lacquer you had on last Saturday is flattering on you, a nice complement to your complexion. Isn't it "Groove" by Lancôme?

Awaiting your reply

E. Schuyler

"Shit, he knows every fucking thing about me," I whispered as I finished the third reading.

Syllabus, sensing my nervous state, jumped up on the table. I startled and knocked over the half full soda can. "Damn you cat," I yelled as I tore off a handful of paper towels from the roll I kept nearby for such emergencies. Syllabus sauntered away, pleased with himself for making me angry. Once more, I considered and discarded the idea of dumping him on some lonely country road. I decided to wait until the first winter snow.

Stay calm. You can deal with this. Most dancers, sooner or later, attract a stalker—some lonely man who leaves flowers, little notes, or cards on their windshields. Usually this guy is retired or recently widowed. Stalking takes a lot of time. Men with real jobs don't have the time to follow a dancer home at two in the morning. I was always afraid someone would follow me from the club. It's one of the few good reasons to have a boyfriend to watch your back. But dancers' boyfriends have a tendency to beat them up, steal their money, and turn them into hookers. Instead of a boyfriend, I bought a pistol—two actually—and learned to shoot.

On screen I highlighted the personal facts. My stalker must have first sighted me at one of the clubs while I was dancing. He watched me leave and wrote down my license plate.

Then he bribed someone at the motor vehicle registry for my name and home address, plus my social security number.

With those, he could get my credit reports, medical records, school transcripts, and employment history from skip trace Web sites. My college loans would be on my credit report. Both handguns were registered with the state.

Harold and Tommie would be easy. If my stalker was watching the house, he could see Harold arrive and get his plate number. Home visits from your married boss signify adultery. I didn't want to, but I downloaded the attached image file. There was my sister, kneeling on her purse while Harold leaned against a tree. I remembered Tommie talking about romantic luncheon picnics in a park near the office.

It was odd that he knew Arnie's full name. Then I recalled that the club's incorporation papers were in the public domain. For that matter, my name was on the incorporation papers for Dolly Madison Systems and Abigail Adams Systems. The papers identified the businesses as Web hosting and electronic mail. I should have lied.

The fact he knew the brand and color of my nail lacquer scared me more than anything else. Had he followed me into Macy's and spied on me at the cosmetics counter? Or did he dig the sales slip out of the garbage. I glanced at the paper shredder in the corner; I make a silent commitment to use it more often.

As a forensics computer specialist, I was trained to search digital databases. Once you had a single piece of personal data, gathering the rest was easy. The staff at ADS says everybody's life story is only three Web sites away.

E. Schuyler's e-mail address was firstlady02@findnot.com, obviously created for his stalking venture. Abigail Adams was the second first lady after Martha Washington. Findnot was an anonymous e-mail server located in the UK. There were dozens of e-mail sites in Europe who specialized in forwarding untraceable electronic mail. You had to be a government agency hunting a murder, terrorist, or pedophile to get their cooperation.

I looked at my watch. I had to start for the club. It was in Rhode Island, an hour's drive. I wrote a rushed reply.

My dear stalker,

My favorite ice cream flavor is Mint Chocolate Chip; however, when it's warm, I switch to Maine Blueberry.

When I dance to "Riders on the Storm," I feel no particular connection to Jim Morrison but obviously one to his music. Other than his overdose and death in France, I know little about him. I will visit The Doors' Web site and learn more.

If any of the dancers were to have an accident, I would prefer it be me. But please, don't hurt anyone.

Hamo

P.S. I see no reason for us not to meet in person. Come by the club and introduce yourself. First dance is on me.

The name E. Schuyler sounded familiar, but odd for a stalker. I went into the living room and searched until I found the two-volume biography of Alexander Hamilton my father gave me when I started high school. He made me read two chapters a day. Each night at dinner we discussed it.

"You should know your namesake," my father said when I balked at reading seven hundred pages about a man two hundred years dead.

I found what I was looking for. Elizabeth Schuyler was Alexander Hamilton's rich wife. My stalker was creepy and clever. I changed "My dear stalker" to "My dear Elizabeth" and clicked send.

Chapter 7

"Watch my back, Tice, I've attracted a stalker," Tice was working the door at Foxy Vixens II. I stood on my toes, wrapped my arms around his neck, and gave him a kiss, brushing my tongue against his lips before plunging it into his mouth. A giant hand squeezed one buttock. The hand holding the metal detector was in the center of my back, pressing my chest to his.

"Is it serious, Alex?" asked Tice, his manhood pressing against my belly. He was well equipped. I melted against his manly frame, all female weakness in the face of danger. "Yes, he mentioned a dancer having an accident."

"What's he look like?" asked Tice.

"Don't know. He sent me a threatening e-mail," I said as we ground together like swans engaged in a mating dance.

"I'll stop anybody with a laptop," Tice said as we uncoupled. He must have thought I was an idiot, but a friendly one. Always be extra nice to security was Gloria's advice, and I followed it religiously.

"How is it inside," I asked?

"Busy," said Tice opening the door for me. "You should do all right."

I danced Friday and Saturday nights, and Sunday afternoon. The clubs are open seven days a week from noon to the local closing time, which can be anytime from midnight to two in the morning. Holidays were never honored. I've celebrated Thanksgiving, Christmas Day, and Easter dancing naked for tips.

I said hello to Gina, the bartender. Gina had worked for Arnie since he opened his first club in Boston's Combat Zone, thirty years ago. She gave me the hand sign for a free spending crowd. That sent me hurrying through the door marked "Employees Only."

Four dancers already occupied the Dressing Room. I dropped my carry bag on a free makeup table. I pulled out the six outfits I'd be wearing that night and hung them on a pipe rack. All the changing is tiring, but the customers like to see you in different looks, and they're the ones with the tips.

I plugged in my hot curlers and ran for the showers. I was soaping up when I felt someone come up behind me. Two arms wrapped themselves around me, tucking under my boobs while lips planted a kiss on the side of my neck.

"Bathsheba, you scared the piss out of me," I said, turning around to face the tall brunette. Bathsheba was my age, exotic as a Gypsy, and decidedly lesbian when she wasn't dancing or escorting.

"Water sports, I've never done that, but with you, precious, anything," said Bathsheba, leaning forward to kiss me full on the lips. She grabbed my ass and pulled our sexes together. Bathsheba loved to trib.

"Ooh," breathed Bathsheba, grinding.

"I've got to get ready. I'm on in fifteen." I shrugged free of her arms.

"Then let me wash your back. Please."

"All right, but quickly," I said, leaning face forward against the tile wall. "How's the crowd?"

"Delilah said the man in the gray suit at the corner of the stage owns a car dealership, but he's a cheap bastard, so don't waste your time."

"Any weirdoes?" I was thinking of E. Schuyler.

"Aren't they all?"

It took another kiss and grind before I made it back to my dressing table. I had to agree we'd dance together during our last set. Bathsheba had a life partner, Carrie, who drove a semi between Boston and Portland.

Fifteen minutes later, I was talking to Rick, the DJ. Every dancer gets four songs. During the first song, I tease off most of my clothes. The second song starts with my boobs showing and ends with me naked. I dance the last two songs nude.

"Do you have anything I could substitute for 'Riders on the Storm'?" I asked. It was normally the first song of my first set.

"Why, getting tired of it?" asked Rick.

"Yes," I lied.

"How about 'L.A. Woman'? Same band, faster tempo."

"Not crazy about it, but it'll do."

I watched Sonja finish her set. It's important to see whose spending money. A party of five in Beacon Electrical T-shirts was feathering Sonja's G-string with tips. Electricians make good money, and they take cash under the table to avoid taxes.

I eyed the deadbeat Bathsheba had mentioned. I wondered whether I should ignore him or treat him as a challenge—or is that "opportunity". As a rule, men in groups tend to be freer with tips to dancers on stage. It's a macho thing. However, loners are more likely to pay for a lap dance.

Foxy Vixens II stood a hundred yards off the interstate just outside Warwick, Rhode Island. The Ocean State has a reputation for tolerance when it comes to vice. The club was easily accessible from Boston, and on weekends it was always crowded.

There was a VIP room in the back where totally nude lap dances were permitted. A dancer could earn a thousand dollars a night rubbing her ass over men's crotches. And if Security made itself conveniently absent, more money could be had giving handjobs and blowjobs to repeat customers.

I resisted the urge to take Rick's microphone and offer five free dances to anyone who knew the maiden name of Alexander Hamilton's wife. The crowd would think I'd overdosed on crystal meth.

"And here she is, the fabulous Alexandra," blasted Rick. I danced onto the stage wearing black mesh thigh high stockings, a black teddy held together by Velcro, a black bra, and two sets of panties. The pair against my skin was a thong, and the outer one French cut. Six-inch platform heels completed my look.

Customers prefer tall, statuesque women, so dancers end up with Achilles tendon problems. I've known dancers who permanently fucked up their legs, dancing in extreme high heels.

At least some of the audience yelled and clapped as I came on stage. I grabbed the brass pole and did a one-armed three sixty. During the first dance, you need to figure out who's interested in spending money for a close-up of your private parts and who's there to brag about his new pickup truck.

The stage was equipped with three brass poles. Some dancers barely use the poles, too much effort. Not me, I love them. My pole stunts open wallets.

By the end of the first set, I'd slipped out of the teddy and bra. I danced around the edge of the stage to give the audience a close-up of Doctor Keller's magic gazing orbs. I used makeup to darken my areola for the men who should be wearing their glasses. The electricians were showing interest, so I stopped and asked the Alpha male of the group his name.

"Ken, honey, what's yours?" He must have been in the john when Rick announced me.

"Alexandra. You guys here to celebrate something special?" I asked.

"Nope, just pussy looking. Are you going to show us yours?"

"That's what I'm here for, Ken," I said as I danced away.

"Beautiful tie," I said to the tightwad car dealer. He looked up at me, startled, but then he smiled. I saw some possibilities. I recognized a couple of regulars, one of whom we call the Method Man.

There are customers who are obsessive. The Method Man, actually Frank Somebody, goes to the bank on Friday and gets one hundred dollars in brand new singles. He arrives at eight on the dot, and gets upset if someone is sitting in his favorite spot. He divides his cash into four equal amounts using paper clips and stays until midnight rationing out twenty-five dollars each hour. His last new dollar bill will leave his hand at exactly five minutes to midnight. I guess it beats staying home watching *I Love Lucy* reruns. I can count on him for ten dollars each set. I passed by and blew him a kiss. I've rubbed my boobs on his shiny skull more times than I can remember.

Tips usually start at the end of the second dance, when I do a little tease thing with my thong. It's amazing how you can stretch nylon without it losing its shape. I pick up the bills as I dance, almost always singles or fives, but sometimes more.

When a customer places a bill on stage, I'll dance close and assume one of several positions that give him a good view of my pussy or asshole, probably both. Hemorrhoids will put a dancer out of work. Your back door cannot look like a cabbage decorating a keyhole.

After the fourth song, I scooped up any bills left on stage, brushed my boobs against the best tippers, and scurried to the dressing room. I threw the money into a security locker and donned another outfit. I'm back working the audience inside of two minutes; lust cools quickly. Mr. Car Dealer grabbed my hand, and we were off to experience passion in three-minute increments at twenty dollars per.

Chapter 8

I spent Sunday morning reviewing the MillProMan documentation. First, I woke to the sound of running feet and laughter. "Don't, Harold, that tickles," my sister wailed from somewhere beyond my locked bedroom door. Harold's flight attendant wife was in London.

I started with the overview. MillProMan cost over two million dollars to develop, and represented sixteen man-years of work. It was designed to manage the most complex construction projects ranging from major roads to skyscrapers. Every transaction related to human resources, engineering, procurement, construction, and financial were supported by the system. If the system met its objectives, Millennium would have a competitive advantage.

I was familiar with project management systems. We use a simple one at ADS to record results and track billable time on each project. After our meeting in Mrs. Kabel's office, John entered 1.5 hours of his time and 1.0 of mine. I still wondered what was discussed in the half hour before I was invited to join them.

Those 2.5 hours put $575 in ADS's pocket, not bad since we hadn't done anything other than agree to do something. My Friday meeting with Saul Ebert was also billable, and I input 4.0 hours. Even the time I spent reading MillProMan documentation was billable. I often wondered why ADS wasn't profitable. Could it have anything to do with Mrs. Kabel's company leased Mercedes-Benz S-class?

I'd finished the System Overview when I heard Harold leave. I got a cup of coffee and moved to DMS World Headquarters. I counted Friday and Saturday's earnings using the currency counter I bought off eBay. I'd made over eleven hundred dollars. I pay whenever possible in cash. Checks leave a paper trail.

After I finished, I searched the Web for information on Millennium, beginning with the official corporate site. Millennium was huge, a ten billion dollar construction behemoth, third largest in the US. Benjamin Sheffield had founded Sheffield Construction in 1946, when he returned from the Pacific. The company grew slowly, reaching only twenty million in revenue by 1975. In the 1980s, Benjamin's two sons, Marshall and Benjamin Junior joined the firm. Benjamin Senior retired in 1990. Growth accelerated a little; two hundred million in 1990 and two hundred fifty five million in 1995. Six years ago, the company was renamed Millennium Construction, and began to pursue international business.

Recent acquisitions were the reason for the exponential growth. They had acquired thirty major companies and many smaller ones. There's nothing wrong with buying up the competition, but exploding into a ten billion dollar company in less than ten years struck me as too much success to be honest.

I decided to call Mark, the financial services representative who handles my 401K. I'd met him twice, when he visited

ADS to answer questions. He would remember me; after both meetings, he called and asked me out. I didn't want to deal with another request and planned to leave a voice mail asking him to email me; but he answered on the first ring.

"This is A.H. Thornton from Andover Data Systems; you said to call if I had any questions."

"Oh yeah, Hamo. Still too busy to go out with me?" asked Mark. God, he was not going to give up.

"Tell me about Millennium Construction," I ignored the question hoping he wouldn't repeat it.

"Hold it a second, need to access the corporate database. Fortunately, you caught me at my computer."

"How's my 401K?" I asked to fill the dead air with a safe topic.

"Good, didn't you get a monthly statement?" asked Mark.

"You lost six percent of my money."

"Market's been tough lately. Oh here it is. If you're looking to buy stock, forget it. It's a private company," said Mark.

"I know that. They seemed to have grown phenomenally over the last few years. Is there any research explaining how they did it?"

"It says here the company is uncommunicative about itself. They've refused requests for interviews. The only thing they announce is their new contracts, and they get a lot of them. Have you tried their Web site?"

"Yes, it's pretty basic."

"You haven't heard anything about their going public, have you?" asked Mark. "That would be very interesting to my boss."

A quick lie, "No, nothing like that. A friend of mine applied for a job there. She asked me to check on the company. I got curious when I saw how fast they've grown."

"I've got a graph here of their revenue. They took off like a rocket six years ago, bought out their competitors," said Mark.

"Where'd they get the capital?"

"Possibly from private resources, no large loans or bond sales were executed," said Mark.

"Isn't that unusual?"

"Not really. There's lots of capital floating around—oil sheiks, dotcom billionaires," said Mark.

"Can you e-mail what you've got to my work address?"

"Consider it done. How about dinner and a movie?"

"I'm a vegan," I said. Being a vegan discourages the hell out of most men. They figure under no circumstances will you put meat in your mouth.

"No problem, I know some places with terrific vegan dishes. Have you been to Regine's Kitchen?"

"No, Mark, haven't been there. Look, I'm just too committed to my career for a relationship. You seem like a great guy, and you deserve time and attention. Unfortunately, at this point in my life, I can't offer those things." That was easy letdown speech Version 2.0.

"Look if you're already involved with someone, I'll stop asking," said Mark.

"No, I'm not involved, but I have my mother and sister, plus a job to look after."

"All right but I'm going to ask again."

"Thanks for the info, bye," I said and hung up.

I don't date by choice. I get asked out ten times a weekend at the clubs. Those are the last men on earth I would want to go out with. Ninety-nine percent are married. The other one percent only want free sex.

Having a normal boyfriend would mean giving up dancing, and my college loans wouldn't be paid till the end of the century. I figure no one's life is perfect, and mine's imperfection is the lack of a man. I can live with it.

Next, I looked at the Careers page on Millennium's site, to see if my job was posted. It wasn't. Most of the jobs were overseas engineering and construction. Millennium's claim to be a global concern wasn't an exaggeration. The Projects page was organized by the five continents and then by country.

Much of the work was concentrated in the Middle East. Recently, the company had won a multi-billion-dollar contract to build an oil pipeline through Iraq to Turkey. Since "Middle East" and "terrorism" are words that go together, I could see why the FBI might suspect that terrorists had targeted an American construction company. But to do what—sabotage the recipe for concrete so everything would fall apart in five years?

I searched Barron's and the Wall Street Journal archives for scandals involving the company. Shockingly, there was nothing. It was hard to believe no one had ever charged Millennium with paying bribes, especially since it operated in parts of the world where bribes are the norm. They'd even rebuilt bridges and overpasses for the New Jersey Turnpike Authority.

I ran the names of executives and the Board of Directors through searches and came up clean. There were two Arab names on the Board. One was a Kuwaiti billionaire, and the other an Egyptian businessman. A Web search revealed that, other than being cursed with enormous wealth, they were scandal free.

Benjamin Junior and Marshall, the two sons, now ran the company. The CEO was properly known as Marshall E. Sheffield, Harvard MBA with an Engineering Degree from Stanford. That was impressive. Benjamin Junior was the Chief Financial Officer or CFO. His education was less impressive. He'd earned an undergraduate degree in Accounting at a state university.

I took a look at the brothers' photos on the Web site. Marshall looked the part of a CEO: tall, distinguished, and well groomed. Benjamin was shorter and on the heavy side. I searched for Marshall Sheffield in the *Boston Globe*. There were a number of hits, so I sorted them by date, oldest first.

There were the usual business stories, interspersed with an occasional society article. Marshall and his wife, Chelsea, had served on the board of several local charities. Pictures of Chelsea, a tall blonde who looked something like me, blessed the *Globe*'s society page.

I read aloud a four-year-old headline. "Tragedy Strikes Millennium CEO." Chelsea was driving home after a board meeting of the Boston Ballet. She got a flat tire and pulled onto the shoulder. A semi-trailer struck her, killing her instantly. The driver admitted to falling asleep. His name was Ebrahim Sayaid, a Pakistani citizen with a green card that turned out to be a fake.

Ebrahim told the EMTs he couldn't move his arms and legs, so they strapped him to a board and took him to Mass General. Ebrahim vanished from the MRI Lab and was never seen again. There was an outstanding warrant for his arrest for vehicular homicide.

The *Globe* archive had pictures of Marshall standing at the gravesite holding the hands of his son and daughter, Justin and Judith. Both children had their mother's blonde hair. Justin looked kindergarten age and Judith seven or eight.

The next article was a wedding announcement. A year later, Marshall Sheffield married Soraya Habib Al-Kuuzaai. The wedding took place in Dubai, one of those Arab countries none of us would recognize if it weren't floating on a pool of oil. Her father was the Kuwaiti billionaire on Millennium's Board of Directors. There were several pictures of Soraya, and to call her beautiful was an understatement.

She graduated from Smith College. I had applied there and was rejected. Soraya did graduate work at Harvard and held an advanced degree in International Relations. I went to Smith's Web site because it had information on alums, especially rich and successful ones.

Soraya was a woman of no small accomplishments. She spoke six languages and had written a book urging the Muslim world to adopt Western attitudes toward women. She was the director of an organization whose mission was to promote human rights for Muslim women. She served on the board of several charities I vaguely recognized.

She's beautiful, rich, has a wealthy and powerful husband, and is ridiculously overeducated. I decided I hated her. I did a search on just Soraya, and there she was, holding the hand of a frail, bald child, boarding a private jet. She was taking a cancer victim to Disney World. I called myself a jealous bitch for hating New England's Mother Theresa.

Still, I thought it strange. Four years ago, Chelsea Sheffield meets her untimely end at the hands of a Pakistani truck driver.

Marshall Sheffield remarries in short order a Kuwaiti. Her incredibly rich father is on Millennium's Board of Directors. A sleepy little New England construction company successfully reinvents itself as an international juggernaut. Some things are too good to be true.

Chapter 9

Millennium corporate had leased a renovated mill, a relic from when Lowell, Massachusetts was the textile-manufacturing center of the United States. That had been before the turn of the nineteenth century. After that, the textile industry moved to the Carolinas. These days it's in Bangladesh.

The huge factory complex had stood abandoned for decades, but the buildings were too expensive to tear down and too well built to fall down. Outside, the building looked dark and ominous, but inside, it was modern and airy.

"Given your late start on the project, we've assigned you to Data Transformation," said Max Elkins, leaning forward to get a better look at my body. Max really meant that Data Transformation was the place I could do the least harm. It was ten thirty and I had been in HR for the past two and a half hours filling out forms. I had gotten an ID badge and watched a boring video welcoming me to the Millennium family.

"I've had experience with Data Transformation," I said, feigning the enthusiasm of a slut given a token job for rendering bedroom services.

"Millennium has acquired over thirty companies. To date, we allowed them to continue operating under their pre-acquisition systems. With MillProMan, that's all over.

Everyone will be integrated, their standards brought up to ours." Max was waxing Napoleonic. "Is your passport up to date?"

"Yes." I'd taken Mom and Tommie to Aruba last year.

"Great, there's international travel involved. You can travel can't you?" meaning Max didn't want to piss off Cock Hound by shipping his piece of ass out of the country."

"Travel is not a problem," I said.

"We like to think of ourselves as a family friendly company, so if you need to take some time off for personal reasons, don't hesitate," Max pressed on.

I resisted the urge to say, "If Cock Hound needs a blowjob at the Lowell Marriott, I won't hesitate." I just said, "That's generous, but I doubt it's necessary."

I had dressed like a person whose sexual availability to an executive got her a job she was in no way qualified to do. I wore a tight, black, knit skirt, cut above the knee; a silk blouse with a bold print, unbuttoned to show some lace; and closed-toe pumps with a four-inch stiletto heel.

Max introduced me to the project team. The manager was a nervous little man with oily skin named Preston McBride. He wasn't thrilled to meet me. Data Transformation had four members, now five. My chain of command was lengthy. I reported to supervisor Doreen Givens, whose boss was Preston, who took orders from Max, who listened to Saul, who pimped for a still unidentified Cock Hound.

Max and Preston introduced me to Doreen and left. Actually, they fled. As we shook hands, Doreen assumed an expression of righteous disapproval. In her view she worked her head off to be where she was, and I got there by giving head.

"Have a seat," she said. "Hamo, that's short for Hamilton?" I had written it on the employment form as my desired moniker.

"Yes, my father wanted a boy."

"Don't they all," said Doreen. There were photos on her desk of her with two teenage girls. I did not see a man in any of them. I was dealing with the most dangerous person on the planet, a single mom with two teenage daughters. I had to win her over, or she would make my life the same, a living hell.

"Mine stuck me and my sister with boy's names and then disappeared, leaving our mother to raise us." Actually, we were in college when dad left, but it didn't hurt to leave out some details.

"Well, I see you got a good education," Doreen said, softening a bit.

"And I need to make it work for me," I replied.

"Well, I wish I had more time to train you, but you're going to have to learn on your own. We're under pressure to get MillProMan installed on schedule," said Doreen.

"Just point me in the right direction, and I'll ask questions when necessary."

That seemed to work for Doreen. She took me to an empty cubicle and told me it was mine. She showed me how to log onto their systems with a temporary password, so that I could create my own.

"This is the specification manual for the data transforms," she said and handed me two thick notebooks. "The standards are in the first section. If you see a problem or don't understand something, come to me. Your assignment is in volume two, section six. That section covers the system they use at G&E."

"G&E?" I asked.

"Grunewald and Ellison, our West African sub—we acquired it two years ago. Ever been to Nairobi?" asked Doreen.

"No."

"Better get your shots up to date. You're going in two weeks. Read the material. I'll be back later to get you started," she said and walked away.

I thumbed through volume one, noting the sections before mine were for subsidiaries in the US, Canada, and Europe. Section 5 was in Rome. I joined one section too late.

My eight by eight cubicle was beige and had the same uncomfortable modular furniture as the ones at ADS. The only way I was going to keep Doreen off my back was to impress her with hard work. Luckily, I had worked with DataScript before. I launched the editor and got busy. I figured, before the assignment was over, I'd be dreaming in DataScript.

Data Transformation is the process of converting information from old databases to new ones. It's a simple concept but difficult and tedious work. My first task was to convert the contract master file. I immediately hit a problem with the customer address information.

MillProMan had a standard set of country codes, but the G&E system allowed you to enter the country name any way you could spell it. Over the years, creative ways to spell "Zimbabwe" had crept into the data. I had to take into account each misspelling and convert them to the correct country code. Stress will have you chewing two Prozacs a day to keep from climbing into a tub of warm water and slitting your wrists. It's a trial and error process. You program the transformation, test it, see what fails, and then modify your script. You repeat this process until the conversion is error free.

Once I had Doreen's trust, she would relax. Then I could search for evidence of terrorist plots. Earl Bowers had given me his latest tools. I had programs that would let me search email and files I was in no way authorized to access.

I tore into the task. Failure meant layoff at ADS. I finished my first script after working through lunch. I was preparing to email my test results to Doreen when my desk phone rang. "Are you the new employee of feminine persuasion?" asked a deep male voice.

"This is A. H. Thornton. I am female, and I did start work today."

"Ben Sheffield here. I try to meet all the new associates, especially the ones who serve under me."

So Ben Sheffield, brother of the CEO, Mr. Chief Financial Officer, was Cock Hound. "Well, that's very nice of you, Mr. Sheffield," I said.

"Ben. I'm just Ben to everyone here. Mr. Sheffield, that's my brother, Marshall."

"All right, Ben it is."

"Now, you walk right out the front door and look for the little blue roadster waiting at the curb. I'm taking you to lunch."

"Can I take a rain check, Ben? It's my first day, and I'm trying to impress my boss," I said.

"No, it's a tradition. I take all new employees out on their first day. Don't you worry about Doreen. Her bark is worse than her bite."

"I really should work."

"Don't make me come in there and get you. I will, you know."

"All right, you're the boss," I said.

"So they tell me, but they lie about many things."

Saul had predicted I would quickly learn the true identity of Cock Hound. Now it was up to me to behave in a fashion that fitted my undercover role. I had to make the rest of the company believe I was sleeping with him. The problem I faced was that he would expect me to put out regardless. I wasn't prepared to screw Ben Sheffield as part of my assignment. At least I didn't think I was. But if it was a question of keeping my day job and health insurance, I might have a tough decision to make.

I emailed my script and test results to Doreen. Then I hurried to the ladies' room to brush my hair and repair my makeup.

Chapter 10

"Just my mom and sister," I said, cutting veal with the side of my fork. I took a sip of pinot grigio. "This is delicious."

"The food's always good here," Ben said. Ben was fiftyish and heavy set, with thick dark brown hair. I was looking at many thousands of dollars worth of hair replacement. He was wearing a tailored, dark gray, pin stripe suit, a white shirt, a designer tie, and oversized gold cuff links that kept banging on the table as we ate. A Rolex kept him on time.

"I can't believe someone as pretty as you don't have a man in her life," he said, fishing for whether I was available.

The Bens of the world are lazy predators, attempting to bag as much game as possible before hunting season is over. They never question the meaning of their actions; they're just taking orders from the brain between their legs.

The moment I stepped out into the bright light of a New England fall day, a car horn sounded. A mid-life crisis blue BMW roadster was parked in the fire lane. "Get in, get in," Ben said as he leaned over to unlatch the passenger door.

Getting into a low-slung car in a skirt as tight and short as mine couldn't be done modestly. I hiked the skirt up past the lace tops of my hose before sliding into the bucket seat. Ben looked at my legs like a hungry barracuda, released the clutch, and laid rubber. I took that as his version of a complement. We revved and zoomed through downtown Lowell to Ristorante de Lucia.

We were seated in a booth at the back. Ben was obviously a regular, and the booth was reserved for him. We didn't order; the waiter just brought food. He immediately started asking about my personal life.

"Only my cat, he's male—at least he used to be," I said.

"I didn't know we had any job openings in IS&T, but I'm thrilled you're with us. We need more attractive, intelligent women at Millennium."

"I am impressed with the company's attitude toward equal opportunity," I said, shoveling bullshit back his way. Ben was a throwback to the seventies, after the sexual revolution and before women's lib, when executives treated female employees like breeding stock. He'd ignored all those silly seminars about sexual harassment. However, I was there to locate a terrorist cell, not determine whether Millennium was in compliance with Title VII of the Civil Rights Act.

"You're so tan. Have you been on vacation?" I asked to change the subject.

"Got back last night from my place in Boca," said Ben.

"Boca?" I know Boca Raton is in Florida, but bimbos aren't supposed to know geography.

"Boca Raton. I have a place on the Inland Waterway. Come by my office, and I'll show you some pictures. Have you ever gone deep sea fishing?"

I'd never fished for anything. "No, is it fun?"

"Hell, yes. My boat's docked there. I fish every day, mostly for pompano and marlin. Marlin's the king of game fish. When a marlin hits the bait, the reel sings. It can take an hour to land a big one." Well, he genuinely loved *something*.

"It sounds exciting," I said. "Do you have trophies mounted on the walls?"

"A few, but these days I catch and release unless the fish is a record breaker," said Ben. "You should come down sometime and I'll take you out on *Ben's Sin III*."

"I don't even know how to bait a hook," I said.

"I don't either. That's what the crew is for. I bet you got a cute little bikini. Of course, you can get an all over tan once we're out of sight of land."

"You mean go naked." I wondered what he'd think if he knew I went naked most weekends. I had a moment's fantasy. It would be nice to be lounging on Ben's yacht with a crew of men in white fetching me drinks. But it would be Ben's yacht, not mine, and he could dump me anytime.

"There's nothing wrong with the human body; a beautiful young woman like you shouldn't be shy."

"Me? Not at all," I said. "Speaking of travel, Doreen mentioned Nairobi. I've never been to Africa."

"You must be working on G&E. That's one of our largest acquisitions. Don't you let old man Grunewald get you alone. Over there, they don't have rules about how to treat women."

"I'll remember to keep him at arm's length. Thank you, Ben. Lunch was wonderful, but I should get back. I don't want to make a bad impression on my first day."

"All right, we've got to keep Doreen happy. But we'll do this again soon," said Ben.

Ben opened the car door for me when we left, but I kept my knees together and swiveled my legs. Limited access increases demand.

"Thanks again, lunch was delicious," I said as we parked into the fire lane in front of Millennium.

"I'm going out of town for a few days, but when I get back, let's go out for dinner." he said taking my hand in his.

"I'd like that," I said giving his a gentle squeeze. My mind signaled that I had possibly mishandled Ben Sheffield. Maybe I should have played harder to get. On the other hand, he might have taken that as a challenge and hung around my cubicle the rest of the day. Who the fuck knows?

Ben sped off as soon as I closed the car door. His workday was over. I hurried in to find Doreen and get her feedback on my programming. She was looking at my script when I tapped on her cubicle.

"How was lunch?" she asked. She looked me over, checking to see if my clothes were rumpled. Maybe I should have left a button undone. Word traveled fast at Millennium. I considered bringing in my spyware, so I could read emails about the new whore. I discarded the idea as premature.

"Excellent. The food was delicious," I replied. "What's the verdict?"

"You did a good job. I made a few minor changes to conform to standards, nothing substantial."

"One down, forty-one scripts to go," I said.

"How is our CFO?" Doreen couldn't resist asking.

"We had a nice talk, mostly about fishing. And he warned me to be wary of Mr. Grunewald's wandering hands." Why had she used the phrase "our CFO"? Was she telling me we shared his body fluids?

"You know, underneath all his bullshit, Ben's a decent type. His father was a real gentleman," Doreen said, wistful. She was establishing her supremacy; she had slept with both generations.

I tried to envision how Doreen looked when she first joined Millennium. A tummy tuck would fix the bulge hanging over her belt. A face-lift would smooth the wrinkles at the corners of her eyes and mouth and give her a firmer jaw line. Collagen would put some fullness back into her lips. Liposuction would slim her butt, hips, and thighs. The saddlebags needed to go. Doreen was only fifty thousand dollars and two weeks of serious pain from being a MILF.

"So, the script looks OK?" She had just said so, but I wanted to move off the topic of Ben Sheffield.

"It's good to go. I gather you've worked with DataScript before," she said.

"I took a course in college and liked it. They say people do best at things they enjoy," I answered.

"Well, if you finish G&E and the rest of your work is this quality, we'll see if your next assignment can be somewhere more pleasant than Nairobi," said Doreen.

When I got back to my cubicle, I attacked the specifications with a vengeance. I finished six more transformations by six p.m., an hour after quitting time. On the commute home, I concluded my first day had been a success. I'd successfully melded into the installation team, impressed my supervisor, and acquired a rich boyfriend. Not a bad day's work.

Chapter 11

My cell phone rang as I pulled into my driveway. It was Bradley Dickerson. "I'm across the street. I need to hear about your first day."

"Damn," I swore to myself, staring at the oversized SUV. I was looking forward to getting out of my uncomfortable clothing. I considered telling him to wait for me to go inside and change, then decided to get it over with.

"Let's make it quick. I've had a long day," I said as I opened the passenger door. The seat was chest level. For the second time that day, I hiked up my skirt, showing more leg than I wanted.

"You've got great legs," said Bradley admiring my thighs.

I decided, as an act of defiance, not to tug my hem down. "Look, I'm tired, I'm cranky, and I need a shower. What do you want?" His comment struck me as inappropriate plus it pissed me off.

"How was day one?" Bradley looked annoyed. He wasn't used to women giving him a hard time.

"Good, I completed six of forty-two data transformations."

"Can we cut the geek talk? What are data transformations?"

"Did it ever occur to you that, just like police officers do not like to be called 'pigs,' computer professionals might not like the title 'geek'?" I said.

"All right, you win. Could you please explain data transformation to this apologetic pig?" Bradley gave me his contrite, altar boy look intended to melt my black female heart.

It worked a little. He was awfully handsome and wearing a gorgeous tie. "The computer department is installing a new system, MillProMan, to replace a hodgepodge of less capable systems used by the subsidiary companies they've acquired in the last five years. The goal is to have one unified system for all company components. As part of the conversion, existing data must be reformatted to work with the new system. Still with me?" I asked.

Bradley nodded, and I continued. "My supervisor is Doreen Givens. She assigned me to the Grunewald & Ellison system, a company headquartered in Nairobi. Today, I completed six of forty two data conversions. I'm going there in two weeks."

"That's a major center for terrorism. The Nairobi airport is on the State Department's watch list. How did you draw Nairobi?" Bradley asked.

"Rome was already taken," I said.

"I have a contact who can watch your back in Nairobi. Anything else?"

"No, I'm working to gain their confidence. It won't be easy, since rumors are flying that one of the executives got me an unbudgeted job for personal reasons."

"You mean as a girlfriend?" asked Bradley.

"Girlfriend, slut, mistress, paramour, bimbo…take your pick."

"Why use that cover? It makes you more obvious."

"It provides a plausible explanation for adding an extraneous person to the payroll. As I said, there was no budget to hire anyone."

"Is it working?" asked Bradley.

"Must be. Ben Sheffield AKA Cock Hound wants to take me marlin fishing."

"I don't get it," said Bradley.

"Marlin is the king of game fish."

"I know that. It's a warm water fish." Bradley had a crease across his forehead and intent eyes. He was still confused.

"Ben is known for adding girl friends to Millennium's payroll. It's an executive perk. He took me to lunch today. We're flying down to Boca Raton and sailing on his boat, the *Ben's Sin III*. He will land a record marlin while I nude sunbathe. After he catches the big one, he'll celebrate by screwing me with the crew watching."

"Are you really going to do it?" asked Bradley, concerned.

"No, but I'm tempted. If I could get him to divorce his wife and marry me without a prenuptial agreement, I could use his millions to pay off my college loans."

"All this in one day," said Bradley.

"Ninety five percent of my time went into writing those six data transformations."

"Of course, this Ben thing could work for us," said Bradley.

"I agree. The CFO's slut du jour has a lot of clout. That's the upside."

"And the downside?" asked Bradley.

"He'll expect to consummate the deal."

"Is that a problem?' asked Bradley.

Did the man think that CSSIP stood for some kind of exotic whore who screwed information out of people? "Hell yes, that's a problem. I'm a forensic computer analyst, not a whore."

"All right, sorry, anything else?" said Bradley back to the contrite look.

"Tell me something that wasn't discussed in our first meeting."

I waited as Bradley thought it over. You could almost hear wheels grinding as he selected the factoid that would do him the most good at the least cost. "Millennium's politically connected. They've got friends in all three branches of the government," he said.

"That's good to know. Someone might rat me out to the terrorists."

"That won't happen," said Bradley.

"Remember, I grew up in Lynnfield. Distrust of the FBI comes natural to me."

"What's Lynnfield got to do with anything?" asked Bradley.

"A Lynnfield FBI agent turned police informants over to the Irish mob. They were executed, died gruesome deaths. I went to school with his son and daughter."

"I remember that. It was a while ago. He was a bad apple. That's bound to happen in a large organization," said Bradley.

"That's very comforting, Agent Dickerson."

"How good are you with the Glock?" asked Bradley, changing the subject. Boston FBI office's collusion with the Winter Hill Gang was a major embarrassment to Hoover's boys.

It occurred to me that I now had both a stalker and a FBI agent looking into my life. That was the last thing I needed. "You've been checking up on me?"

"Gun ownership is a matter of public record."

"But you took the trouble to look," I said.

"I like to know who I'm working with."

"Twice a month I shoot at a gun club. I'm fully qualified with the right hand still working on the left. Find out anything else?" I asked.

"Honors student, athlete, went to a private college, master's degree, professional certification in security," he said.

"Get a look at my GPA?"

"Yes, it was there," said Bradley.

"Better than yours?"

"I don't remember mine," said Bradley.

"Liar."

"Are you always this charming?" asked Bradley.

"Try me when I have PMS." On that note, I left.

Chapter 12

I rushed upstairs, showered, and dressed in my most comfortable running suit. Mom was waiting and primed for me when I walked into her place.

"Who was that nice looking young man, Alex?"

"It's work, Mother. I'm on a new assignment. He wanted to know how my first day went."

My mother was not going to let it go. "So he works for ADS?"

"No, the FBI, but don't tell anybody, including Tommie. It's company confidential."

"You don't trust your own sister." She worried that after she was gone Tommie and I would never see each other again. There was a good chance she was right.

"I trust Tommie. I just don't trust Tommie with Harold. Where is she by the way?"

"She's working late."

That brought up an image of Tommie in her hygienist chair with Harold between her thighs drilling.

"What's for dinner?"

"There's salad in the refrigerator. I've already eaten," said Mom. When I returned, she said, "I thought the FBI man was handsome."

"Handsome is as handsome does," I said wondering if she got his plate number to run a registry check.

"He's not nice?" asked Mom.

"Mother, it's a professional relationship. We exchanged information related to my assignment. Since you didn't see me bend over to suck his cock, just assume it was business and stay out of it."

Mom stood up and left the room. "I'm sorry. I didn't mean to pry."

I've done it now, I thought as I put my plate down and followed her. She was in the kitchen loading the dishwasher. I came up behind her and gave her a hug.

"I'm sorry, Mom, I had a stressful day but that's no excuse to take it out on you. I wore a short skirt to work, big mistake. I spent the day keeping men from checking out my underpants."

"You have beautiful legs, Alex. I remember when you played field hockey. You had the most beautiful legs of any girl on the team. Your father was so proud of you."

"I got them from you. Dad's relatives have legs like tree stumps." I ignored the father pride remark. Normally, he's a taboo subject.

"I worry about you. I don't want to see you old and alone like me," said Mom.

"You're not that old, Mom. I bet men are buying handbags just to look at your legs and check out your underpants." She worked at Macy's. She smiled and I figured I was forgiven.

"Don't push men away because of what your father did. There are good people in this world, and a few of them are men," she said.

"I won't," I said. "As soon as I make my first ten million, I'm going to find an Italian stallion with a killer schlong, sign him to an iron clad pre-nuptial, and screw his brains out. I'll drop two gorgeous bambinos for you to spoil."

"You're incorrigible, Alex," said Mom laughing and hugging me.

Once again, I thought I was home free, only to be jerked back.

"You won't get mad if I ask one more thing," asked Mom? I decided she was an expert at playing people and would have made a fortune as a dancer.

"Of course not." What else was I going to say?

"Is he married?"

"Bradley doesn't wear a ring," I said.

"Bradley, that's a nice name."

Back in my duplex, I poured myself vodka on the rocks and repaired to DMS world headquarters.

Curious, I did a Web search on "Nairobi and computers". The first site on the list was the University of Nairobi. I checked out their Institute of Computer Science. It wasn't MIT or Berkley, more on a par with a junior college in the US.

Next, I scanned through the Bureau of Tourism's official site. There were the usual American hotel chains. I breathed a sigh of relief. When Doreen mentioned Nairobi, I pictured myself sleeping in a hut with a mud floor.

I searched for articles on terrorism. Bradley was right. The Nairobi airport *was* on the State Department's list of places to avoid. I went to the CIA Web site and selected Kenya from its World Fact Book. It reported widespread government corruption, a border war with Sudan, drug trafficking, money laundering, and an AIDS epidemic. I considered calling Allison Kabel and telling her to get someone else, and then discarded the idea. I needed the paycheck and health insurance. Google returned zip on nude dance clubs in Nairobi.

Curiosity satisfied and mindful of my backlog, I began putting the finishing touches on Miranda's site. An hour later, I transferred the site from my test server to the production one. I was now making an additional two hundred a month. Any John with Internet access could view Miranda's naked body, learn that athletes turn her on, purchase a pair of recently worn underpants, and arrange for a "date".

I looked through my Webmaster e-mail for anything from E. Schuyler. I'd been too busy Sunday to check it, so there were two hundred sixty five messages.

My favorites are the ones for Lorna's site. Lorna serves a niche market. Men hire her to treat them like infants. Her homepage has a picture of a large, hairy man wearing nothing but a diaper and baby bonnet, pacifier in his mouth, lying in an oversized crib. Lorna is standing by the crib in a June Cleaver outfit with removable flaps covering her milk-laden breasts. She charges seven hundred fifty a session, and that includes one breast feeding. If the guy messes his diaper, that's another two hundred fifty. Per Lorna she changes more diapers than a new mother with twins.

I was almost scanned through when it appeared, "Greetings, Alexandra Hamilton Thornton."

My dearest Hamo,
Saturday night, when you faced that filthy masturbator, I realized how brave you are. You hesitated a moment, but

quickly overcame your fear. You bested him at his own game. I was right to choose you as my life partner.

I wish you hadn't substituted "LA Woman" for "Riders on the Storm." Please as a favor to me return to our old song.

I tried Ben & Jerry's Mint Chocolate Cookie, but still prefer Chunky Monkey. Have you tried Cherry Garcia? According to their Web site, it's their most popular flavor. I recommend New York Super Fudge Chunk if you're a chocolate lover.

There are so many things I don't know about you, Hamo. You have no idea how much joy I get out of learning even the smallest details of your life. I visited your mother at Macy's. You two bear a strong resemblance. She is such a gracious woman. I look forward to calling her Mom someday.

Tommie's Harold is definitely a problem. What should we do to make the poor girl see he's not the right man for her? As your sister, she deserves better.

It's terrible about Bathsheba. Drugs are the Black Death of our age.

Please indulge me. I have more questions:
1. What is your favorite flower and why?
2. Have you ever been to the opera or the ballet?
3. Do you follow any sport?
Looking forward to hearing from you soon.

Lovingly,
Elizabeth S.

P.S. I see you discovered the significance of my nom de plume. Clever girl, I congratulate you.

"Shit," I whispered while dialing Bathsheba.

"Hello?" said a voice that sounded familiar but wasn't Bathsheba.

"I need to speak to Bathsheba. This is Alexandra," I said.

"It's Carrie, Alex. Have you heard? She OD-ed" Carrie is Bathsheba's life partner. She's very butch; I'm talking Doc Martens, flannel shirt and a buzz haircut. For a tough bull dyke who liked to brag that no man had ever been inside her, she sounded very upset. Her voice kept cracking.

"Yes, is Bathsheba going to be all right?"

"Yes, the EMTs say they got her just in time."

"I didn't think Bathsheba still used drugs." She'd told me months ago, she had given up weed.

"Just a little coke when she's dancing. She says she needs the energy. The police say it was uncut. A customer gave it to her. They're charging her with possession."

"Bathsheba's strong. She'll be okay," I said recalling that Bathsheba had once before gotten drug charges dropped.

"I screwed the right people," was her explanation.

"I pray to God she will be," said Carrie.

"What hospital?"

"Saint Vincent's."

"If there's anything I can do, let me know."

I hung up and ordered flowers from a Web site. Then I went to the kitchen, poured myself another drink, and picked up Syllabus. He was in a giving mood, so he allowed me to carry him back to my computer and stayed in my lap, purring.

Furious, I responded to E. Schuyler.

Motherfucker,
You could have killed Bathsheba. When I find out who you are, I'll put out a contract on your sorry ass. I'll pay extra for them to cut off your cock and balls and feed them to you.

"Don't be stupid." I deleted the message and waited for the vodka to calm my nerves before starting another reply.

My dearest Elizabeth,
A good relationship is based on mutual respect. To gain mine, you have to treat the people around me with care. If you harm them, you are harming me. Harold is not good for Tommie, I agree. That said, Harold is very dear to Tommie, and if anything happened to him, she would be devastated. I'm sure a person of your sensitivity understands this. Your respect for my friends and family will help to forge a bond between us.

Ice cream, I love it, but my dancing career depends on my remaining a size 6. (Did you know I was a size 6?) I visited the Ben & Jerry's Web site. They make Cherry Garcia as a low-fat yogurt. I'll give it a try.

To please you, I'll go back to "Riders on the Storm."

I've always been proud of my mother. She is kind and gentle, and I wish I had more of her good qualities. When I was growing up, she always planted daffodils. When we saw the little green blades in the snow, I knew winter was losing its grip. I love daffodils.

When I was a little, my parents took me every year to the Boston Ballet's production of the Nutcracker. Those were my only trips to the ballet. I have never been to an opera.

I played field hockey and soccer in high school. Sometimes I watch a few minutes of soccer on television. Sorry, I'm not a Red Sox fan, if that's what you were hoping.

In friendship,
Hamo

I read it through twice before I pressed send. If I kept up the bullshit, he would eventually tell me something that could identify him. I created a spreadsheet and entered a list of possible clues. I considered hacking Ben & Jerry's e-mail list. Elizabeth seemed the type to sign up for new product announcements.

I had no idea what to do when I found him. Having him beaten to a pulp was appealing, but if the police got involved then ADS would fire me. If he hurt Mom or Tommie, I wouldn't just have him beaten up; I'd kill the motherfucker.

Chapter 13

I was finishing up my part of G&E conversion when disaster struck. The fact that matters had been going well should have warned me that something bad was about to happen.

Bradley had not reappeared. Mom had asked me twice if I expected to see him again. I told her only if my job required it.

Dancing had been profitable. I made twenty five hundred over the weekend, most of it from one customer. He liked my VIP Room performance so much that he tipped in one hundred dollar bills. I liked his tips so much that my right hand brought about a happy ending.

I was making progress on the E. Schuyler front. We had exchanged three more sets of chatty emails. I added rows of facts to my spreadsheet. If I could get him to reveal enough about himself, I could identify him. Tice could handle him from there.

Bathsheba's overdose was history. According to Carrie, she woke up hungry and horny. She avoided prosecution by having very kinky sex with a member of law enforcement and his wife. A newly minted convert to the war on drugs, she announced she would never touch blow again.

I was seated in my cubicle when an envelope landed on my desk. What's this? I asked looking up at Marshall Sheffield's administrative assistant, Stacia McClain.

"An invitation, attendance is mandatory unless a member of your immediate family has died." Her look and the way she said that made me think she would have been happy if my Mom had just passed away.

My brain went into overdrive trying to concoct an excuse that would convince this fashionable, model-thin, thirty-something woman.

I had never been to a charity gala, and I had no idea how to comport myself at one. It was Thursday, my ninth day at Millennium. The forty-two G&E data transformations were completed. Sunday night, Doreen and I, along with three other members of the installation team, were flying to Nairobi.

"I don't have anything to wear," I lied. I was stalling hoping something more believable would materialize.

"If you don't have appropriate evening wear, then take the afternoon off and buy something," Stacia said, coolly batting the ball back into my court.

"There are two tickets," I said upon opening the envelope.

"You are required to bring someone; otherwise there will be an empty seat," said Stacia. "You must know a man—or even a woman if that's your preference."

After Stacia clicked off in her high heels, I stared at the invitation. "Black tie" was printed at the bottom. I visualized my closet. I had a dress I bought for dancing. I hadn't altered it yet, to allow me to slip out of it easily on stage. I'd bought the dress with the idea of re-creating a burlesque striptease. I'd found a Web site with video clips of a famous stripper named

Sally Rand. Sally ended her performances wearing more than I started in. In exotic dancing, you are always looking for an edge, a way to set yourself apart from the other dancers. It was an expensive evening dress from a clearance rack. It fit me perfectly.

I called Tommie to see if she was available. "Need a favor, sis. You free tonight?"

"No, sorry, I have my final class on sonic cleaning. If I don't go, I won't get certified."

I tried Mom next.

"I always work Thursday night," she said.

"You could call in sick."

"I've used up all my sick days. Besides, you should go with a man. Who goes to a gala with her mother?"

"I don't know any men to ask."

"Bradley would look very handsome in a tuxedo." How could she be so keen on a man she had never met?

"That's a professional relationship," I said.

"So he should take you since this is work related," said Mom who can be terribly quick witted when you least need her to be.

After I hung up, I consider other options. I could hire one of the club security guards to escort me. Showing up with a three-hundred-pound gorilla wasn't a good idea I decided.

I could call Mark, since he was always asking me out. No, he'd leech on, and I'd never get him off. Mother had a point. Bradley had a professional obligation to help me out. It would be business and nothing more.

As soon as he answered, I launched into the invitation. "This is A.H. Thornton. I'm required to attend a Millennium charity function tonight. I need an escort, dressed in tuxedo. Pick me up at my house at six."

"In the past, has this worked for you when you need a date?" asked Bradley.

"This is *not* a date. It's part of my assignment. You said you were my backup. So back me up."

"What's the occasion?"

I said more calmly, "It's a Charity Gala for Learning from History, whatever that is. It's at the Four Seasons."

"Oh, one of those, couldn't you find something more romantic?"

I blew him off. "Undercover assignments are always romantic, if you believe the movies. Have you been to a charity gala before?"

"Yes, cocktails at seven, dinner at eight, boring speeches at nine, dancing from ten to midnight, then home to bed," said Bradley, sounding worldly.

"Good, you know the drill. See you at six o'clock." I hung up, furious at myself for some reason.

At three p.m., I stopped by Doreen's cubicle to tell her I had to leave early for an appointment with the hair stylist. I asked her why the company invited me.

"To fill the table," said Doreen.

"I don't understand," I said.

"Soraya, Marshall's wife, is on the Board of Trustees for Learning from History. Millennium is a corporate sponsor, so the company buys two or three tables at every event," she said.

"I still don't understand."

"Each table seats ten. Each seat costs five hundred dollars. If the company buys three tables, they have thirty seats to fill. They invite employees to occupy the seats."

"That's how charity works?" I asked.

"Yes, the charity gets the proceeds, after cost—about two-thirds."

"Three tables equal fifteen thousand dollars, and the charity gets ten thousand. Why not simply write a check for fifteen thousand?"

"Then no one would get to play dress up, wear their jewels and furs, and appear in the society section of the newspaper."

"You seem to know a lot about this," I said.

"Years ago, I helped plan those events for Sheffield Construction. Of course, the company was much smaller then."

"Why me? You deserve it more than I do."

She shrugged. "You're young and attractive. Ben and Marshall want to impress other companies with beautiful people doing beautiful work."

"Thanks for the compliment, but it's so fucking superficial of them. This is a construction company, not a modeling agency."

"It's run by men," she said simply. We were starting to get along. Then she tilted her head. "There could be one other reason. You said Stacia invited you?"

"Yes, she practically threatened me with violence if I didn't come."

"Hmmm, perhaps, Marshall is playing a joke on his brother. But go, enjoy yourself. It's their expense."

Chapter 14

"They're a 36D. They're constructed of an outer layer of flesh with a core of sterile saline solution encased in a silicone pouch. The surgeon moved my areola higher, for reasons of symmetry and aesthetics. I wanted perky tits. Now that we have that out of the way, please look me in the eye when you speak to me," I said using my arms to lift my boobs in his direction.

I was trying to make a point but when I looked down I realized to my embarrassment that I'd caused a nipple slip. Putting my boob back in the dress did not improve my attitude. In the darkness I wasn't sure what Bradley saw.

Bradley had shown up precisely on time in a brand new sedan. I was pleased he wasn't driving the tank. Mom was right. He did look very handsome in a tuxedo. But his eyes had been laser focused on my chest since I stepped into his car.

The moment I tried on the dress, I knew it was perfect. You can try on a thousand dresses; most look awful, some are okay, and once in a blue moon you find an absolute stunner. You look in the mirror and say, "Damn girl, you look good." My reward was a man who mumbled something about my looking nice then fixed his eyes on my breasts like they had him in a trance. When I'm dancing that's acceptable because it increases revenue but I wasn't trying to sell Bradley anything.

I hoped the dress wasn't too daring for the gala. I was showing serious skin. According to the magazines at my hair stylists, bare was in. The neckline plunged, and I had a deep canyon for it to plunge into. It was backless and slit almost to the hip on one side. Underwear was limited to a pair of sheer panty hose. The shade of blue was perfect for my hair and complexion and the jewelry worked. Bradley's lack of appreciation for the total package annoyed the hell out of me.

"I thought they were real. They look real," said Bradley, trying to confirm that he had seen what he thought he had.

"Do you want to see the scar where the surgeon made the incision, or are you willing to take my word for it?"

"I prefer to see the scar," Bradley said with a grin.

"Not in my fucking lifetime," I said, wondering if it was a federal crime to punch an agent.

"Are you always so nasty?" he asked, impressed.

"Are you always so shameless?" I snapped.

He was smiling. Bastard.

I turned my head to look out the window and decided to ignore him for the remainder of the evening. Why had I listened to my mother? Asking him was a mistake. What I needed was a tuxedo clad cyborg. I could charge him up for occasions like this, and then stuff him back in the closet when they were over.

"I've alerted our embassy in Nairobi of your trip. Here's a global cell phone," he said.

I felt something touch my shoulder and reached up for the thing, a slick little Motorola. I took it as a peace offering. "Thank you." I deigned to look at him.

"The first number in the Speed Dial is your contact at the American Embassy. The second number is mine," said Bradley. "It's a satellite phone. You can call anywhere in the world."

"I won't get voice mail or be put on hold?" I asked.

"No, I guarantee Winston will answer. He'll be nearby in case of trouble. I briefed him on your mission and faxed him a copy of your itinerary. Also, here's a Bureau pamphlet on how to be less of a target for international terrorists. It's mainly common sense. Lastly, there's a confidential report on places and people to avoid in Nairobi." He handed me a manila envelope.

"Thanks, I've never been to Africa. Actually I've never been anywhere," I said.

"Didn't spend your college summers in Paris or London?"

"I worked summers in order to afford college," I said.

"You went to good schools. I checked," he said.

"You know all about me and I know nothing about you. I am going to do a background search on you, to make us even. Is this your car?" I asked. His Audi was new enough to still have that new car smell.

"Yes, I've only had it since the first of the month. What do you hope to learn?"

"Education, family history, ex-wives, what sports you played, financial status, medical history, etc, I'll hack into the bureau's computer and look at your fitness reports."

"There are no ex-wives. And it's a felony to hack the FBI," said Bradley.

"It's suspicious that a lowly FBI agent drives such expensive cars. Where's your Crown Victoria?"

"The Crown Vic belongs to the government," said Bradley. "I thought you'd be more comfortable in this."

"It's very nice and comfortable. Tell me why you're qualified to be the agent in charge of counterterrorism."

"Just for the Boston office but that does cover all of New England except for Connecticut. The New York office handles that," he said mildly.

"What did you study in college?"

"Accounting, and I have a law degree," said Bradley.

"Just what I need in case terrorists try to kill me: a fucking lawyer."

"I completed counter terrorism training at Quantico."

"Any practical experience?"

"Yemen, Jordan, UAE, Indonesia…I investigated attacks, interrogated suspects, caught some bad guys," said Bradley.

"And you speak fluent Arabic and know the Quran backwards and forwards?" I asked.

Bradley released a torrent of what I suppose was Arabic.

"And that translates to?" I was no longer teasing.

"Men are the protectors and maintainers of women, because Allah has given the one more strength than the other, and because they support them from their means. Therefore, righteous women are devoutly obedient and guard in the husband's absence what Allah would have them guard," said Bradley.

"I'm impressed," I said and I was, although his quote was misogynistic as all hell.

"I'm also a man of independent means, and I like cars," said Bradley as we pulled up in front of the Four Seasons. He sounded a little put out. We had a knack for pushing each other's buttons.

We gave the car to a valet, checked our coats, had our picture taken, and found our assigned table in a glittering ballroom.

I recognized Soraya from her Web images. She was on the dais leaning over an older woman discussing something, perhaps last minute changes to the agenda. In spite of the glasses perched on the end of her nose, she was beautiful, more beautiful than her pictures online.

Millennium's three tables clustered together near the front. Saul Ebert and his wife were at the next table. While Bradley was getting our drinks, I went to say hello to Saul and meet the missus. She said she absolutely loved my dress. Saul introduced me to the others who seemed eager to meet the strumpet Cock Hound had added to the payroll.

When I returned, Bradley handed me a glass of wine then whispered in my ear, "We have a problem. There's someone at table twenty-two who knows I work for the Bureau."

Bradley's cover story was that he was an accountant who had recently set up his own practice. When I looked toward table twenty two I saw a brunette waving. She immediately stood up and began walking in our direction.

"Let's meet her halfway," I said, grabbing Bradley's hand. Moments later, I was shaking hands with Natalie. I could tell she was an ex girl friend.

"Did Bradley tell you we were friends at Yale?" asked Natalie.

I didn't know Bradley went to Yale." I tried not to look impressed. I had applied to two Ivy League schools, Dartmouth and Brown, and been rejected.

"No, he didn't mention it. But he can be so secretive sometimes."

Natalie was pretty in an aristocratic way. I could picture her foxhunting across daddy's estate.

"Hamo? I just adore your name," said Natalie.

"Short for Hamilton."

"What do you do, Hamo, when you're not keeping Bradley company?"

"Computer programmer," I said, resisting the urge to add, "When we're not fucking like rabbits."

"For the FBI?" asked Natalie.

She was certainly curious. I wondered if she had a tens card on her, to take my prints. I said, "No, Millennium Construction."

"Then you must know Soraya. I tell you, the woman is a saint." Natalie gushed.

"No, I haven't met her yet. I only started at Millennium two weeks ago."

"Well, she is a wonderful person, so generous and giving. She and I serve together on the board of the foundation, and it's a privilege to work with someone so dedicated to the less fortunate."

"I've heard wonderful things about her." I tried to sound enthused.

"Are you involved in any of our good work projects?" asked Natalie.

"No, this is all new to me." The only philanthropy that interested me was the A.H. Thornton Foundation for the Repayment of College Loans.

"Well, let me give you my card. Call me if you're interested." She pulled a card out of her purse. "It's hard work, but very rewarding, and you get to meet attractive young men—like Bradley."

"Well, if you can promise me a steady stream of Bradleys, I'll definitely call." That ended our conversation. Bradley had to promise Natalie a dance.

"She's still got a thing for you," I told Bradley as we approached the buffet.

"I suppose." Bradley was thoughtful.

"What was the problem? She's pretty, rich, went to the right school. It must be those B cups," I said.

Bradley laughed aloud and shook his head.

"So you're a Yale man, Skull & Bones I presume?"

"If I were, it would be a very deep secret," he said.

"I'll ask Natalie."

"She doesn't know," he said.

"I'll hack their computer and find out," I said.

"I'm not sure Skull & Bones have one." he said. Bradley wandered off to another section of the buffet.

I was placing shrimp on my plate when I felt a hand on my shoulder. "Has anyone told you, you're the most beautiful girl here?" asked Ben Sheffield.

"I think that title belongs to your brother's wife," I said.

"Soraya's all right, but you surpass her in every category. My heart almost stopped when I saw you in that dress. I'm going to cancel my travel and stay in the office, just so I can look at you," said Ben.

"And who'll catch all those marlin?"

"The ocean can keep them for now," he said. "Who's your date, one of your admirers?"

"No, Bradley's just a friend from my old job. He's here as a favor. I only got the invitation at noon."

"My brother's idea of a joke, Marshall has an unusual sense of humor."

Bradley arrived so I introduced him to Ben who kept the complements coming.

"You do realize you're with the most beautiful women here?" Ben asked Bradley?

"I'm lucky she asked me to accompany her," said Bradley.

"Guess I better get back, Nice meeting you, Bradley," said Ben before rejoining his table.

Bradley and I had barely sat when Stacia arrived with Soraya. They were an odd couple. Stacia was a tall blonde and Soraya a petite brunette.

"You said you didn't have anything to wear," said Stacia after I introduced Bradley. "Soraya and I think you have the most beautiful dress at the gala."

"I'd forgotten I had this," I said.

"Beautiful, is it Carolina Herrera?" asked Soraya, unaware that couture is not sold at the mall where I shop.

"I don't know. It's just something I grabbed it off the clearance rack."

Aren't we women supposed to foster the illusion that spending time on our appearance is the least of our concerns?

"We should go shopping together, never pay retail is my mantra," said Soraya.

"Marshall tells me you're a computer programmer," said Soraya.

"And according to her supervisor, a very good one," added Stacia.

After dinner, Soraya introduced a local television personality as the MC. There followed some tired jokes and a slide show depicting the good works resulting from our generous donations. It was after ten when Soraya finished reading a seemingly endless list of people who worked to make tonight's gala a success. She thanked them all profusely, and then, finally, announced it was time to dance.

"Let's dance," said Bradley, pulling me to my feet.

We danced three fast songs. Then the band switched to a slow, sultry something, and Bradley gathered me in his arms.

"I didn't think programmers could dance," said Bradley. "You're terrific."

"You're guilty of stereotyping," I said. What would he think if he saw me sliding naked down a brass pole?

Later, as we were catching our breath, Natalie showed up to claim her dance. It was a slow song. I quickly diagnosed Natalie's problem with Bradley. She wasn't a good dancer, and she was a non-stop talker. I was watching them, when someone beside me cleared his throat.

"Marshall Sheffield," said Marshall, extending his hand. He had the unsteady look of too much alcohol.

"Hamo Thornton, I work in IS&T," I said.

"I know. May I have this dance?" said Marshall.

You don't turn down the CEO, so I said yes.

"Ben's taste is improving," said Marshall, once we were dancing to something Sinatra.

"Taste in what?" I knew what he meant, and didn't like it one bit. I was risking life and limb at his company while working my ass off.

"You're a definite improvement over his last special hire," said Marshall.

"I still don't understand. Maybe you better explain it to me," I said, getting angry.

"Look, everyone knows why Ben gave you a job," he said.

"For your edification I am not fucking your brother." I spoke loud enough for the couples dancing near us to hear. Marshall glanced around. He was drunk, but not too drunk to be embarrassed.

"Not so loud," he whispered.

I was losing control; something had started and was gaining momentum. Maybe it was the smug look on his face. Wiping it off became my mission. "And you want sloppy seconds," I said, nearly at the same volume.

"Please keep it down," said Marshall.

"Tomorrow, ask my supervisor, Doreen Givens. You'll find that Millennium is getting an honest day's work out of me," I said quietly.

"I apologize. I was misinformed," said Marshall, looking genuinely contrite.

"Apology accepted. And I apologize for my outburst. This is all new to me and I'm not handling it well. Let's put it down to office gossip and forget it ever happened. Your brother has been nice to me. I know what he wants. But I'm not sleeping with him."

"Understood, I'm very sorry. That was rude and unforgivable," Marshall said as the song ended.

For the sake of appearances, I smiled and said thank you.

Bradley was still dancing with Natalie. My conversation with Marshall left me deflated. Being considered a worthless whore is not easy to endure. I needed a quiet moment to recoup, so I headed to the ladies' room.

There was a line stretching out into the hall. Good thing I didn't actually need to go. I saw a dark alcove crowded with stacks of spare chairs. I stepped into the back, leaned against the wall, and began giving myself a lecture.

I'd just done something stupid. I should have rubbed my boobs on Marshall, and played dumb. I was fucking up my cover story, and Allison Kabel wouldn't like that one damn bit. What had gotten into me? Somehow, Marshall's easy and plausible assumption that I was his brother's whore hit a nerve. Maybe I hadn't done any real harm. Millennium's employees would continue to see me as a bimbo, even if I took out a full-page ad denying it.

I took a deep breath and squared my shoulders, preparing to exit my sanctuary. As I was about to take a step, someone ducked into the alcove, blocking me.

I felt a little foolish hiding there. I saw the illuminated face of a cell phone flipped open. I stepped further back into the shadows and waited.

"I'm almost done here," said Soraya. I recognized her voice. I had been listening to her all evening. In spite of Smith, she still had a slight accent.

"It's taken care of. I've arranged everything."

Listening to half of a conversation was frustrating.

"She'll be out of the picture for a while, nothing too serious... Understood, just a few love taps... They probably will... Too bad you can't be there. You'd enjoy watching... See you Sunday at the Savoy. I've reserved a suite for us. I have to go." Soraya flipped the phone shut.

I don't know whether she heard me breathing or it was a sixth sense. She turned toward me and stared into the darkness. I held my breath. After a few seconds, she gave up and left. I counted to one hundred, like a child's game of hide and seek, then peered out. I saw her back as she returned to the ballroom. I congratulated myself on my patience. She had waited outside, to see if anyone came out. That was odd for an innocent phone call.

The crowd for the Ladies Room had dwindled. I went into a stall, took out pen and paper, and wrote down Soraya's side of the conversation. After repairing my makeup, I rejoined Bradley. Natalie reluctantly said her good-byes.

"It looks like you missed out on a sure thing. I could get a cab." I said.

"My father taught me to always leave with the girl I brought," said Bradley.

It was getting late, and the band was almost finished, so we left.

"Thank you for being my escort," I said when we arrived back at my place. Then I pulled him into my arms for a kiss that surprised him. Recovering quickly, he returned it.

Bradley was an excellent kisser. We made out. I let him satisfy his curiosity whether breast implants feel and taste natural. My hand did some investigating, too. He had a large package and it was fully erect. However, I put off showing my appreciation the usual way noting movement in my mom's living room window.

"I should go," I said

"Yeah, it's late. Let's go to dinner when you return. I'll need to hear about your trip," said Bradley.

"As long as it's only dinner—we need to maintain a professional relationship," I said before kissing him again. I scraped together enough self-control to extricate myself from his embrace, return my breasts to their hiding place, and say goodnight.

Mother insisted on hearing about my evening. It was one o'clock before I climbed in bed. However, I couldn't sleep for wondering about what I'd overheard.

I got up and performed a Web search on the Savoy Hotel. It was a five-star establishment in London catering to the super rich. Soraya may be a living saint on the charity circuit, but she was also an adulteress arranging a fuck. I felt better about not liking her.

Chapter 15

"This is living," said Doreen, taking a sip of her appletini. "I wonder if Tariq would like to induct me into the mile high club." Doreen was referring to the darkly handsome—and much younger—cabin attendant. He had mentioned that he was born in Amman, Jordan. Given my concerns about terrorists, I would have been happier if Tariq were named Mike and from South Boston.

We had just taken off from a small airport serving corporate jets. Getting to fly on a private plane was novel. The cabin was roomy and comfortable, totally unlike the sardine can commercial airliners I had flown.

Preston, the team leader; Dave, the systems administrator; and Sanjay, the database administrator, were nearby playing computer games.

"Normally, we nerds fly coach, but MillProMan is a high profile project. They're letting us taste the executive life," said Doreen.

The way her eyes followed Tariq's ass each time he walked past, I wondered if the executive life included getting laid. I couldn't blame her. Between job and family, there couldn't be much sex in her life that didn't require batteries.

Doreen and I would be sitting together for the next sixteen hours; it was a good opportunity to learn about Millennium. There was no reason to rush into it and be obvious, so I began on a personal level. "How are your girls getting along?"

"Mandy, she's my sixteen-year-old, is the easy one. Kim, she's fifteen, doesn't get along with the world."

"I didn't get along with my father. We fought all the time. Still, I was his favorite," I said.

"Mothers are supposed to love their children equally, but I'm partial to Kim, in spite of everything."

"My sister, Tommie, was the good child. She's closer to our mother."

Doreen looked sad as she spoke. "Kim refers to me as 'pathetic loser' or 'the PL.' There's no man in my life. I am forty-eight years old, overweight, and don't make enough money to buy her everything she wants."

I made a pledge to never again say anything that would make my mother sad. "It's just a stage she's going through. I was hard on my mother when dad left. I blamed her. Kim will grow out of it."

"Kim's latest grudge match with me is over dating. I told the girls they couldn't date until they were sixteen; so Mandy's allowed to date and has a boyfriend. He's very polite and treats her like she was made of glass."

"And Kim does not want to wait?" I asked.

"Behind my back, she's been seeing a boy named Quince. His parents work, so Kim has been going to his house after school. His mother called me two weeks ago, screaming at me. She said to keep my slut daughter away from her son."

"What happened?"

"The Mother found the two of them in bed. She gave me a very graphic description of what they were doing."

"That must have been embarrassing," I said.

"It embarrassed the hell out of me, but Kim laughed it off. She said all the girls in her class are having sex. She also informed me that she has been giving blow jobs since the eighth grade, and was better at it than I would ever be."

"What did you do?"

"I got her a prescription for birth control. I'm too young to be a grandmother," said Doreen.

"My dad never allowed me to date. He was very strict, watched us like a hawk. We had to account for every minute we were away from him. Not that it mattered, in my case. Nobody ever showed interest."

"You're kidding, with the way you look," said Doreen.

"My awkward stage lasted longer than most. I didn't learn how to handle men till after Dad left and I went to college," I said.

"I married right out of college—a church wedding, bridesmaids, and a reception for two hundred. It practically bankrupted my dad. Hank and I lasted five stormy years. We didn't work from day one."

"Men are such bastards," I said. I wondered if it was true or if women expect too much. I was also starting to feel the effect of my drink.

"They're only good for one thing, and after forty, most of them need a little blue pill to do that right."

We sipped our drinks and were quiet. I was considering how to steer the conversation to Millennium when Doreen provided the opportunity.

"I heard you outclassed everyone at the gala, including Soraya. Even your date was movie star handsome."

"Soraya is very beautiful. So I doubt that. Bradley is just a friend, but he is very good looking."

"Is it true, what you told Marshall?"

"What did you hear?" I tried to sound disinterested, but alarms were sounding.

"You had an argument, something about sloppy seconds," said Doreen, like laying a trump card on the table.

It was time to lie. "That's absurd. I'd never say a thing like that to Marshall. He's the CEO. And it wasn't an argument, just a misunderstanding about my work ethic. He apologized, and so did I. We parted on friendly terms."

"Speaking of work ethic, yours has surprised me. Honestly, when you were hired, I was furious. I had been asking for more help for months and been refused for budgetary reasons. Then all of a sudden out of the blue without any input from me, you show up."

"It must have pissed you off. I would have been if I were you," I said.

"At first, I planned to assign you a difficult task and provide no help. I figured you would become frustrated and quit, proving my point. When you promptly submitted your first working DataScript and then left for lunch with Ben Sheffield, I was flummoxed."

"The whore can program. Who would have thought it?"

"You're not what you seem, Hamo," said Doreen.

I ignored her remark. Doreen was shrewd and something about me didn't add up in her mind.

I composed an ambiguous answer. "Just because Ben gave me a job doesn't mean we're sleeping together," I said. "Nor if I were banging him, does it mean that I can't program."

"In the past, Ben has saddled the department with some real losers," said Doreen.

"Someone at the gala told me that Soraya was Marshall's second wife. His first was killed in a car accident. Everyone was surprised he married so soon," I said attempting to move beyond the current topic of discussion. It worked.

"Chelsea Sheffield was a woman of character. Everyone liked her. We all took it hard when she was killed. Marshall almost went crazy with grief. He lost it for a while."

"Soraya had a hard act to follow," I said

"Did you meet her?" asked Doreen.

"Briefly, everyone says she's very nice, that she spends all her time raising money for charity," I said.

"That's not what everyone says."

"You have a different opinion," I said.

"Let's just say that Soraya has more control over her husband than most wives," said Doreen.

"I'm not sure what you mean,"

"Have you met Stacia McCain, his Administrative Assistant?" she asked.

"Yes, I've met her kind before. I work for the CEO, so everyone's my bitch." I did my best Stacia impersonation.

"Before Stacia arrived, there was Sue. Sue was Marshall's girl Friday for a decade. She was indispensable to Marshall.

After he married Soraya, Sue was terminated, and Stacia replaced her. Soraya made it happen," said Doreen.

"Maybe they were getting it on, and Soraya found out."

"Sue Wilkins is one of my best friends. We grew up together. She wasn't screwing Marshall."

"Maybe it's her best kept secret," I said.

"Sue is a lesbian who's been in a committed relationship for the past ten years. She's very proud of the fact that no man has ever been inside her."

"What Sue's explanation of what happened?" I asked.

"Sue says Soraya replaced her with Stacia because Soraya wanted someone who reported to her. Firing Sue wasn't Marshall's idea. He gave her six months' severance and found her another job."

"That does seem strange. It implies that Soraya is the real CEO of Millennium. Marshall doesn't strike me as the type to go along with that," I said.

"According to what I hear, Marshall is not happy. He works seven days a week so he doesn't have to be with Soraya," said Doreen.

"What could possibly be the connection between Soraya and Stacia?"

"Preston saw Stacia getting out of Soraya's limo two blocks from the office. It was seven o'clock in the morning. They were down a side street, and the two exchanged a kiss that, in his opinion, went way beyond friendly."

"Marshall replaces Sue with another lesbian who is having lesbian sex with his wife. Sounds very Sodom and Gomorrah," was my only comment as we finished our drink and decided to call it a night.

Before I dropped off, I added an Internet search on Stacia McCain to my To Do List.

Sometime during the night, I sensed movement near me. It was Doreen returning to her seat. Tariq was right behind her. He helped her into her seat and covered her up. He even leaned down and gave her a kiss. Kim was more like her mother than she realized.

Chapter 16

"How safe is Nairobi?" I asked Tom Weatherby, G&E head of security, as we drove out through the airport gate.

Tom was a Brit, at least his accent was. He met us on the tarmac as soon as our plane stopped. He was armed with an assault rifle and the three natives with him carried shotguns. The guns and the fact that Tom smelled of gin was not reassuring.

"Safe enough, if you don't do anything foolish," he said.

"Define 'foolish.' Driving into town from the airport?"

"You're safe here, Love, bulletproof glass and titanium side armor," said Tom, tapping the window of the Land Rover.

"And in the hotel?" I asked.

"It's in a safe part of the city, but under no circumstances leave the hotel without one of my bunch."

"I don't suppose you have a spare gun to loan me?" I asked.

"Hear that, Mebeki, our lady visitor plans to shoot someone," Tom said to the Kenyan driving. He replied in his own language, but I understood his laugh.

"Only if it's necessary," I said. "I'm trained in the safe handling of firearms."

"H&K or Glock?" Tom reached into a door panel.

"Glock," I said, surprised I had a choice.

I checked the safety before slipping it into my purse. Doreen and the others were watching me, wide eyed. I didn't care. I felt much safer with a gun.

"Anybody else require armaments?" asked Tom.

"No, guns scare me to death," said Doreen.

"We'll delegate Hamo to do all the killing," Preston said nervously.

By the time we got to our rooms; it was close to ten. The Somerset Essex was an elegant old hotel that had undergone recent renovations. There were armed guards in the lobby. A sign at the reception desk announced that rooms with an Internet connection were available.

I was anxious to check on DMS. I had just established a mutual support arrangement with a college classmate. Solomon was attempting to build a hardcore porn Web empire from his parents' basement. We'd agreed if one of us had to go out of town, the other would play substitute Web Master. I supported Solomon last summer, when he was serving in the army reserves. It was his first time to support DMS.

"Does my room have an Internet connection?" I asked the desk clerk.

"No, I'm sorry. Mrs. Givens has the last one," said the clerk.

"Take my room, Hamo. I don't need Internet. I can check my e-mail when we get to the office tomorrow" said Doreen.

"Are you sure?" I asked as we switched keycards.

"If Kim burns down the house, I'll hear about it soon enough," she said.

It was late, and we went straight to our rooms. The next morning Tom and his constables delivered us to G&E headquarters. We met the head of IS&T; he was none too happy about having the project management system he'd developed and maintained for the last ten years scrapped for something from corporate. The programmers who supported the old system would probably lose their jobs. That's job security in the age of information technology.

It was noon before Dave got the servers up and running. I executed a final test of my data transformations and fixed some minor glitches. The installation schedule was tight. Tomorrow at noon, the old system would be shut down and its database frozen. Doreen and I would spend the afternoon converting data. At six p.m. Nairobi time, MillProMan would become the official project management system for G&E. We were scheduled to depart Nairobi at nine p.m. If we encountered problems, our departure would be delayed until next day. Delays would impact G&E, so it was important for everything to go smoothly. If there were problems, management would complain to Corporate, and shit would flow downhill to IS&T.

By mid afternoon, jet lag struck me. Coffee was effective at first. Later, it only worked because I had to run to the ladies' room every ten minutes. By force of will, I survived the rest of the day and made it through dinner then begged off joining Doreen in the lounge for a nightcap.

I crashed when I got to my room. I was even too tired to check on DMS. I undressed, brushed my teeth with bottled water, and crawled into bed. I was asleep in an instant.

A loud thud woke me. The illuminated dial on the clock read eleven thirty. Doreen's room was right beside mine. The closet door was a slider. Doreen must be drunk, because she'd opened it with enough force to slam into the wall. Sounds of muffled voices came through the wall along with more thumps and another loud noise.

"Thanks for nothing, Doreen," I whispered to myself, trying to get back to sleep. Then I heard a regular thumping sound and more voices. She must have gotten lucky. Mindful of the CIA's comments about AIDs I hoped he was using a condom.

I told myself to be patient. Her partner would soon blow his load, then roll over and go to sleep—or more likely dress and leave.

"Thank you, Jesus," I whispered when the thumping stopped. I followed that with, "Fuck," when the thumping started again.

Maybe he had staying power and they were switching positions. Doreen was on top for this round. It was a young boy, a bellman, and he was good for a double.

"Finally," I whispered when the second round of thumping stopped. A half minute later, it resumed. "This is fucking ridiculous," I said to myself. I considered banging on the wall and screaming, "Hold it down, I'm trying to sleep." Not smart, given she was my supervisor. Be reasonable, I told myself. An overworked, stressed out, single mom was having some well-deserved sex.

Then I heard a muffled scream and more noises that sounded like slaps punctuated by sobs. "What the fuck," I said mindful of the possibility that my imagination was running away with me.

I sat on the edge of the bed trying to think of an innocent explanation. The possibilities weren't that innocent. Her partner wanted anal or water sports or for her to play his Rusty Trombone and she refused. He'd gotten pissed and was slapping her around to get what he wanted.

That was when I recalled a trick from my college days. By holding a drinking glass against my dorm room wall and my ear against the mouth of the glass I could listen to foul mouth Mindy screwing her date.

It took a minute for me to make the glass work. I could distinctly hear male voices, definitely more than one. They weren't speaking English but at one point one of them laughed. A dozen loud slaps interspersed with sobs followed. That was followed by the head board resuming the thumping.

Doreen was unlikely to have invited several of the locals to her room for a gangbang and beating. If it turned out that I was wrong, I would apologize.

I threw on my robe, grabbed my borrowed Glock, chambered a round, and ran into the hall.

"Open up, hotel security," I yelled as I banged the butt of the Glock against the door, marring the wood not that I gave a shit. I yelled and pounded again.

It was quiet for a moment; then I heard someone turning the dead bolt. I jumped to the opposite side of the hallway, crouched down, and took aim. The door flew open, and a black man emerged. There were two more behind him. The first man out the door looked at me in shock. I guess he expected a man. The three ran down the hall and took the stairwell.

I didn't shoot. I would have if they had moved toward me. Looking back, that was the right decision. Blowing away three locals even in self defense was probably frowned on by the authorities.

Her room was dark. I waited before I reached in and switched on the light. The place was a mess. The mattress was hanging off the bed. I heard a muffled sound coming from the other side of the bed, under the mattress. I considered the possibility there was a fourth man who hadn't the nerve to escape. I shoved the mattress back onto the bed with the side of my leg.

Doreen was on the floor, naked and gagged. Her hands were tied behind her back. There was blood on her face and several nasty looking bite marks on her breasts. I took the precaution of closing and locking her door before I set the Glock down.

They'd left a knife on the night stand. It was razor sharp and made short work of the ropes.

"Are they gone?" asked Doreen as soon as I removed the gag.

"Yes, they're gone."

I helped her to her feet. She immediately took several steps toward the bathroom. I put my hand around her waist to steady her. A few more steps and Doreen fell to her knees and vomited into the toilet.

"I'll get the police and EMTs," I said.

"No, don't!" yelled Doreen who had just emptied her stomach.

"You need medical attention."

"I don't want the police. I don't want anybody to know about this," sobbed Doreen.

"But you're hurt. They beat you. They might have given you some STD." I didn't want to say AIDS.

"Just my ribs and my jaw—it's not that bad. Please, I don't want anyone to know." Another fit of retching interrupted her sobbing. I stood over her, holding her head. The vomiting stopped after a while.

"You need stitches," I said, examining a small gash on her lower jaw. Bruises were starting to show on her cheekbones.

"I don't want the police involved," she repeated, adamant. She said it like she was the boss, and I was to do what I was damn well told.

"Maybe I can get some help that won't involve the police," I said. There was Bradley's mobile phone. "I need to go back to my room for a second and get something."

"No, don't leave me, don't leave me," Doreen wailed frantic and grabbed my arm.

"I have a friend who can help, but his number is in my briefcase," I said.

"Let's go to your room. I don't want to stay here," she said.

I grabbed one of the hotel's robes and helped her into it. When she got to my room, she insisted on taking a shower. I followed her into the bathroom, concerned she would pass out and hit her head on tile floor. She stepped in the shower turned the hot water as far as it would go, grabbed the handheld showerhead, and directed the flow right into her vagina.

"You'll scald yourself," I said, turning the faucet back. I knew what was on her mind, but if she had an STD the damage was done.

While Doreen was in the shower, I made my call. Bradley was right about no voice mail.

"Speak," said someone with a New England accent.

"A.H. Thornton. There's been an attack. We need a doctor."

"How badly are you hurt?"

"It's not me. It's a co-worker. She was raped and beaten in her hotel room."

"I'm only supposed to help you."

"Listen, asshole, she's an American, and she needs a doctor. She doesn't want to make the trip down to police headquarters where they'll want to inspect the damage. Get off your ass and do something about it."

"Bradley said you were something else. My name is Winston. I'll be along within an hour."

"Make it half an hour," I said and hung up.

Winston and a Doctor Reynolds arrived forty minutes later. The Doctor looked old enough to be retired. Winston and I went to Doreen's room to talk while Doctor Reynolds examined Doreen. I gave him a detailed account of the attack while I straightened the room. Winston looked of an age with Bradley. He looked preppy in khakis and a sweater. He certainly didn't look lethal

"Did they take anything?" Winston asked.

"I don't know. I'll have to ask Doreen. They didn't take her laptop. It's on the desk."

"Let's see if we can find her purse," said Winston.

After a few minutes of searching, I found it. It had gotten kicked under the bed.

"Let's see what's missing." Winston dumped the contents of the purse on the bed.

"Wallet's still here," I said, flipping it open, "Money and credit cards are in it."

"You interrupted them or they would have robbed her, even if rape was their objective.

"So why did they beat her?"

"Because she's white. Bradley won't be pleased when I tell him that you confronted the rapist. You could have been injured. You should have called hotel security."

"You can tell Bradley to go fuck himself. I am an excellent shot. I should have blown their dicks off. I could have kept them as souvenirs."

At that moment, the telephone rang. It was Doctor Reynolds. He'd finished with Doreen.

"I gave her a sedative. Her injuries are not serious; however, there is the possibility of venereal disease," said the doctor.

Doreen was sleeping peacefully in my bed.

"She'll be tested as soon as we return," I said.

"I don't think there are any broken bones, but her face and ribs should be X-rayed," said Doctor Reynolds.

"I'll tell her," I said

Winston decided to spend the night standing guard. I thought the chances of Doreen's attackers making another try were remote, but I welcomed his presence. Plus after my initial adrenalin rush passed, I was exhausted. I climbed into bed with Doreen, leaving Winston to the couch.

The young bellman who delivered morning coffee, toast, and jam seemed a little shocked to find the three of us in one room.

"Ménage a trois," I said to him as I signed the check.

We'd decided to tell the project team Doreen had slipped in the bathroom, landed face first on the floor and been badly cut and bruised. A doctor had treated her and advised rest. They'd assume alcohol was the cause of her mishap.

Chapter 17

The remainder of my trip was uneventful. Before we left for the airport, I applied makeup to Doreen's face. A dancer knows how to hide bruises.

I returned the Glock to Tom on the tarmac, after I ejected the cartridge from the firing chamber. "Thanks, I would have cleaned it, but I didn't have my kit."

"Shoot somebody, Love?" he asked, noting I had chambered a round.

"Came close, but no." I glanced at Doreen.

"Someone put their hands on your knockers," said Tom, putting his arm around me and pulling me close. He smelled of gin.

"Yes, a horny Brit grabbed my boobs."

"So why didn't you shoot?" Tom one handed my butt grinding his groin against mine.

"He ran away so fast I couldn't get a bead on his cock," I said, giving Tom a steamy kiss reinforcing my cover as the resident whore.

Exhaustion caught up with me when I got to my seat. I fell asleep as we were taking off, woke up in London and then immediately went back to sleep. It was dark when we landed so I walked Doreen to her car.

"Thanks, thanks for everything," said Doreen.

"Are you going to be all right?" I asked.

"Yes, I'm feeling much better. You did a good job at G&E. Take tomorrow off. None of us are going into the office," said Doreen before turning serious and hugging me. "I really appreciate what you did for me. You saved my life."

"I'm just sorry I wasn't able to save you from a fate worse than death."

"If you hadn't stopped them, they would have beaten me to a bloody pulp," said Doreen. She leaned back against her car and started to cry.

I'm not good at comforting people, but I put my arms gently around her. It made her start sobbing.

"It wasn't the first time I was raped. It happened at a party. There were three of them also," She slid down the car to huddle by the fender. "I didn't report that one either."

I had no idea what to say so I mumbled, "You'll be okay. You're a survivor."

After a few minutes, Doreen pulled herself together and drove off. I found myself thinking about E. Schuyler. What did he want with me? Maybe he was some harmless troll with a passing fixation. With time, he'd lose interest. No, he was not going to quit until I stopped him or he had me. I pictured myself chained up, naked in a basement. Elizabeth was feeding me oatmeal between anal rapes. I hate oatmeal.

I was confident my approach was correct, keep him writing until I figured out who he was. Before I left, I sent him a message informing him I'd be out of the country and wouldn't be answering e-mail. I didn't want him to think I was ignoring him.

Since I was behind on my ADS paperwork, I didn't get a day off. At eight prompt, I arrived at work to catch up on my reports. Mrs. Kabel discovered I was in the building and sent Marie to fetch me. This time there was just the two of us.

"Bradley reports you're doing an excellent job. He speaks very highly of you," said Mrs. Kabel. "I hope his glowing reports of your work aren't grounded in the wrong reasons."

"I don't understand. I haven't even begun my research. My efforts are focused on gaining their trust," I said wondering what she meant by wrong reasons.

"And apparently you're enjoying yourself," said Mrs. Kabel as she pulled an eight-by-ten photo of Bradley and me from a manila folder. It was the one taken at the charity gala. We were standing together smiling, and he was holding my hand. The photographer posed each couple as they entered.

Several thoughts ran through my head as I glanced at the photo. The dress was definitely a winner. I made a note to wear it at the club that weekend. Bradley looked more than okay, too. How in the hell did Mrs. Kabel get our photo?

"There's obviously a side of you, Hamilton, we don't see here at ADS," said Mrs. Kabel closely examining the photo and glancing at me. She was having trouble reconciling the woman standing beside Bradley and her prim employee.

"Attending the charity gala was essential to my undercover assignment. Millennium's CEO invited me. He insisted I attend," I said.

"And you chose to invite Bradley, a client. Surely, you have a male friend who could escort you?" said Mrs. Kabel.

"As a matter of fact, I do not. I needed someone on short notice, and who was aware I was working undercover," I said.

"Couldn't you have asked a member of your ADS team?"

"It was black tie."

That stopped her in her tracks. Allison Kabel considered all of her staff sartorial disasters. She doubted they owned a decent suit.

"So your attendance was strictly professional?" asked Mrs. Kabel.

"Absolutely, I have no romantic interest in Bradley Dickerson." I wasn't really sure that was true but it was the right thing to say.

"Good, I'm glad. We need to keep our professional and business lives strictly separate. I could understand the attraction. Agent Dickerson is an eligible young man from one of the best families in New England."

"May I ask how this photo came to your attention?"

"Bradley's mother, Bunny, is a friend of mine. She saw the photo. Bunny and I went to school together."

"And how did Bunny trace the photo to ADS?" I asked, genuinely curious.

"Your name is on the back," said Mrs. Kabel, turning the photo over. "Cleveland and Bunny are not without resources."

"And what is her concern?" I said wondering why she went to all the trouble, before remembering how my own mother had reacted to Bradley.

"It is normal for a mother to be curious when she sees her unmarried son with a beautiful girl, and has no idea who she is. When Bunny learned an A. H. Thornton worked for ADS, she sent me a copy of the photo. I was able to confirm to her you were the one in the picture."

"And what did she want to know? I'm concerned that my assignment remains confidential."

"Of course, I told her nothing about your work here at ADS, nor that you were working with Bradley. I merely informed her you were a forensics systems analyst who'd been with us for three years, extremely diligent, and a young lady of sterling reputation."

"Thank you, Mrs. Kabel," I said.

Having satisfied Mrs. Kabel that I was not screwing Bradley, we had a brief chat about Millennium. Mrs. Kabel did not appear the least bit concerned that one of my co-workers had been attacked. Her only comment was about the lax security found in overseas establishments. Marie interrupted to say that Mrs. Kabel had an important call. I was dismissed with a "put everything in your reports and I'll read it later."

Damn Bradley, he was turning out to be more trouble than he was worth. Bunny was worried her precious son was seeing some trollop. As the abandoned mutt of an undistinguished college professor, I was decidedly déclassé. I was beginning to worry my FBI handler was a trust fund baby who would go yachting if things got rough.

I had barely gotten back to my cubicle when the telephone rang. It was Bradley calling to establish the time and place of tonight's dinner.

"I just want you to understand this is strictly professional. It's not a date. In fact, I'm paying," I said once we agreed on particulars.

"It wouldn't be my first date where the woman paid," parried Bradley.

"Well, a free meal is all you're getting. And by the way, say hello to Bunny for me," I said as I hung up. I figured my comment might add a worry line to his forehead.

I caught up with my paperwork by mid afternoon. I'd written more than enough to justify ADS's exorbitant billing. I switched to my laptop and launched the electronic form for my Millennium expenses. It wasn't much—mileage to and from the airport, airport parking, and the hotel bill.

"Shit, I got the wrong bill," I whispered when I examined the hotel bill. At express checkout, I'd grabbed the envelope labeled *A. H. Thornton* and handed Doreen the one with her name. The three room service breakfasts I'd ordered were missing. We'd swapped rooms because I needed an Internet connection. My next thought sent a cold chill down my spine.

"They were hiding in the closet. They jumped out when I opened it. I was so frightened I couldn't move. One of them held a knife at my throat while they ripped my clothes off and tied me up," was Doreen's tearful description. "Between rapes, they beat me with their fists."

It should have been me, I thought while trying to calm my racing heart. I told myself that I was younger, stronger, and tougher, a veteran of strip clubs where facing down drunks with rape on their minds was all in a day's work. I would have broken free, grabbed the Glock and blazed away. Or would I have reacted like once raped Doreen and frozen when I felt a knife pressing against my Adam's apple.

I took a deep breath and shoved all those thoughts out of my head. Don't go there, I told myself. There was nothing to gain but fear. I put off completing my expense account.

As I put the hotel bill back in the Millennium folder, I noticed the scrap of paper with Soraya's one-sided cell phone conversation.

Something clicked in my mind. I started to imagine what the person on the other end was saying. It was easier now, after Nairobi.

Chapter 18

"Winston was a perfect gentleman, very professional," I said to Bradley. He frowned. Was it possible he was jealous or merely competitive? I was feeling playful and rested for a change.

Winston told me he and Bradley had gone to the same prep school before Yale. "Winston said you fagged for him at Groton."

"We were in the same class. It's the lower classmen who do the fagging," said Bradley.

I wasn't in the mood to act restrained. "Good to know for the day when my son goes off to prep school."

Bradley and I had met at my favorite Italian restaurant where the osso buco was to die for. If he had picked me up at the house, Mom would have started buying my trousseau.

"He and I roomed together at Yale," said Bradley.

"Yes, he told me you were Skull & Bones together. He loves working for the CIA. Quite a chatterbox for a spy," I said.

"He wouldn't have told you that," said Bradley, dismayed. "It would break every oath he swore to uphold."

"Maybe he didn't, but you just did," I said with a smile.

"Oh hell, who cares anyway? If there's anything else you want to know, just ask it outright."

"Who's got the bigger cock, you or Winston?"

"Me. I don't know. You said this was going to be a strictly business dinner. So let's leave the size of my penis out of it," said Bradley.

"Agreed, let's move on. I was supposed to be the one raped and beaten in Nairobi. Doreen was a mistake. We swapped rooms because hers had Internet and mine didn't. We just traded keys, thinking it made no difference."

"Winston mentioned there was something odd about the attack. They didn't take anything. He thinks somebody on the inside was bribed to let the attackers into the room," he said.

"Given that she locked her room before she left and they were waiting for her inside, that sounds highly probable."

"How is Doreen coping?"

"I called her this morning and she sounded okay. Her big concern is AIDS," I said.

"Terrible thing, still, I'm glad it wasn't you," Bradley said.

"I'd be in a Nairobi jail for shooting three rapists."

"Winston said you had a gun. How did you get it?"

"The G&E Security Director loaned me one. But first I had to let him feel my boobs."

"Good, I was worried you brought your own," said Bradley.

"I'm not dumb enough to go through airports with a semi-automatic in my handbag," I said. "Someone at Millennium knows about me and decided to take preemptive action."

"It's possible but it could have been a coincidence. Let's see what Winston turns up."

"I have something to show you." I reached into my purse to retrieve two sheets of paper, handing one to Bradley.

"What's this?" he asked.

"While I was in the lobby at the charity gala, I accidentally overheard Soraya Sheffield making a call on her cell phone. I wrote down her end of the conversation. I felt creative this afternoon and wrote up the other end of the conversation. I call him Mr. X."

"Mr. X, not very creative. How do you know she was talking to a man?"

"Tone of her voice, it was a man or a lesbian lover," I said. "I'll read Soraya. You be Mr. X."

"Seems a stretch, but I'll play." He cleared his voice and lowered it. He thought the mysterious Mr. X was a baritone. "Hello?"

"I'm done here," I read for Soraya.

"Is the Thornton problem under control?" Bradley read.

"It's taken care of. It's all set."

"Terrific looking piece of ass—tell them to make sure she's not so pretty when they're done."

"She'll be out of the picture for a while," I read.

"I don't want her killed. It has to look like an ordinary mugging," read Bradley.

"Understood, just a few love taps," I read.

"They'll rape her for sure." Bradley's frown deepened.

"Naturally," I read.

"She deserves it. Wish they'd make a sex tape."

"Too bad you can't be there. You'd enjoy it," I read.

"We could watch it in bed at the hotel. Where is your reservation?" read Bradley.

"London, the Savoy, see you there Sunday." I put down the paper.

"You have an active imagination, or just a dirty one. This could be right, but it's also possible she was arranging to meet her lover and it had nothing to do with you," said Bradley.

"I agree its conjecture," I said. "But it fits. Can you find out who she met in London?"

"I'll try. That might be more difficult to do if she was using an alias. What's lacking is motive? Why would Soraya Sheffield, daughter of one of the world's richest men and a highly educated, Westernized woman, be a terrorist? Granted, she's having an affair. That's not surprising. She's married to a workaholic," said Bradley.

"I thought Osama Bin Laden was rich and educated. Wasn't his second a medical doctor?"

"Bin Laden is the exception to the rule. We investigated Soraya and her father when the possibility of terrorism first surfaced. We came up with nothing."

I wasn't going to accept pushback. My ass was on the line. "I agree it's circumstantial, but I'm the one who woke up to the sounds of a coworker being raped and beaten in what was supposed to be my room. I expect the matter to be taken very seriously."

Bradley temporarily conceded defeat. "Understood, I'll have another look at Soraya Sheffield and ask our people in London to check on the Savoy. If you feel like you're in danger, use this to call me. It's encrypted." Bradley removed a very small cell phone from his pocket and handed it to me

"I won't get your voice mail?"

"No, it's a special number."

"Even if you're at home in the carriage house and Natalie's sucking your cock?" I said.

"God, you've got a filthy mouth. Natalie doesn't come around anymore. That's over," said Bradley, annoyed.

"What did Bunny and Cleveland think of Natalie?"

"None of your business; I see you've done your research. Are there any gaps in the information that you'd like me to fill in?"

"Actually, I didn't have enough time or interest to look you up. I got my intel from Mrs. Kabel this morning," I said.

"You've lost me," said Bradley.

"Mrs. Kabel called me to her office. She had a copy of the picture that fat little photographer took of us at the gala. She got the picture from Bunny. Somehow they're acquainted."

"Bryn Mawr," said Bradley. "But how did Mother know you were the one in the picture?"

"My name was printed on the back," I said. "They must have checked on every A. H. Thornton in new England. I doubt there are very many."

"Only two, you and an Alice Hilliard Thornton who lives in Brookline. She's in her seventies, a retired English teacher," he said.

"I didn't know that. And when your overprotective mother saw there was an A. H. Thornton working at her BFF's company, she sent the picture along for verification."

"Mother and I are going to have a serious talk about respecting my privacy. The mail always comes to the main house, and Walter walks mine over to the carriage house. Somehow, she must have seen the envelope with the photographer's name and decided to open it. Damn, it's hard to believe she'd do that."

"It's also a federal offense but don't be too hard on her. She's just a mother trying to make sure her blue-blooded son doesn't hook up with some cur bitch and pollute the bloodline," I said.

"She's not like that. I'm thirty, unmarried, and not seeing anyone. She'd like to see me settled," he said.

"Maybe she worries you're gay. She was probably thrilled you were with a woman," I said.

"She knows I'm not gay," said Bradley.

"She's seen Natalie sneaking out of the carriage house in the morning," I said.

"Yes, she knows that Natalie stayed over. For your information, Natalie Aimes was not the only woman in my life. So, how did Allison react?"

"She was concerned. The employee handbook expressly forbids screwing clients," I said.

"And what did you tell her?"

"I said I'd only given you a hand job, and that was only after you begged me. I pointed out you aren't my type. I have an aversion to early balding," I said.

"I am not going bald," said Bradley with some heat. He reached toward his forehead, thought better of it, and jerked his hand away.

"Actually, I told her our relationship was strictly professional. I assured her I was behaving myself like a lady and you were being a gentleman. I had to explain you were the logical person for me to invite to the gala."

"So what is your type?" asked Bradley.

"One that hasn't been created yet, but I'll settle for you if you're as rich as I think you are and willing to marry me without a prenuptial."

"And that's all it would take?" asked Bradley.

"True love is willing to go halves when true love disappears," I said.

"You'd marry me strictly for my money," said Bradley.

"Receding hair line and all—tell Bunny to schedule the caterer. We can have it in the spring. A tent on the lawn would be nice. I'll just move into the carriage house after the ceremony. No point in making a fuss. I don't plan to hang around that long."

"Why not move in before the wedding? We could go there tonight," said Bradley.

"Then I wouldn't be a virgin on my wedding day. I plan to wear white and deserve it," I said, as I snatched the check away from the waiter, took a quick look, and handed it back with the cash.

"Let's do this again next Thursday." Bradley took a PDA from his coat pocket.

"You are a glutton for punishment," I said.

"You could try to be nice to me," he said.

"Abuse is my attraction, Bradley. You've lost interest in eager to please femmes dying to suck your cock."

"Who says I'm attracted. This is business; but I'm paying next time. There is such a thing as an expense account at the Bureau."

Chapter 19

I was parked in the Millennium garage, waiting for Stacia McClain to arrive. So far the only thing I'd learned was that coffee and surveillance are incompatible. People on stakeouts in the movies never had to pee.

Work didn't start until eight, but at seven thirty a cream colored Lexus slipped into a reserved space, and Stacia stepped out. That she had one of the few reserved spaces spoke volumes. Administrative assistants don't merit reserved parking unless they're letting the boss park on them.

I was playing a hunch. The Soraya-Marshall-Stacia relationship intrigued me. Maybe Soraya was just being smart. If a husband was going to stray, his secretary was a likely temptation. At the least, she'd have the comfort of knowing where his cock had been.

I watched as Stacia exited her car, showing a lot of leg. She could have been a dancer. She was tall and her legs were nearly as good as mine. She was dressed in a business suit and carrying an expensive briefcase. She looked more like an executive than a worker.

I watched her through my dad's well-worn Zweiss binoculars. That and his *Birds of North America* were the only things of his I kept. As I zoomed in on Stacia, I wondered whether he still drove out to bird sanctuaries to capture bragging rights on rare species.

Stacia was too well groomed. Her eyebrows were absolutely symmetrical, professionally waxed. Every blonde hair was in place, makeup perfect, and her nails lacquered. She must start her morning at a salon.

There was also the matter of her wrist watch. I noticed hers at the gala but hadn't thought about it until later. It was a brand I recognized because I owned one like it but with fewer diamonds. I'd bought mine from a customer at the club who assured me that it had fallen off a Swiss air flight at Boston Logan.

That was back in my free spending days and I had paid a weekend's earnings. I'd worried it was a fake but when I took it a jeweler he assured me it was genuine.

"I don't carry the brand, too expensive for my customers. Did you buy it around here?" was his comment, as he eyed me suspiciously.

"It was a gift from a generous friend," I answered the nosy bastard implying a rich lover was rewarding me for services rendered.

I wondered what salary she got for being Marshall Sheffield's administrative assistant, not enough to buy a watch like that. Perhaps she was like Bradley, someone with a trust fund. Or she had a rich husband. That seemed more likely, and all the more reason not to pursue a career of getting the boss's coffee.

At the gala, Marshall sat between the two. I tried to remember the man seated beside Stacia but came up blank.

I had a thought. Maybe Bradley could flash his FBI badge at the photographer and get their picture. I dialed Bradley on the high tech phone he gave me.

"Hamo," said Bradley sounding like I woke him. I barely recognized his voice. It sounded like he was talking through a steel drum.

"You sound weird. Am I talking to you or your avatar?" I asked.

"Avatar? Don't speak geek at me in the morning."

"Your avatar is a software-based persona representing you inside the computer. It's derived from the Sanskrit name for the human incarnation of Vishnu."

"The phone is digitally encrypted. That's why it sounds weird."

"I need you to visit the photographer who took our picture at the gala," I said.

"I had a talk with my mother. I made her cry. I hope you're happy," said Bradley.

"Did you mention our getting married in the spring?"

"It slipped my mind. Other than harassment, is there a reason for calling me this early?"

"I want to know who Stacia McClain's date was at the gala."

"Who is Stacia McClain?"

"You met her there, tall blonde, attractive; you mentioned she gave you a hard on. My boss told me something interesting. Stacia got her job through Soraya Sheffield, the woman who planned my rape in Nairobi. I think Stacia and Soraya are lesbian lovers in addition to being terrorists."

"Using the Bureau's resources to investigate corporate gossip is not considered good form. You're totally off base. Soraya and her father aren't involved with terrorists."

"Be more open minded." Bradley was having trouble believing his social class could ever do anything to endanger their wealth. I didn't have a trust fund, so I couldn't imagine how having one would alter my thought processes. "Will you just do it?" I asked.

"All right, but I still think it's a waste of taxpayer money."

"You're already wasting two hundred dollars an hour for ADS," I said.

"ADS bills two hundred and fifty an hour. You're getting rich," said Bradley.

I started to say something but stopped. If ADS was billing at the rate for Computer Forensic Specialist II, I should be making another ten thousand dollars in annual salary. Mrs. Kabel was cheating the FBI and me.

"I only get half," I lied.

"You said Stacia McClain, right?"

I spelled the name as he wrote.

"I'll pay a visit to the photographer. I'll bring her picture and ours when we have dinner."

I heard paper rustling in the background. "You must have our photo on your nightstand. You've been using it to whack off and it's covered in pecker tracks. I should be flattered."

"You have the filthiest mouth of any woman I've ever met," he said.

"I'm only trying to keep you from getting carpal tunnel."

"You don't affect me that way."

"Then Bunny's right to worry about your long term sexual preferences."

"I should marry you to convince her of my heterosexuality."

"If it's on my terms, set a date. Invite Winston to be best man. We can have a threesome on our wedding night."

"I'll give it serious consideration," said Bradley.

"I've got to run. See you Thursday," I said, feeling a new surge of bladder pressure.

"Be careful, Hamo. If they're on to you they'll make another attempt. And this time, they won't screw up."

"Watch my back," I said as I hung up.

I wrote down Stacia's plate number then grabbed my digital camera. I got out of my Acura and walked slowly toward her car, making sure there was no one around. I placed the camera against the windshield, checked to make sure I had the VIN number, and clicked off two quick images.

I reached my cubicle, grateful for an empty bladder. The first thing I did was enable the software that would record communications between Stacia's desktop and the network. Every image and keystroke would be copied to a surrogate log file. If one of the Network Administrators happened to notice the file, which was highly unlikely, he'd find it was password protected and encrypted.

I'd barely finished when Doreen appeared, looking much better than when I saw her last.

"You're in early," she said.

"Couldn't sleep," I said.

"I'm assigning you to the Weber conversion team. Specifications are in Section Twelve."

"And the work will take place where? Kabul, Baghdad, Moscow, Manila?" I asked.

"Worse than that, Los Angeles, Weber's customers are primarily in the Middle East, but headquarters is in LA."

"How are you feeling?" I asked.

"My doctor sent my blood off to the lab. I won't hear anything until tomorrow. If things are okay, I have to be tested again in three months, and six months."

"Six months, that's a long time to be concerned."

"If the first test is negative, the chances of a subsequent positive are very small," said Doreen. "I've decided not to tell anyone about what happened."

"My lips are sealed."

"Thanks. I owe you," she said.

"Forget it, until you're doing my annual review," I said.

After Doreen left, I grabbed the specification manual and turned to Section Twelve. They had a more sophisticated system than G&E. There were sixty-five sets of data to transform.

My work load was overwhelming. Between my job at Millennium, dancing on weekends, and DMS, I was full out. Arnie had called to inform me he was opening a new upscale club in downtown Boston, and wanted to discuss my designing and hosting its Web site. I was also dealing with a potentially lethal stalker. A terrorist attempt to rape me had only failed by chance. There was no one to complain to; Syllabus didn't care.

Chapter 20

"May I please join you?" Marshall Sheffield politely interrupted my working lunch.

I was sitting in a coffee shop near Millennium's office, using their wireless Internet connection. I was about to search on Stacia's license plate and VIN number when he appeared. What the hell does he want popped into mind; but you don't refuse the CEO. "Of course, please sit down."

I looked around but didn't recognize any Millennium employees. If anyone saw us, "Both brothers fucking Hamo," would be the corporate news of the day.

"I wanted to apologize once more for what I said. It was unforgivable," Marshall said as he sat.

"Untrue, since I've already forgiven you," I said, as I closed my laptop. After what happened at the gala, I hadn't expected Marshall to ever speak to me again. But there he was and for some reason I was glad.

At first I put it down to my weakness for men in suits. Marshall's navy blue worsted with just a hint of a stripe fit him perfectly. He certainly looked like a CEO. Build wise, he was the opposite of his brother. Based on how we fit when we were dancing, he was an inch or two over six feet and lean, not even the slightest hint of a paunch.

Classically handsome, his coal black hair had the slightest touch of grey, and he had the most beautiful blue eyes.

"I'm not disturbing your work, am I?" asked Marshall.

"Not at all, just catching up on my e-mail."

"It's hard to remember life before e-mail," said Marshall.

"Was there life before email? I got my first e-mail address in grammar school."

"You don't look like the average computer wizard."

"I'm hardly a computer wizard."

"Not according to your co-workers. They say you did an excellent job in Nairobi when Doreen had her accident. Doreen's a fan of your by the way."

"She's been a great boss. I'm lucky to work for her. I'm not sure they all feel that way."

"They're misinformed, and so was I until you set me straight," said Marshall.

I didn't want another apology. Marshall must have a reason for searching me out. I needed for him to talk about himself not me.

"Did you enjoy the gala?" I asked, changing the subject.

"I'm a little worn out with philanthropy these days."

"Have you been doing it long?" I asked.

"I started with my first wife. She made it fun and rewarding. Now, it's become tiresome."

"I'm told Soraya is very active in charity work."

"Oh, she's active all right," he said, frowning.

Philanthropy sounded tiresome to me, but that wasn't what was bothering Marshall. "I've never been married. You were married before?"

"Yes, her name was Chelsea. We met in college. It was love and lust at first sight. She was killed in a car accident," he said.

"Children?"

"Two, Judith and Justin, they're away at school."

"College?" I knew Marshall's children were too young for college, but I was playing dumb.

"No, that's still a few years away. They're in prep school. Soraya thought it would be better if they had a cosmopolitan education. They go to school in Switzerland."

"You must miss them."

"Every day," said Marshall, unhappy. "Did *you* enjoy the gala?

"As my first time, it was interesting. Honestly, it would get old quickly if I had to do it often. Why was I invited?"

"I'd heard the rumors about you. Ben's penchant for putting girlfriends on the payroll annoys the hell out of me. It's bad for company morale. We're supposed to be a meritocracy. I thought if Ben's wife, Sarah, learned about you, she would give him some grief. I told Stacia to make sure you were invited."

"Stacia practically threatened me if I didn't show up."

"Stacia does not take 'no' for an answer," said Marshall. I got the impression that also applied to him.

"She strikes me as overqualified for the position." I was dying to find out more about Stacia, enough to go out on a limb.

"Stacia's very competent," Marshall hedged.

"She's also very beautiful, and she certainly knows how to dress."

"You seem impressed with her," he said.

"Impressed enough to form an opinion," I said.

"Care to share it?" said Marshall.

"Too upscale to sit outside the CEO's office and answer the telephone," I said.

"So you think there must be another reason Stacia is willing to serve in such a position."

"Yes I do. While we're discussing company rumors, the one I've heard is that Soraya picked Stacia." This was risky. Marshall might tell me to mind my own business or go look for another job.

"Unfortunately, that rumor is true," said Marshall. "But don't tell anyone I confirmed it."

"I won't say a word. Any conversation between us is strictly confidential."

"Soraya's from a different culture. She has different ideas about what helps or hinders a husband," said Marshall.

"And selecting someone you trust to screw your husband, but not run off with him, is part of her culture," I said.

"You think I've slept with her," he said, looking surprised.

"She projects availability. Yes, I think you have. But she's not your type."

"And what is my type?"

"Chelsea was." I skipped Soraya, and he didn't blink. He didn't deny sleeping with Stacia either.

"You remind me of her. In spite of all her education, she had a mouth on her that would have make a sailor blush. She didn't care who heard her, either. When you made your comment about sloppy seconds, I had a flashback to one of our first dates."

"I'm flattered. I saw her picture on the Web when I was deciding whether to take the job. She was very beautiful." Actually, it was kind of creepy thinking he was attracted to me because I reminded him of his dead wife.

"Some people are beautiful inside and out. She was one of them."

"Doreen assigned me to the Weber installation. I understand it is Millennium's largest acquisition." We were slow dancing from topic to topic until we got there, wherever there was.

"Weber was larger than Millennium when we acquired them. They have important connections in the Arab world," said Marshall. "With all the petrodollars pouring into the Middle East, it's turned out to be a very smart acquisition."

"How does a small company buy a larger one?" I asked.

"We raised the necessary capital from investors," Marshall said.

"Soraya's father?" I asked.

"Yes, he's arranged for infusions of capital. You seem to be well informed about how we've financed our acquisitions," said Marshall.

"I researched Millennium before I accepted the job. I wanted to work for a company with a future." I hoped he bought the lie.

"I know this sounds all wrong, but I would like for us to get together occasionally to discuss the company and other matters. I get so little feedback beyond my immediate staff. You are perceptive and not afraid to speak your mind. Let's have dinner tomorrow night at Teatro's in Boston, meet you at seven."

Now I knew why he was there. His invitation sounded rehearsed. Given that he was married and I have an unbreakable rule against going out with married man, I quickly accepted.

"I'd like that, as long as you understand I'm not going to jack you off, suck your dick, or fuck you." That came out naturally, but I wondered if it was something Chelsea would have said.

"I'll leave my dick at the office. This is my private number," said Marshall, writing the number on the back of his business card.

I wrote down my cell number and handed it to him.

"Hamilton, be careful," said Marshall as he turned and left.

What the fuck was that all about, I thought as I watched Marshall walk away. Was that a serious warning, or was he just telling me to keep my mouth shut about dinner?

Maybe I was not being sufficiently paranoid. What if Marshall was the one Soraya called about the Savoy? There could be a very nasty surprise waiting for me tomorrow night. My instincts told me it was all right, but I decided to take the Glock anyway. I liked Marshall, and I felt sorry for him. The term "maternal instinct" came to mind, and I immediately dismissed it. A. H. Thornton was not maternal.

There was something beaten down and sad about Marshall Sheffield. For some odd reason, he was reaching out to me. Why? Because I looked like his first wife and had her skill with expletives.

More likely, he would try to talk me into spending the night in a Boston hotel. The really odd thing was that I wasn't certain I'd refuse.

I glanced at the clock. It was past lunch hour, but I decided to make one attempt to learn something about Stacia. It took only a second for Earl Bower's software to hack into the DMV database. Under vehicle owner the screen read "McClain Foundation."

Chapter 21

"Now, Syllabus, let's see who this bitch really is," I whispered. Syllabus looked away to hide his contempt for people who talk to cats.

It wasn't until after work that I found time to research Stacia McClain. Her VIN revealed that her car was leased to the McClain Foundation. According to their Web site, the foundation's sole purpose was to operate the McClain Museum. The museum was located in a small town in the Western end of the state. I'd never heard of it, but I'm not much for art museums.

The site contained a brief history of the founding family. Ryan McClain was the family's Horatio Alger story. Scottish immigrant arrived penniless in New York in 1895 and amassed an enormous fortune in real estate. Ryan began his path to riches in Hell's Kitchen and eventually moved on to blocks of Manhattan.

Ryan's only son, Branson, married Cora Hedrick, and surprise: the Hedricks owned more real estate than the McClains. Adding to the perfection of the marriage, Cora was the only heir.

The two honeymooned in Europe for a year, where they became obsessed with collecting art, specifically French

Impressionists. Over time, the McClains acquired the nation's largest privately held collection of Impressionist art.

Branson and Cora, continuing the family tradition of under breeding, had two children, Lydia and Ryan II. Lydia died at age fourteen of an infection from a bite by her pet macaque. Ryan II survived to father one son. Branson II, the current chairman of the McClain Foundation Board.

After Cora died, Branson went off the deep end. It was the period in American history when ordinary folks built backyard shelters again nuclear Armageddon, and vowed they would shoot any neighbors who attempted to enter. Convinced New York City was first in line for destruction, Branson purchased a huge tract of land in the Berkshire Mountains. There, he constructed a museum, then built a castle nearby, to keep watch over the precious art he considered far more important than his fellow New Yorkers. His will established the McClain Foundation.

Stacia McClain was not listed as a member of the board, even though they had leased her Lexus. The board included prominent politicians, academics, business executives, and—surprise of surprises—Soraya Sheffield and her father.

The McClain Foundation site linked to the site of the McClain Museum. I took a virtual tour of the museum, hoping to learn something I could apply to Arnie's new club. Images on the home page showed McClain Castle overlooking the museum. Museum hours were posted, along with a notice that there was absolutely no admission to the castle or its grounds. The Web site was enormous, with hundreds of pages displaying its collection.

Searching of local newspaper archives revealed Branson II married Stacia in London five years ago. She was a former model turned art dealer. I suppose that made sense. Branson II was also on the board of three charities that provided art education to inner city children. In one instance, Soraya Sheffield was also a board member. Credit checks showed Branson II was very rich and paid his bills on time.

I'd not learned much about Stacia other than she did have a wealthy husband connected to Soraya via the boards of charitable foundations. According to the Berkshire Gazette, Branson II had relocated to Key West, the Provincetown of Florida, after a scandal involving one of the museum's male interns.

Assuming Stacia's husband was gay, it wasn't a shocker that Stacia was relying on Marshall for straight sex and Soraya for the other kind.

Left unanswered was why wealthy Stacia chose to work a menial job in Lowell, not the most exciting city in the US, when she could be in the Key West watching her husband sodomize boys.

I made a note to research foundations. Maybe I could recast DMS as a foundation for the betterment of nude dancing and avoid taxes forever.

Next, I relocated my search to Millennium's Human Resource database. Earl Bower's tool kit allowed me to slip past their firewall protection in a matter of seconds. That afternoon I compromised the firewall by installing a trapdoor. I could come and go untraced.

I displayed Stacia's personnel records. There were no reprimands or warnings. Her reviews were all "outstanding" and written by Marshall.

Stacia's marital status was "M" and the next of kin was "Branson R. McClain." Her address was in a small town just across the New Hampshire border. Lowell was less than five miles from the state line. Her annual salary was $47,589, almost the same as mine. She was thirty-three years old. She looked damn good for thirty-three. I wondered who did her plastic surgery.

I made copies of her human resources records for my case file. There was one more place to check—MillProMan accounting. It would show the account codes Stacia could charge and any projects where she could authorize expenses. In business, the authority to spend actual money is restricted to a crucial few. I had zero authorization to spend ADS's money. When I scrolled through the list of personnel who could issue a purchase order or sign a contract, there was Stacia with exactly the same power of the purse as Marshall. I was amazed to say the least.

"The bitch is running the company." Syllabus gave me another disparaging look for speaking to him.

My research had produced more questions than answers. Frustrated, I exited Millennium's system and began checking my DMS emails. I deleted hundreds of SPAM before I came to a message from Elizabeth Schuyler wanting to hear about my trip to Nairobi. My reply included a detailed and graphic description of Doreen's rape. After an internal debate concerning the wisdom of discussing rape with your stalker I sent it. Maybe, a lurid account of rape would excite him enough that he would get careless and reveal something I could use.

Chapter 22

"Tell me about Hamo," said Marshall after the waiter had delivered our drink order and recited the specials.

Marshall suggested we start with the antipasto. "It's delicious and it will give us something to sample while we get to know each other."

We were in a small private room at an Italian restaurant named Teatro's, located in Boston's North End. The North End was an ethnic Italian neighborhood. The Irish were concentrated in the South End. According to my dad, between the two they controlled the state's two largest criminal enterprises, the mob and the government.

It was a moment my mom had warned me about when I first started dancing.

"When you meet someone you're interested in, you'll have to either lie to them or tell the truth. Either way, it won't be easy."

The fact that she was right didn't make it any easier either. I wasn't about to tell Marshall the truth about my dancing or that I was working under cover. Lying to him bothered me more than usual. Maybe I was interested.

"Where would you like to start," I asked?

"High school, you dated the captain of the football team?"

"Wrong, I doubt Tommy Edmonds knew my name."

"Tommy must have been gay. You were the most popular girl in your class?"

"Let me summarize my high school career. I was the only female member of the Math Club. There were two other girls in the Computer Club. I was studious, well behaved, and not allowed to date. My father was very strict. Boys in his view equated to loss of reputation, pregnancy, and venereal diseases."

"It's hard to believe that boys didn't seek you out," said Marshall.

"A few did, but I wasn't allowed to respond."

"So your social life began in college," said Marshall.

"No, not really, I worked my tail off to pay my way. No time for either sex. My college was filled with coeds whose rule was lesbian until commencement."

"But that wasn't you," asked Marshall looking concerned about my lesbian remark?

"No, but I was tempted. Some of them were terrific kissers."

"For a woman who claims never to have had a social life, you seem very confident and self-assured. Why did you have to work so hard?"

"My dad disappeared right before my freshman year, leaving me destitute. I was forced to become an 'all work and no play' girl."

"He just disappeared?" Marshall leaned forward.

"Yes, after he emptied the bank accounts including the one containing my tuition. I'm indentured to a local bank for college loans."

"Wow…" There was a pause as he searched for polite conversation. "What does your sister do?"

"She's a dental hygienist. Mom works in a department store. She used to work in a circuit board factory before they moved it to Taiwan."

Marshall was given to rapid changes in the subject. I was happy he moved away from me. I had too many secrets.

"What's your evaluation of Millennium's IS&T department?" asked Marshall.

"MillProMan is impressive. It should give the company a competitive advantage."

"And what is your opinion of my brother, Ben?"

"Garden variety whore monger," I said, deciding it was time to cut the bullshit and really say something.

"You've dealt with them before?"

"They are as common as leaves on trees. If I were willing to blow him after he caught the Guinness Book of Records marlin, he'd keep me around until someone new caught his eye."

"I can't fathom how his wife Sarah deals with it."

"I imagine they met in college, and Sarah was the hottest piece of ass he had screwed to date. After they married, the lust failed to last and Ben began to roam. Sarah focused on home and children while enjoying the privileges of being a rich man's wife."

"She could leave him and take half."

"Then she'd become a middle aged divorcee, an object of pity, expected to fuck any man who bought her dinner. Sarah's considered her options and made her choice."

"You're right when I think about it," said Marshall.

"And what is your excuse? You have an attractive administrative assistant sitting outside your office door and your wife is an international beauty. Even though the two of them are servicing your cock, you'd still fuck me on this table if I was willing which I'm not."

"Let's finish dinner before do it on the table. Why do you think I am sleeping with Stacia?"

Once again he didn't bother to deny he was screwing Stacia or he wanted to screw me.

"Rumor has it that Soraya pimped her for you," I said, walking out on the end of a very thin limb.

"For some who had been at Millennium for only a few weeks, you know a lot. I'm not going to lie to you. Soraya did force me to hire Stacia and from day one she declared her availability. She has the sexual appetite of a billy goat."

"Just to satisfy my female curiosity, how did she make her declaration," I asked? I have no idea why I asked the question.

"She wasn't subtle about it. Right after lunch, she came into my office, locked the door, and lifted her skirt. She tossed me the panty she had been wearing. She told me that I could have her anytime, starting now. At first, we did it every afternoon on my office couch, or I went to her condo in Nashua if she wanted me to do certain things to her."

"Soraya knows but does not care," I said stifling my curiosity about certain things.

"Correct," said Marshall.

Marshall hesitated before he spoke further. I could tell he was debating how far he could trust me. "I'm telling you things that could cause both of us a lot of grief, even put you in danger."

"No one, not Doreen nor anyone will ever hear anything you tell me. My lips are sealed." That sounded corny but he needed to hear it. "Who's the best fuck of the two? My guess would be Stacia."

"You're right again. She taught me things."

Exactly what things would have to wait for later. But I was dying to know.

At that moment, the waiter arrived with our main course. I decided it was smart to redirect the conversation in spite of the fact that I was intrigued with Marshall's situation. None of it made much sense based on what I knew but I knew very little.

"How did you meet Chelsea?"

"It was the summer after I got my Engineering degree. I'd been accepted to Harvard's MBA program. The company won a subcontract to erect the steel for the Whitmore Life Building in Hartford. When we got up to the twenty-sixth floor, I looked across at the building beside me, and there she was. I spent more time watching her than welding. She had a summer internship at this radio station. I decided to wait in the lobby to ask her out. She called security and had me banned from the building. I was smitten, but she wasn't. Next day, I had a florist deliver a dozen roses."

"And you got your first date?" I asked.

"It wasn't that easy. When the delivery guy pointed me out, she stood in the window and dropped the roses in the trashcan, one by one. Two dozen the next day, same result, I kept at it. At five dozen, she put them in a vase and told the deliveryman she would meet me for lunch downstairs."

"What did she say at lunch?"

"I'm only doing this to get rid of you. I don't want any more fucking roses. I hate roses, and I don't date construction workers. You're only interested in getting laid, then bragging to your buddies that you've screwed me."

"But she did agree to a second date," I said.

"Yes, it was one of those 'I'll meet you at the restaurant because I don't want you to know where I live' dates. After that, things got intense, and stayed that way until the night she was killed. God, I still miss her."

"You married Soraya thinking she would take away the pain," I said. What the hell was I saying? Talk about getting personal on a first date. Then again, it wasn't a date.

"Something like that," said Marshall. "Plus, I thought Justin and Judith needed a mother. I'd become a workaholic and was neglecting them."

It was time to lighten things up. I felt a twinge of jealousy toward Chelsea. I suppose we're all after something real, and few of us ever find it. Having that kind of relationship seemed far beyond my capacity.

I'd learned from others in my department that Marshall was the driving force behind MillProMan. So I switched to shop talk and spent the rest of the evening conversing about construction systems. I knew barely enough to hold up my end of the conversation, but once I got Marshall started, all I had to do was nod.

It was after eleven when we finished our cognac and called it an evening. He helped me into my coat, allowing his hand to rest on my shoulder longer than necessary. He surprised me by holding my hand as we waited for the valet.

"Can we do this again soon?" asked Marshall when my car finally arrived from some distant lot.

"Yes, I'd like that." I don't understand what happened next. I wrapped my arms around his shoulders and kissed him. He tensed at first. Then he relaxed, embraced me, and we had a long, slow kiss while the valet stood there, holding my car door open.

Chapter 23

"Danceable," I said to myself as I transferred the song track to my MP3 player. I was multitasking, using driving time to search out new music I could use on stage. I'd decided to take the day off and do something stupid. I was stressed from work and needed a break. The weather was not helping to lighten my mood. It had rained earlier and the sun had taken the day off.

According to my GPS, driving one hundred forty-eight point six miles would get me from home to the McClain Museum in Lenox.

Driving the interstate gives you time to think and I had more than my share of thoughts.

I flipped the vanity mirror down to examine my forehead. To Botox or not to Botox was the question—to suffer the wrinkles and crow's feet of outrageous frowns, or to take a syringe of poison and erase them.

"Not yet," responded Doctor Keller after he examined my eye sockets and forehead.

"Are you sure?" I asked. Dancers five years younger than me were Botoxing.

"Maybe in a few years."

He sent me on my way. That was what I got for having a board certified plastic surgeon, not a money hungry butcher eager to carve me up like topiary.

Matters at home hadn't been uplifting either. Harold had taken the wife to Hawaii for a two-week vacation. His absence left Tommie in a funk that had me feeling uncharacteristically sisterly.

"You must miss him," I said, giving her a hug. I had not said the obvious, "See, it's the wife who goes to Hawaii not the mistress."

"I do," she said, looking unhappy. "I've lost five pounds. Can you tell?"

"Yes, you can really see it in your hips," I lied.

I wondered if it was the right thing to say. My dad always said if you tell people what they want to hear, you are an enabler. That was his rationale for being brutally frank about any shortcomings he perceived in me.

"It's my role as your father to be critical and never sugar coat anything. I want you to grow as a person," was something he liked to say after he took me to the brink of tears.

I was wearing the black wig and baseball cap that I wore to my banks. Tinted glasses completed my disguise. In my backpack, I had binoculars, notebook, and *Birds of North America*—in case I wanted look like I had a purpose other than snooping. I'd also brought the Glock and a spare magazine just in case.

I should have been home working on DMS. My backlog was out of control. I'd placed a small ad in a trade magazine catering to strip clubs. I reasoned that if I got a single customer for my two hundred dollars, I was ahead. Two days after the magazine hit, I had eighty-five emails from dancers. DMS had outgrown a part time programmer. I needed help.

There was one other issue bugging me. Why did I kiss Marshall Sheffield? Even more disturbing, my heart skipped a few beats when I did.

Marshall was twenty-five years older than me. He had two children. He was married to an educated, wealthy, beautiful woman with whom I could not compete. Socially, I was one step above white trash. Any beauty I possessed was the result of Doctor Keller's skills, not my DNA. Mrs. Kabel would fire my ass in a heartbeat if she learned I was personally involved with an executive in a company ADS was investigating.

And the one thing I wanted was for Marshall to ask me to dinner again. My lack of judgment was appalling. If I had any brains, I would be trying to snare Bradley. He was my age, no kids or wives. He was handsome, rich, and a good dancer. Moreover, he seemed to have a thing for me. I could marry him and use a month's income from his trust fund to pay off my school loans.

Chapter 24

Two hours and twelve dollars later, I'd suffered through my museum experience. The paintings were nice, and I even recognized some of them. Twelve dollars to look at art seemed absurd. The millions Branson Senior had left to operate the museum had not been enough to keep the admission reasonable.

I parted with more money in the museum's gift shop. I'd spent twenty four ninety five on a book titled *History of the McClain Museum* and thirty seven fifty on *Great Art of the McClain*, a birthday gift for my mother. A chef's salad and diet soda from the museum café was nine fifty. The place is a rip-off.

I was in the museum parking lot studying McClain Castle through my binoculars. Who lived there? Not Stacia, she had a condo in Nashua where she and Marshall went to fuck. Now why did that bother me? Who Marshall screwed was his and Soraya's business. Stacia's husband, Branson McClain, was in South Beach practicing his sodomy.

One might assume it contained the offices of the administrative staff that operated the museum. But the museum guide I got when I paid the admission fee contained a map showing an entire wing of the museum building was dedicated to administrative offices.

There was a rocky outcropping half way up the mountain that looked down on the castle. An old logging road led partway there. The outcropping would provide a vantage point to spy on the building and grounds.

I glanced at my watch. It was a few minutes after noon. I didn't have to be at the club until seven for a meeting with Arnie to discuss the Web site for his new club.

I drove to the entrance of the logging road. I ignored signs reading "Private Property—No Trespassing." Vandals had broken the chain blocking the entrance, so I drove in.

I didn't get far on the logging road before the ruts became too much for the Acura. I slung my backpack over my shoulder and began to hike. As a dancer, I thought I was in shape, but inside of five minutes, the steep climb had me dripping sweat and breathing hard.

The climb got steeper and muddier as I went up. I scratched my hands and wrists, pushing through bushes and grabbing tree limbs to pull myself up. I told myself this couldn't possibly be worth it. I could learn more from the Internet in five minutes than I could on this crazy hike.

Finally I reached the outcropping, and clambered up onto the flat granite and collapsed. I was soaked with perspiration and covered with mud up to my knees. I slipped off my backpack and lay there for a good five minutes staring at passing clouds. Just hours from now, I'd be on stage and expected to dance. I made a mental note to select slow music.

I took an energy drink out of my backpack and gulped it down. When I managed to drag myself to the edge, I saw that

I had been right about the view. I was looking almost straight down at the castle and grounds.

Somewhat restored and determined to be methodical and thorough, I got out my notebook to make a rough sketch of the grounds. I started with the main gate, maybe a quarter of a mile from the castle itself. The gate was closed, and there was a guard standing in front of a small guardhouse.

"Something isn't right," I whispered to myself. Rich people have fences and gates surrounding their property, but damn few are willing to pay for a guard. I panned my gaze slowly along the fence that completely enclosed the grounds. A massive stone wall faced the front, but sides and back fencing was chain link. The chain link looked new and had multiple strands of razor wire along the top.

I followed the fence around and back to the gate where, at the moment, a scene was playing out. An RV the size of a city bus had stopped at the gate. The guard was making angry gestures at a man taking pictures. A woman in the RV's driver seat was yelling. A tourist couple asking if they could take a tour was the logical assumption. They obviously hadn't visited the Web site.

The man walked back to his RV, and the women handed him a camera with a telescopic lens. The guard rushed into the guardhouse emerging seconds later with an automatic rifle. The visitors fled. But not before the ballsy woman gave him an Italian salute. The guard put his weapon back, then came out and lit a cigarette.

A foreigner, I decided based on the odd way he held the cigarette.

I studied the grounds. Something was missing. A quick check showed my mobile had Internet access. Images from the Lenox historical society's Web site gave me my answer. The stand of magnificent oak trees had been cut down. Trees do die, but not all at once. Oaks would provide cover if someone slipped over the fence to spy.

In the back, there was a swimming pool, tennis courts, and a garage. My attention was drawn to a set of satellite dishes. They were partially concealed behind tall hedges, impossible to see unless you were looking down from above. There were two large dishes and two small ones. The large ones reminded me of the ones installed outside of Channel 5. The castle had commercial satellite communication capability. That was something I could research.

I pulled my camera out and began snapping images. I was busy making notes when I heard a sound behind me. Whipping around, I slipped my hand inside my backpack to rest on the grip of my Glock.

"Beat you," shouted a young boy, jumping up onto my boulder top.

"Unfair, you pushed me," yelled a girl close behind him. The girl looked like his sister. She was older, early teens. The boy I guessed was twelve. I took out not the Glock, but my birding manual, just as the two noticed they were not alone.

"Hello there," I said. I gave them the smile I use on potential lap dance customers.

They looked at me open mouthed. Then the boy spoke, "You're not supposed to be here, lady. You can get in trouble."

"I'm just birding." I held *Birds of America* up for them to see.

"What kind of birds?" asked the girl?

I don't know squat about birds in general and the birds of Lenox in particular. "All kinds, this region is habitat to many of our feathered friends."

"They won't like you being here," said the boy. He said it in a way that made it sound like my transgression was very serious.

"My name's Tommie, what's yours?" I wondered who "they" were.

"Tommie, that's a boy's name," said the boy.

"Not always."

"I'm Brent," the boy said after a moment's hesitation. I'd seen a look of concern cross his sister's face. She relaxed as soon as the boy said his name. It crossed my mind that I had just exchanged aliases with a child.

"And yours?" I said to the girl.

"Barbara," she said.

Brent and Barbara, what kind of a sadist would name their children that? Then I thought about my sister and me.

"Do you live in the castle?"

"Yes," said Brent.

"We're not supposed to talk to strangers," said Barbara. "Let's go Brent."

"I'm harmless." I said in my most reassuring voice. I lifted my camera and clicked off several images of the two.

"Why'd you do that?" asked Barbara.

"You've very pretty, Barbara. Are you a model?"

"Come away, Brent, we're going to get in trouble," said Barbara, stepping toward her brother to grab his arm.

"You're all muddy," said Brent shrugging of his sister's hand and stepping closer. Whatever scared the shit out of Barbara didn't faze Brent.

"But you're not. You must know a better way."

"We came the back way," said Barbara.

"What's it like to live in a castle?"

"Creepy," said Brent.

"Brent, be quiet," said Barbara.

"Well, it is creepy, and we never get to go anywhere. I hate it," said Brent.

"We'll get in trouble if they find us talking to her. Remember what happened last time," said Barbara.

"I don't care," said Brent.

"Trouble with your mom and dad," I asked?

"Our mother's dead and our Dad's not here," said Brent with a touch of bitterness, surprising for a twelve year old.

"Be quiet, she's coming," said Barbara, alarmed.

I heard someone struggling up the side of the outcropping.

"Who's coming?" I asked.

"Alisha, our nanny," said Brent. "I hate her, too."

The way he said it, I believed he meant it.

"You two are going to be punished for running ahead," said a hard breathing, heavyset woman clambering onto the bolder top. She was carrying a picnic basket. When she saw me she gave me a look to make the sky go dark.

"Hello," I said, holding the bird book in front of me like a shield. I gave her a big, disarming smile.

"This is private property. You are trespassing," Alisha said. Then she scolded Brent and Barbara in a foreign language. I'm not a linguist, and I don't know Arabic, but it sounded to me like what I expected Arabic to sound like.

"I'm sorry. I didn't see any signs. There is a rare falcon that nests in this area," I said, resisting the urge to tell her to fuck off.

"You are breaking the law. You must go immediately." Alisha stepped towards me. I moved away from the ledge. The thought occurred to me that the fall would kill me, and it would look like an accident.

Alisha looked down at the castle then at me; she noticed the camera hanging around my neck.

"Pictures are not allowed. I must check to be sure," said Alisha, gesturing toward the camera.

"I haven't taken any. No falcon," I replied.

"The camera, I need to check," said Alisha sticking out her hand insistently.

"I said there are no pictures," as I moved back.

Alisha pulled a radio-intercom out of a holster on her hip. She pressed a button and spoke a rapid burst of what I assumed was Arabic. An equally rapid burst of angry words crackled back from the small speaker.

I leaned down slowly to pick up my backpack.

"Stay, we have to make sure there are no pictures," said Alisha, reaching for my arm.

"No, sorry, I have to be somewhere," I said, moving away.

Alisha spoke into the radio-intercom again, more urgent this time. I could see movement at the back of the castle. Four figures emerged, headed in my direction. Two of the figures were men, and the other two were dogs, big dogs.

"Run, lady, run," yelled Barbara.

I was off. Before I'd gotten two steps, I heard a loud slap and a cry of pain from Barbara. I wished I had time to turn around and put a nine-millimeter slug in each of Alisha's chubby knees. But I had a feeling I was going to get worse than a slap if they caught me.

I went down much faster than I went up. I fell once and almost brained myself on a rock. That made me slow down. Set a steady pace and sustain it, I told myself as I ran. I figured if the men had to come up their side of the hill and over the outcropping, like Barbara and Brent, then I would be long gone before they arrived. I was wrong.

Chapter 25

I was jogging along when I heard someone shout, "Stop," behind me.

It turned out there was a gate in the fence, parallel to the logging road. When I looked back I saw men and dogs emerge from the trees. The dogs were choking themselves on their collars, eager to catch me.

I ran as fast as my dancer's legs would carry me. Another glance over my shoulder informed me they had unleashed the hounds. I ran for my life. I could see my car in the distance. If I could get there before the dogs and get inside, I would be safe.

The car was a good two soccer fields away, and the dogs sounded close. Another look and I realized I was not going to make it. I recognized the breed—Alsatians, long limbed bastards with a nasty temperament. When I was growing up, one of our neighbors had an Alsatian named Bullet. When a car hit Bullet, the neighborhood kids threw a party.

I saw a fallen log by the road and made a decision. I jumped over the log, slipped off my backpack, and took out the Glock. I was breathing so hard my chest hurt as I pulled the slide back and chambered a round. The only thing I had ever shot was a paper target. I assumed the stance they taught at the firing range. The hounds looked happy. The rabbit had quit running and was standing there, waiting to be eaten.

I had spent a fortune sculpting my body to look the way it does, and no damn dogs were going to ruin my investment. I squeezed off the first shot, and my initial thought was how loud it sounded without noise protection. One dog pitched forward in an awkward roll. I got off four more rounds before the second Alsatian leaped the log and grabbed the sleeve of my gun hand.

I panicked and dropped my gun. The Alsatian had a bullet hole in his shoulder that was pumping blood as we struggled. Luckily, he had only sleeve in his fangs. If his jaws had been crushing my wrist, I'd have been in too much pain to do anything other than scream.

Survival instincts took hold. I pushed my arm forward, taking the Alsatian along as I reached down and picked up the Glock with my other hand. He had a puzzled look on his face when I placed the muzzle between his eyes and pulled the trigger. The impact almost ripped my arm off. I ignored the splattered dog gore, picked up my backpack, and ran.

The Acura started on the first try. Off I went sliding over the rutted road as the men came into view. Looking in my rear mirror, I saw one of the men raise his automatic rifle. But he lowered it without firing. I must have been too far away, or they realized a fusillade of rifle fire near a main road might draw attention.

I left Lenox as fast as the Acura would go. Later, I realized how dumb that was. If a trooper has pulled me over, he would have found me covered in dog blood with a recently fired handgun in my backpack.

Halfway home, I managed to calm down. I stopped at a rest stop to clean up. The sleeve of the jacket was shredded, so I dumped it in the trash. The wig had slipped to one side, revealing blonde curls. My face was flecked with dog blood. Better his than mine, I told myself as I washed. I removed the wig, and combed my hair out. With luck, someone looking for a brunette would ignore the blonde.

There were half dozen fast food establishments in the rest stop and the aroma made me realize I was starving. I treated myself to a diet drink and a double cheeseburger plus fries. Between the hike up the mountain, the run down, and the struggle with the Alsatian I had burned enough calories to compensate. Eating gave me opportunity to think about what had happened.

My trip to the McClain Museum had been a learning experience. I learned that great art is difficult to differentiate from not so great art and that museums are ridiculously expensive.

McClain Castle had also been a near death experience. Possibly I was exaggerating but I was happy my pursuers hadn't gotten close enough to read my license plate. The castle was downright hostile toward outsiders and appeared to have something to hide. The castle's residents included two unhappy children, who I suspected were Marshall's by his first wife. He told me they were going to school in Switzerland—so much for honesty in our relationship. Their nanny spoke a language I suspected was Arabic. Brent and Barbara hated her, and so did I.

The next time Marshall and I dined, I'd ask to see pictures of his children, and the proud father would oblige me. Then

I had the unhappy thought that he wouldn't ask me again. I'd been too nosey about his relationship with Stacia.

The satellite dishes needed to be researched. Why were their four of them? What was their purpose? Earl Bowers could find out for me.

In spite of the fact that the Stacia-Soraya-Marshall-Castle connection seemed all wrong, I didn't have any hard evidence to give Bradley. Satellite dishes and high levels of security don't translate into terrorism. It could mean the residents are paranoid but have a strong desire to communicate with the outside world. Bradley would think I was acting unprofessional and tell Mrs. Kabel to take me off the case. ADS had laid off another ten employees Friday.

You are going about this all wrong; I told myself as I sat there shoveling French fries into my mouth. I had lost my professional detachment, and was rushing about the countryside crashing into situations for which I wasn't trained.

What would have happened if they had caught me? A terrorist cell would have tortured and killed me. Upstanding art collectors would have had me arrested for trespassing. Having a weapon on my person even though I was licensed would have made it worse. They could charge me with criminal trespassing and assault. I know dancers who spent time in correctional institutions; they said they were not spa-rated.

Chapter 26

"That's how it's going to look, for real?" asked Arnie, staring at the screen. He was sitting at his desk, and I was leaning over him, guiding the mouse.

"Yes, it's called a virtual walkthrough. It provides a simulated tour of the club," I said. "It'll make the site interactive and appealing."

"I've got to make some changes," said Arnie before he screamed, "Maureen, get that asshole Mark Cummings on the phone!"

"It's Sunday," Maureen called back calmly. Maureen was Arnie's assistant. I was never sure what office hours Arnie kept, but if he was at his desk, she was at hers.

"Call the motherfucker at home!" yelled Arnie.

"What's wrong?" I asked.

"I don't like it," said Arnie.

"You don't like it?" I exclaimed, not hiding my disappointment. I'd just spent the last half hour showing him a preliminary version of Boston Gentlemen's Web site. I thought I had done a fantastic job. I'd gone to the expense of hiring a talented graphic designer.

"No, darling, I love what you did, but I don't like what Cummings did," said Arnie. He was referring to the architectural firm who designed the club's layout. To reassure me, he slipped his arm around my waist and gave me a hug, then reached down and squeezed my butt cheek.

"Are you sure you like it?" I asked, needing more reassurance than having my ass pinched.

"It's fantastic, sweetheart," said Arnie repeating his squeeze. "I just saw some things I don't like about the layout. I'm lucky you showed me this. I'm going to call that son of a bitch architect and tell him he fucked up. Maureen, where's that goddamn call?"

"How about the rest of the site," I asked, looking for meaningful feedback?

"Your Web thing is fucking fantastic. Tell me again why a computer genius like you is working here for tips," he said.

"I'm not a genius. Because there's more money in exotic dancing than computers," I said.

"You going to dance at my new place?" asked Arnie.

"You know I can't. Someone from ADS would find out, and so long day job."

"You're missing out on a lot of cash. There are five hotels within six blocks, charging three hundred and up for a room. The place is going to be packed with convention guys tipping twenties and hundreds."

Left unsaid was what I could make if I visited those hotel rooms. "I'm thinking long term. I can't dance until I'm eligible for Social Security."

"You got another five years…maybe seven."

"Thanks, but I figure no more than three." Lately, every time I looked in the mirror, I saw another sign of aging. I'd started drinking water to keep my skin hydrated, but it was wearing my legs out running to the restroom.

"All the more reason to make it while you can. Have you thought about my other offer?" he asked.

"Yes, I am seriously considering it." Arnie had offered to let me join management, starting with weekend daytime shifts. His club managers made a good living. Kurt, the manager of Foxy Vixens II, was putting two kids through college.

"Cummings on line one," yelled Maureen.

"I'll show you more, later," I said, closing the laptop.

I stopped at the bar for a soda. I wasn't scheduled to dance for another hour. I had planned to spend more time with Arnie, but he wasn't interested in the finer points of Web design. I took his reaction to mean he trusted my judgment and was leaving it up to me.

Arnie was someone I respected. With only a high school education, he had made himself rich operating clubs in New England. He had been married thirty-two years and probably held the New England, possibly the United States record for adultery. The couch in Arnie's office belonged in the Museum of Fornication, if anyone ever built such a place.

The second Wednesday night of every month was amateur night at his clubs. It helped girls break into the business. It was very competitive; as many as fifty girls would show up to audition. He expected the winners to show their appreciation for the opportunity. On slow days, he had Maureen. I'd never met his wife, and had no idea what his personal life was like. He had two grown children and was a grandfather.

Arnie drove a three-year-old Buick and lived in a modest three-bedroom home in Roslindale, not Boston's wealthiest suburb. Out of curiosity, I once ran a credit check on Arnie. Arnold Rothenberg Entertainment paid him the lordly sum of $125,000 for being president and CEO. Intrigued at how little that was, I took a look at his corporate tax filings. Revenue was wildly understated. Clubs handle cash for the most part. You can't pay for a lap dance by check or credit card. Owners skim cash off in the backroom.

I was sitting at the bar, working on a dancer's Web site, when Bathsheba put a hand on my shoulder. She'd recovered from her drug overdose and was working every shift Arnie would give her. She'd spent a fortune staying out of jail. I got the usual long, lingering kiss, with lots of tongue. Bathsheba is a good kisser. And while she hasn't turned me on to the point that I'm ready to hop in bed with her, she gets me to thinking about it.

"You have the softest lips," Bathsheba breathed, breaking the kiss for a moment. Did I mention she's also good with words? She can talk a customer out of his last nickel.

"You're looking great," I replied, letting her kiss me again. Lately I put more into kissing back.

"You're early. You're not dancing for another hour," she said, her arms still around my neck. Guys love to see girls get it on. Homophobic men get hard watching women kiss.

"I came early to show Arnie the Web site for the new club. But we finished sooner than I planned."

"You're always working. Why don't you come over to my place after work and relax? I'll give you a back rub." Bathsheba gave me a preview, rubbing my shoulders.

"I have to be at work tomorrow at eight in the morning. I need to go home and sleep," I said.

"Carrie's on an overnight haul to Bangor. We'd have the place all to ourselves."

"I'd definitely be up all night."

"You could call in sick, take the day off."

"I'm on a big project. I have to finish a program and go out of town for a few days." I was leaving for Los Angeles on Monday night.

"All right, but Carrie and I want to have you over for dinner, just dinner," said Bathsheba.

"As long as it is just dinner," I said, and immediately wished I had not agreed. I'd spend the evening fending them both off. Maybe I should give in and get it over with.

"Chance is doing her freakazoid thing. Let's watch," said Bathsheba.

I wasn't going to get any work done at the bar; so I closed my laptop and followed Bathsheba to the dressing room.

Chance, a highly tattooed Goth, was delivering a tutorial on body modification. I stood close, since the studs in her tongue made her hard to understand. Alligator clamps, secured by nylon straps around her thighs, spread her labia. She was filling a syringe when we arrived.

"This is sterile saline solution. You can order it online from a hospital supply warehouse," announced Chance, tapping the syringe and squirting a spurt of clear liquid to clear any bubbles. She handled the syringe like a head nurse, or someone with speedball experience. I watched as she pinched the top of her inner labia, stuck the needle in, and pushed the plunger. The labia began to swell immediately.

"Ten CCs in the top, middle, and bottom," said Chance grimacing in pain.

"Six shots," I said amazed and horrified. I don't have the nerve to stick *one* needle in my vulva.

"Seven, I do my clit," she said, refilling the syringe. We all groaned in unison. She injected herself six more times. The result was a vagina that resembled boneless sirloin. Her labia minor were an inch thick and protruded past her outer labia. Her sex turned bright red, and her oversized clit stuck out like a parrot's beak.

"How often?" asked Bathsheba.

"Every six weeks," said Chance.

"Are there any side effects?" I asked.

"My boyfriend says it feels weird when we fuck," Chance said very seriously.

I wandered off to check my phone messages. There was a voice mail from Marshall. The message was brief.

"Hello, Hamo. Marshall here, I really enjoyed our dinner. Can we do it again, same day, time, and place? Please call."

I immediately started to reply then decided to wait a minute or two and think about what I would say. I didn't want to sound as excited as I felt.

When I did call I got his voice mail. I decided to be equally brief.

"I had a wonderful time. I'd love to see you again, next Tuesday, at seven, Teatro's, Ciao."

Then I started thinking about what to wear.

Chapter 27

I was in my hotel room in Los Angeles on the phone with Earl Bowers.

"The small dishes are for television reception. The large ones are VSAT," he said.

"You need two for television?" I asked.

"Yes, if you subscribe to two satellite direct services," said Earl.

"Why do that?"

"Maybe they watch European or Asian television in addition to American TV. It's not that unusual. My neighbors from Pakistan have two dishes. They're soccer nuts."

"And VSAT, what the hell is that?"

"Very small aperture terminal, basically it's leasing the capability to communicate through satellites," said Earl. "Google VSAT and you'll find a dozen companies who provide satellite communication services."

"What does VSAT buy you?"

"The ultimate in high-speed communications: private network, secure voice or data, video, Internet, Web, whatever," said Earl.

"Why have two VSAT dishes?"

"Backup, each uses a different satellite. If one fails, you can still communicate," said Earl.

"Can the government listen in?" I asked.

"Sure, the NSA has a backdoor into all the satellites we launch. My guess is they've figured a way to listen in to the others. Europe, Russia, China, and Brazil are in the satellite business," said Earl. "VSAT is super expensive. Are they in the boonies?"

"Yes, the Berkshires."

"It could be difficult to get a reliable land line, so they chose satellite. Is there electronic commerce on their Web sites?"

"Nothing substantial, you can order art books and T-shirts at the museum site."

"Serious overkill, but maybe they have money to throw away," he said.

"So, how are things at ADS?"

"Fair to shitty, they let George go Friday?"

George was a member of my group.

"Yes, Delia emailed me the list," I said.

"I've been thinking about going out on my own. I got some ideas I'd like to develop. If I program them here, ADS owns them. Would you be interested in joining my startup as CEO? You would be responsible for the outside stuff."

"What do you consider outside stuff?"

"Talking to customers, finding investors, running the business while I'm left alone to program," said Earl.

"I'd be interested although I'd like to hang on to ADS a while longer," I said. I make it a practice never to say no to any business opportunity until I have a chance to think about it.

"Well, I'm not ready either. How are things at Millennium? Discover any terrorists?"

"Nothing so far, Millennium will soon decide it's a waste, and I'll join George and Delia in the unemployment line."

"Well, the VSAT thing is intriguing, but what's a museum in the Berkshires got to do with Millennium Construction?"

"That's a very good question, and if I knew, I might wrap this up," I said.

"Then get laid off."

"No good deed goes unpunished," I said. "I have to go, Earl, thanks for the info."

"Sure, miss seeing you around here, Hamo."

After I hung up, I considered the possibility that Earl was Elizabeth Schuyler. He certainly had the computer skill to find out about my alternate careers. He could have slipped some spyware on my PC. I regularly ran a program to detect spyware; but Earl wrote the detection program.

In five minutes, I was meeting my installation team for dinner. The weekend installation had gone off flawlessly. Tomorrow, Sunday, we were flying back to Boston.

Monday I was meeting Bradley at his place where according to my best guess, he would be make a serious attempt to get in my pants. I planned to provide everything short of actual penetration.

Tuesday, I was back at Teatro's meeting Marshall where he would probably not attempt to seduce me. I wasn't sure how I felt about that. I had a feeling that I'd do anything he wanted.

Chapter 28

"A. H. Thornton. I have an appointment with Bradley Dickerson," I spoke into the speaker by the gate to the ocean front estate. Bradley's parents' home was in an old money town, north of Boston.

The reason I agreed to meet Bradley at his place was that it offered privacy where secret matters can be discussed in secrecy. From Bradley's perspective, it also offered a bedroom he could coax me into.

"Good evening, Ms. Thornton. Drive in and park in front of the carriage house, please," replied a male voice. It was a servant's voice. I have no idea how I knew that.

The mansion was enormous, with an incredible view of Cape Anne. There was a postage stamp sized, sandy beach that probably washed away each winter to be replaced in the spring by sand from someone else's beach.

I should marry Bradley I thought for the fiftieth time as I pushed the buzzer to the carriage house door. I pushed it again, hoping to annoy this rich kid who'd decided to play FBI agent and thought every woman on the planet was eager to sleep with him.

I'd made a point of including in my ADS report that I was meeting Bradley there on his recommendation. If Bunny complained to Mrs. Kabel, I had documentation.

"I'm coming," said a woman's voice. "Bradley, warm up the plates in the microwave." The door opened to reveal a woman who had spent ten times what I had on cosmetic surgery.

"Bunny Hargroves, you must be Hamilton," said Bunny, extending her hand as I stepped through the door. Like Mrs. Kabel, she called me by my full middle name. Did they drum into your head at Bryn Mawr that nicknames are gauche? But then again, I doubted her birth certificate read Bunny.

"It's a pleasure to meet you," I said.

"And I you. You know Allie and I were at school together."

"Yes, Bradley mentioned that." I resisted the urge to say, "I heard the two of you got drunk one night and pulled a train over at the Sigma Chi House."

"She told me you're just the smartest and hardest working girl on her staff."

Actually, I was the only girl in my group. "That's so kind of her, but I still have a lot to learn." Oh the false modesty, I was lying down and rolling over for the rich woman. If she'd thrown a Frisbee, I'd have caught it in mid air and brought it back for her to throw it again.

"I understand your father is a college history professor. You must be very intelligent. The children of intellectuals always are."

I wondered how thorough Bunny Hargrove's research on A.H. Thornton was. Her last remark implied Bradley and I could breed a pack of Einsteins to carry on the family name.

"Mother, Hamo's here on business," Bradley said as he walked in from the tiny kitchen. He was wearing black slacks and an iron gray turtleneck. Why is it men look so sexy in turtlenecks, and we women look like we're working security at a lesbian mixer? With tassel loafers and no socks, he belonged in a Ralph Lauren ad.

"Hello. Hamo," he said, awkwardly stepping toward me. He couldn't decide whether to shake my hand or kiss my cheek.

"Hello, Bradley." I stepped forward to put my hands on his shoulders and brush my lips against his cheek.

"She's a take-charge girl, Bradley. They're the best kind," said Bunny. She got a gold star for reading body language. From my alternate career, I was good at it, but Bunny had been at it longer.

"Mother, say good night," said Bradley.

"Goodnight, Hamilton, enjoy your dinner. I'll leave you to your business meeting," said Bunny.

"Do you want me to walk you back, Mother?" Bradley asked.

"No, I can make it," said Bunny.

Bradley watched for several seconds as she walked in slow halting steps toward the main house.

"She's not been well," said Bradley. There was genuine concern in his voice and expression.

The wine was French and the hors d'oeuvres weren't anything I'd had before. The black, fishy-tasting beads on smoked salmon were my first taste of caviar. Regardless of the fancy food, I stayed on message. "So, what can you tell me about Stacia McClain?"

Bradley handed me a thick folder. "I have quite a bit to tell you." Sabihah Harashaba, AKA Stacia McClain, was born thirty-three years ago in London to Azadeh Harashaba. She is an only child. Her mother belonged to a wealthy Egyptian family that settled in the UK in the 1960s. Here is the mother's photo." He handed me a black and white photo that looked like something from a tabloid.

"I suppose all the fur and diamonds are real," I said. Stacia's mom dressed in an evening gown and ermine coat was being helped out of a Rolls Royce by a gentleman in evening wear. Diamond rings, earrings, and a necklace sparkled at the camera.

"She married three of the richest men in England, Lords with titles that still meant something."

"Is that Stacia's father?" I asked referring to the distinguished looking man in the photo.

"That is Lord Worthington, but as far as we know, is not her father. In fact, Azadeh never revealed Stacia's father. That's why Stacia has the same surname as her mother."

"Stacia's a bastard," I said.

"Having an illegitimate child isn't that damaging when you have money and connections," said Bradley. "Sabihah went to the best private schools, not that she was much of a student. She dropped out at seventeen. She changed her name to Stacia, became a model and a member of London's party set," said Bradley, handing me a stack of photographs.

I thumbed through portfolio style shots of Stacia. There were several artsy nudes, nothing pornographic. She was a beautiful woman. I pushed away thoughts of her standing in Marshall's office offering sex.

"Pretty like her mother, but more serious," I said after examining the photos.

"These were taken later."

One was of Stacia sitting in a restaurant with friends. She had a cigarette in one hand and a drink in the other. Everyone was smiling at the camera. There was a touch of sadness; the look of a party girl, tired of it all, too many men, too much booze and drugs.

"When modeling played out, she went to work for an art gallery. She'd studied art in school, and she had the right connections. She was capable enough to be promoted to assistant manager. Along came Branson McClain on museum business. He met Stacia, both beautiful and knowledgeable. Stacia racked up a few hundred thousand frequent flyer miles visiting the US before Branson asked her to marry him. Marriage made her eligible for US citizenship. She became a citizen two years later."

"Branson is gay and lives in Key West. Why did he get married?"

"Maybe he was still hetero or trying to be hetero. Perhaps he thought that marriage to a sexy ex-model would change him. I really don't know, but he wouldn't be the first gay man to take a wife," said Bradley.

I knew dancers who were married to gay men. If you hated cooking and were lousy at home décor, it was an option.

"How did she meet Soraya Sheffield?"

"Soraya's father is a collector of art and was a friend of Branson's father. Stacia and Soraya most likely crossed paths in the art world. They have other things in common: both are wealthy, foreign born of Middle Eastern stock, and married to Americans."

"So, as a favor, Soraya gets her friend Stacia a job as her husband's assistant," I said, leaving out the part that Stacia was screwing Soraya's husband.

"Getting a friend a job is common enough," said Bradley.

"You're right, but that still doesn't explain why a rich former London party girl is willing to answer Marshall Sheffield's phone. Why didn't she open her own art gallery, or take a management position in the Museum?"

"Those are valid questions, but the answers don't necessarily make Stacia a terrorist," said Bradley.

"Stacia's not part of the IS&T Department. Why does the FBI think the terrorists are in the computer department?" I asked.

"Honestly, I cannot answer."

"Cannot or will not?"

"Cannot, this was passed on by the CIA. One of their sources picked it up. They never reveal sources."

"Did you find out who Stacia was with at the gala?"

Bradley handed me their photo from the gala. Stacia's escort appeared to be in his twenties and was extremely good looking. "His name is Steven Wagner. He works in the financial district as a broker."

"Paid escort?"

"No, a matter of mutual convenience—he gets to meet potential wealthy clients and she gets a handsome escort for the evening."

"Can I keep this for a few days to look it over?" I asked, referring to the folder.

"Sure, as long as you don't share it with anyone. Are you finding anything of interest?" asked Bradley.

"I haven't found any evidence of terrorist activity. We finished the Weber conversion this week. That was the last. Now that the big push is over, I'll have more time to search."

"Let me know the minute you find something," said Bradley.

"What's in the Bureau's dossier on Soraya and Marshall Sheffield?"

Bradley handed me a second folder.

"Marshall met Soraya when he was in Kuwait negotiating a contract with her father. Soraya worked for her father in public relations. According to rumor, he and Soraya had an affair. Marshall was still married at the time. Soon afterward, Marshall became a widower. His wife was killed in a car wreck."

Marshall hadn't mentioned sleeping with Soraya while still married to Chelsea. I wasn't sure I wanted to know.

"So Soraya was able to step in when Marshall's wife was conveniently killed."

"My mother informs me her female friends are perched like vultures, waiting for my stepfather to become a widower."

"I can't imagine a casserole widow here," I said.

"I don't get it," Bradley said.

"Women who read the obituaries and immediately deliver a casserole to the widower are called 'casserole widows.' The smart ones deliver it in a good dish, so they can come back for it later."

"I hadn't heard that. I'll have to tell Mother. Soraya must have shown up with a casserole during the wake. She and Marshall were married a year later. Soraya's father is a major investor in Millennium Construction. He arranged to bankroll a merger and acquisition binge making it one of the top US construction companies," said Bradley.

"Soraya's dad is on the board of both the McClain Foundation and Millennium Construction," I said.

"Along with the boards of dozens of other companies in the Middle East and Europe, he's a billionaire many times over."

"How long will the FBI continue to support this project if I don't find anything?" I asked.

"That's up to me. Terrorists are patient, so those who pursue them must be too."

"Based on the number of recent attacks, they seem very busy," I said. The day before, a bomb had gone off outside the American Embassy in Amman. My assignment had sparked my interest in world news.

"Yes, things have gotten active, again" said Bradley looking concerned.

"Some are happening in countries where Millennium has a project. The company has the logistical capability to deliver terrorists and explosives anywhere they have contracts."

"I agree," said Bradley. "Millennium would make an excellent cover."

Our business discussion was interrupted when an elderly servant named Walter arrived wheeling a cart containing enough food for a party of twelve.

I didn't know what you liked so I had cook prepare several different dishes," said Bradley as Walter set up a buffet then served a bottle of what I took to be a bottle of expensive French Bordeaux. It was a Grand Cru something or other.

I started with the seafood crepes then moved to the Beef Wellington. Everything was delicious and I ate far too much to be considered ladylike.

"My complements to the chef. If I ate this much all the time, I would weigh a ton," I said taking a bite of an awesomely intense piece of chocolate cake that Bradley informed me was a Sachertorte.

"I'll tell Myrna you approve of her cooking. Let's move to the living room and have a cognac.

It was almost too perfect a seduction: comfortable setting, delicious food, expensive wine, and forty year old cognac. We were in the living room in front of the fire place resting on a rug made from a tiger skin. Bradley's family obviously wasn't too concerned with the good opinion of PETA.

"Interesting rug, you shoot this yourself," I said resting my head on the tiger's.

"My Great Uncle Wyatt was the last of the great white hunters. His life's goal was to kill at least one of all the trophy animals. I should get rid of it. It's not politically correct."

"Don't, it suits you," I said reaching up to pull Bradley into my arms.

We kissed. When it got passionate, he lifted my sweater up over my bra and slipped his hand inside the cup. His hand was very warm and I had to fight for control.

"Stay the night."

"I can't. I've got to work tomorrow. Terrorists have infiltrated Millennium and I must stop them," I said.

"I said our plan is a patient one," said Bradley. His other hand was rubbing my crotch.

"And I don't want your mother thinking I'm just another one of your whores," I said. I was also aware staying over could get back to Mrs. Kabel and I would be fired.

"She'd understand," said Bradley.

"She'd pretend to, but she's old school. If my Acura is parked here in the morning, I'm a tart in her book. I have to leave but I want to take care of you before I go," I said, reaching for his zipper.

I took my time undressing him. He was well equipped and fully erect when I took him in my mouth.

I take pride in my blowjobs. At the club, I never rush even when it costs me money. I took Bradley to the edge a half dozen times before I brought him to a Las Vegas finish.

"That was incredible, awesome, you're a woman of great talents," said Bradley. "Are you sure you won't stay?"

"Positive, Besides, I've already got your best shot," I said.

He ignored the jibe.

"Mouthwash and a spare toothbrush are in the bathroom cabinet," said Bradley who still hadn't moved.

Visiting the Ladies Room after a blowjob cost a dancer revenue. Semen like Scotch is an acquired taste.

"Mouthwash is for the Natalie's of the world. I like the taste," I said leaning down to kiss him. He didn't object when I shared his essence.

Bradley walked me to my car. "If you stay I'll fuck you until sunrise." His hands grasped my bottom and pulled me against his restored erection.

"Sorry but I have to go or my reputation will be ruined. Don't tell Bunny I sucked your dick. If it's any consolation, I plan to use my vibrator when I get home."

Chapter 29

"So what's it like to live in a ménage a trois?" I asked Marshall as soon as the waiter brought our cocktails. We were back in the private dining room. It was nice not to have to worry about the next table overhearing.

I'd left work early to get my hair and nails done; then attacked my closet like a mad woman searching for the perfect thing to wear. I'd finally settled on a straight wool skirt that was short and tight but not overly so. I was wearing a powder blue cashmere sweater I'd bought at the mall on the way to the restaurant. I'd started out in a silk blouse, and then decided it was all wrong the minute I left my driveway.

My efforts for Marshall far exceeded those for Bradley. I knew what that meant but decided to think about it later.

"What's what like?" asked Marshall. He was still dressed from work, an expensive looking banker's gray suit and a tie I loved. His pheromones are a perfect match for my hormones.

"Having an office wife, it must pose challenges."

"For example?" He was amused, pleased that I started the conversation.

"There are two wet spots to sleep in. How do you decide, rock-paper-scissors?"

"Rock-paper-scissors, that brings back childhood memories. But nothing that elaborate, Soraya keeps a spreadsheet on her PC," said Marshall. "Now, since I've told you about my sex life, let's hear yours."

I didn't think it wise to say that I had give Bradley a blow job the night before so I made something up.

"I ran away from home when I was eleven. I caught the bus to Manhattan where I met a pimp at the Greyhound terminal named Mellow Man Ace. I became his number one outcall girl working midtown. I charged three hundred for a half and half and another hundred for the backdoor."

"Forgive my ignorance, but what is a half and half?" asked Marshall.

"Oral followed by vaginal intercourse, I specialized in CEO fantasies. Having serviced the entire Fortune 100, I became bored and returned to Boston to resume my middle school education."

"Are you still in touch with Mellow Man Ace?"

"Of course, he came to my high school graduation. Mellow Man is like a father to me. That reminds me I need to buy a birthday card. His is next month."

"Final question, what was your favorite CEO fantasy?"

"An auditor named Hamilton catches the CEO overstating corporate profits. She strips him naked and whips him till he orgasms on the SEC rulebook. Then she forces him to commit unspeakable acts against nature while he restates profits for the last two years."

"Sounds delightful, but Millennium's auditor is named Edward. I have a feeling getting to know you is not going to be easy. Let's start with the little things. Do you live alone?"

I decided to be serious. "No, I live with my older sister, Tommie. She's a dental hygienist. I have a neutered tomcat named Syllabus, whose loyalty to me is suspect. I live in a duplex in Saugus. My mother lives in the other half."

"Is Tommie involved in a relationship?" asked Marshall.

"Yes, a bad one. It's incredibly one sided. He doesn't return an ounce of the affection she lavishes on him. His booty calls flatten her self esteem."

"I'm going to need a slang dictionary. Explain booty calls?"

"A 'booty call' is arriving at a woman's house solely for purposes of sex. Tommie's inamorata spends all of fifteen minutes unloading his gun before he's back out the door."

"I thought good manners dictated a half hour. Is he married?"

"Yes, he's a married sleaze ball."

"How uncomfortable," said Marshall.

"You being married is not an issue, because ours is not a sexual relationship. You're my CEO using a social occasion to better understand the mindset of the company's newest female employee."

"Yes, that's exactly what we're doing," said Marshall.

"But for your information, my position on booty calls is that for every minute of penetration, I expect an hour of undivided attention. For that matter, you have no need for additional sex. Between Stacia and Soraya, you're getting more than you deserve."

"The only Sheffield who's getting more than he deserves is my brother," said Marshall.

"Speaking of Ben, I expected to be sailing the Florida Straits seeking trophy marlin."

"I asked him to back off where you were concerned," said Marshall.

"So your poor brother has forsaken female companionship at his brother's request."

"Just yours, his latest can't legally drink but she does have a learner's permit to drive," said Marshall.

"For the Bens of the world, the women get a year younger every time he has a birthday."

"There must be someone special in your life. You were with a young man at the gala," said Marshall.

"He's just a friend who was helping me navigate the tricky waters of high end charity galas. I panicked when Stacia commanded my attendance. I didn't want to look foolish or out of place."

"I can't forget you in that dress," said Marshall. "Not that you look any less beautiful tonight."

"Thank you," I said, suppressing a simper.

"I bet you were a rebellious teenager." Marshall kept the conversation from melting with my knees.

"Wrong. Dad was a dictator and we never questioned him," I said.

"Why did he leave?" asked Marshall?

"I'm not sure. Maybe he looked into his future and didn't like what he saw. I was leaving for college. Tommie was in her final year of school."

"Was there another woman?" asked Marshall.

"Not as far as I know, but it's hard to imagine him without some hapless female to order about."

"Most parents reconcile themselves to their children growing up and leaving the nest," said Marshall.

"And some parents can't be bothered and send their children away." Jesus, why did I make such a nasty remark? You're being a first class bitch I told myself. The look on Marshall's face indicated I had hit a nerve.

"Yes, some do." Marshall looked on the verge of tears. I hadn't meant to be nearly that mean.

"I'm sorry, that was a rotten thing to say." I reached over and put my hands in his. "Forgive me. Talking about my father brings out my inner bitch."

"It's not my choice," said Marshall. We had an awkward fifteen seconds while he held on to my hands so tight it hurt. As penance, I suffered in silence. I wondered what he meant when he said it wasn't his choice. Recovery over, we resumed my departed dad story.

"There were no signs he was unhappy?" asked Marshall.

"None, and that's something we discussed endlessly after we learned he left on his own."

"Do you have hobbies," asked Marshall.

"No, but I have a side business designing and hosting Web sites. I stay very busy. There's no time for a social life, which is okay since I would probably make a terrible life partner."

I was fighting the urge to tell Marshall everything. I wanted to put my head on his shoulder and tearfully dump it all into his lap. I pictured him holding me while I told him I was an ADS employee working undercover at Millennium, an exotic dancer, and a Web designer for soft porn sites, and that someone named Elizabeth Schuyler was stalking me. Thank God I kept my mouth shut.

"I've read stories about people starting life under a mountain of college loans," said Marshall, bringing me back to reality. "I was lucky that my father believed in education and had the means to provide a good one."

"The end is in sight. If all goes well and Millennium doesn't lay me off, I'll be debt free in ten months. Then I'll come here and wait patiently to meet a marriageable professional."

"I can't picture you waiting patiently for anything. How's the MillProMan implementation progressing?" Marshall seemed to sense I had something building up, and changed the subject.

"Installation is complete. Weber converted without a problem. It's a great system," I said.

"Good news, you have no idea how difficult it's been to measure progress looking at reports from different systems."

"I'm very attracted to you," I blurted, like a twelve-year-old who just can't keep quiet any longer. My heart stopped while I waited for Marshall to say something.

"And I to you," he replied, smiling at me. "You have no idea how much I was looking forward to tonight."

After my Veal Marsala arrived, I blundered on, "I know there are issues. I want to get to know you. And I need to understand where you are with Soraya and Stacia." Lucky Tommie had only one wife to contend with.

"I can't tell you everything. After Chelsea was killed, my approach to grief was working twenty-four hours a day. I figured if I worked every waking minute then I wouldn't have time to think about her. I ignored my children and became someone who slept on the couch in his office."

"You concentrated on growing your company," I said.

"A lot of business was up for bid in the Middle East. Governments were awash in oil money. I'd already met Soraya and her father. He offered Millennium profitable sub-contractor work."

"I understand Soraya's father is in a class with Bill Gates," I said. I wasn't going to pursue Bradley's gossip that Marshall was sleeping with Soraya before Chelsea was killed.

"Yes, he has homes on three continents, fabulous apartments in New York, London, and Paris. Azul's the prototypical global businessman. He speaks seven languages, does most of his business from a jet with more electronics than I've ever seen in one place. He's a very charming and powerful man. He can pick up a phone and be put through to a dozen Arab rulers."

"You admire him?" I asked.

"Who wouldn't? I was flattered he took an interest in the company. We weren't exactly a big player. Soraya worked in public relations. She was beautiful and charming and she made the pain go away. She took an interest in Justin and Judith. I began to realize what an awful father I was. I convinced myself that my children needed a mother. Ben said I had such a great marriage with Chelsea, I just assumed marriages were like that."

"Taking marriage advice from Ben, you must have been really fucked up," I said.

"Everything seemed right at the time. Her father was looking to invest in an American construction company. Soraya was acting like my two children were the most important people in her life. So I asked her to marry me. Everything was terrific for a while. Then I realized Soraya had an agenda. She lost interest in the children the day we returned from the honeymoon. The one thing our marriage did produce was a much larger Millennium. Her father and his friends arranged financing to acquire premium companies. His business connections brought more work than we could handle."

"And life with Soraya, what's it like?" I asked.

"I can go a month without seeing her. When I do, it's a social occasion like the gala, where my attendance is needed to keep up appearances."

"Divorce her," I said.

"Some people appear civilized, but they're not. Divorce is not an option."

"Because she has Justin and Judith, she's taken them away, and you don't know where they are," I said, certain they were in McClain Castle—unless my blundering had gotten them moved.

"My God, you're perceptive. I can't talk about it. I'm sorry," said Marshall.

"And Stacia, how does she fit into this?" If Marshall was knowingly aiding terrorists, I needed to know.

"I'm not exactly sure. Stacia met Branson when she worked for a gallery in London. Soraya's father collects art and he's on the Museum's Board of Directors. Azul's donations saved the museum when it was going through financial difficulties. Branson's no longer involved with the museum or the foundation. Soraya's father controls it."

"And Stacia sits outside your office and answers your telephone," I said.

"Not true, Maria Cavetti does most of the day to day work."

"Why did you hire Stacia?"

"After Soraya and I were married, she instructed me to replace my Administrative Assistant with Stacia. I said hell no. That's when I learned how far she was willing to go to get her way."

"She took the gloves off?" I asked

"She said if I didn't do as she said, something horrible would happen to Justin and Judith. God I shouldn't be telling you this. I've carried it around a long time and not telling anyone is driving me insane. You can't tell anyone."

"Not a word, I promise. Where are Justin and Judith?"

"I don't know. I'm allowed to speak with them once a month on a cell phone."

"How are they doing?"

"Unhappy, they blame me and they should," said Marshall.

"What excuse did Soraya use to make you hire Stacia?" I asked.

"She told me Stacia needed a reason to stay in the Boston area, but that was a lie."

"Does Stacia do anything suspicious at work?" I asked.

Marshall thought for a moment before he answered. "Yes, she performs certain favors. Soraya made me give her a free hand. What drives me insane is that it's never anything significant. She'll call a project manager and, using my name, direct him to hire someone."

"Large numbers of employees?" I asked.

"No, just one or two. The financial impact is almost negligible. We wind up with an extra employee. Some of the people she's forced us to hire have been good workers."

"How did you find out?" I asked.

"I was talking to the manager of an oil terminal project in Equatorial Guinea, and he told me how pleased he was with the two guys I sent him. I had to pretend I'd forgotten."

"Anything else?"

"A few thousand dollars to consultants no one ever heard of. Some of these projects are in the hundreds of millions of dollars. Ten or twenty grand to a consultant doesn't make a ripple. Also she arranges shipments on company jets," said Marshall.

"What kind of shipments?"

"According to the manifest, charitable donations to a local mosque, copies of the Quran, medical supplies, all very innocent," said Marshall.

"Is either of the two a devout Muslim?" I asked, although it seemed a stupid question.

"Not unless Gucci sells veils. They never mention religion."

"What do you plan to do?" I asked.

"Get my children back, and then run as far away as possible. I shouldn't have told you any of this. It might put you in danger," said Marshall.

Top shelf liquor and expertly cooked veal are as bad as cocaine, they make you do say stupid things. "Together, I promise we are going to come up with a plan to get Justin and Judith back."

Chapter 30

I'd promised Marshall I would get Judith and Justin back. Was I out of my mind? Actually what I had said was I'd think of something, or *we'd* think of something. I'm not sure what I said. He looked so dejected, I couldn't stop myself.

He didn't discourage me by telling me it wasn't my problem and far too dangerous. He actually expected me to do something. Did that mean we were in a relationship?

One option was a commando raid on McClain Castle. That brought to mind an image of me sliding down a rope from a helicopter wearing body armor and night vision goggles. Unfortunately, the only thing I'm capable of sliding down is a brass pole.

However, I was capable of computer research, and I was working furiously to finish my search before I left for my Friday shift at Foxy Vixens II. Thursday night, I'd loaded the complete MillProMan database onto the server intended to host the Web site for the Boston Gentlemen's club. The hard drive now contained tens of millions of transactions generated during ten years of construction projects.

I scanned through the data, making sure everything loaded properly. I took a thorough look at an ongoing project for an aqueduct providing water to Los Angeles. Most transactions detailed the delivery of concrete.

I'd borrowed a copy of the MillProMan database from Millennium's fireproof vault. In doing do I violated every rule in the employee handbook. I could be fired and even prosecuted if someone found out. Taking a copy out of the data vault had been easy. It wasn't locked during the day. I walked in, located what I wanted, slipped it in my purse and left. Monday, I'd put it back.

Loading the database had taken eight plus hours, even on my new super fast system. The data format allowed transactions to be searched in endless ways. You could retrieve all the transactions for a particular project, or all transactions made on a certain day regardless of project. The data could be sliced and diced until you lost your mind.

Still, I didn't have everything I needed. I required detailed information on every terrorist attack in the last ten years. I Googled my way to a database at Stanford University, created by something called the Center for International Security and Cooperation. I downloaded and reformatted it to fit in the MillProMan database. It included the date, time, and location of each terrorist attack. It also included whether the attack was considered major. I decided to consider only large scale attacks, the kind that would require Stacia to lend a hand

I entered Stacia's date of hire as the start date of my search, and filtered it to look for projects underway at the same time, in the same countries where attacks occurred. A dialog box estimated the search time as twenty-two minutes.

ON THE POLE

While I waited for the progress bar to fill, I rushed around getting ready. The fucker hung at ninety nine percent forever before finally clicking over to complete.

Since Stacia started, there had been forty-seven attacks in countries with an active Millennium project. Unfortunately, there were also three hundred and five projects where there was not an attack, and fourteen attacks in countries where Millennium wasn't present.

I scanned the forty-seven. An attack in Equatorial Guinea caught my eye. Marshall had mentioned Stacia was involved in getting two men hired. I was out of time. I saved everything so I could resume the search later.

Chapter 31

"You've got to be able to work any job," said Avery, the manager of Club Lido. That was why I was helping Gina behind the bar. The scheduled bar back failed to show.

It was late Saturday afternoon. I was half way through a long day. Ten in the morning to six in the evening I was acting assistant manager. From six to closing I was entertainment.

Avery had only been club manager for a couple of years. He was young enough not to be too bent out of shape at the prospect of a female manager.

On stage, a dancer named Persephone was bent like a clothespin, her face smiling between her ankles at a group of men seated at the tip line. The crown of her head touched the dance floor as she flexed her buttocks to show off her gaped open back door. Bills were falling like autumn leaves.

"I almost forgot to mention it. Thursday night, a dude was asking about you," Gina said.

I looked up from emptying a bucket of ice into the bar well. "What did he want?"

"He wanted to know when you were scheduled to dance. I checked the schedule and told him."

I had my share of regulars. It wasn't unusual for a customer to want to know when a particular dancer was working. When things are slow and they've spent all they have, you sit and talk to pass the time. You get to know them, and they think they get to know you. Once they're comfortable, they'll ask for you over and over again.

If not for Elisabeth Schuyler I wouldn't have been concerned. "What did he look like?"

"Short, dumpy, ugly bastard, his head was shaved," said Gina.

My mental picture of my stalker was of a tall thin New England Yankee, a former school teacher based on his writing style. Still I was curious given everything else that was happening.

"How long did he stay?"

"He hung around a while. He asked me if I knew you."

"What did you tell him?"

"Nothing, I know the rules. I said you were a hot piece of ass with a thing for ugly little creeps like him."

"Thanks Gina, you're sweet," I said before giving her a kiss. I make it a point to keep club personnel on my side.

After the crowd dwindled, Avery showed me how to take inventory for the beer and liquor and prepare the spirits reorder.

Management shift over. I took a shower and got ready to dance. Things got busy, and I was either on stage dancing or crotch polishing in the VIP Room.

I just returned from the VIP Room with a Ben Franklin in my bag. It was a customer who had gone commando in slacks made out of the thinnest material imaginable. Seale was on Security and his give-a-shit index was low. I glanced over at Persephone, who had a customer's mouth attached to her nipple. She looked back at me and shrugged.

"Don't bite," I whispered, as Mr. Commando saw what Persephone's guy was getting away with and imitated him. Since each song's duration is less than three minutes, you don't have to put up with anything for long. I concentrated on working my ass against his cock. He surprised me by getting off.

You don't see that often. Most often, we send them home to finish the job by hand. He paid the club tab and handed me a hundred. I wet wiped my breasts, put my top and bottom back on, and returned to the pit.

I arrived just as six newcomers took seats near the stage. It was a denim, T-shirt, and ball cap group of twenty-somethings. Based on the company names on their shirts, they worked construction. I walked over to introduce myself. I was next on stage but I wanted to prime them for later.

"I'm Alexandra,' I said offering them my hand.

A look passed among the six. That should have me warned that something was wrong, but I was concentrating on revenue.

"I'm Ron, We've heard about you, Alexandra," said the alpha male enveloping me in beer breath.

Dealing with drunken horny men is part of the job I reminded myself.

"What have you heard, Ron?" I asked as I placed my arm around his shoulders. He put his hand around my waist and pulled me tight against him. As he did, his buddy, Sam, sandwiched me then slipped his hand inside my top. He squeezed my boob then grabbed my nipple. He wasn't gentle about it. I looked around for Security but they were absent.

"We heard you have big zickers," said Sam pinching hard.

My nipples are sensitive to the callused hands of men who do real work. But there was an air of menace about them. There are happy drunks and mean drunks and they struck me as the latter, the kind who beat the shit out of wives to prove their manhood.

"Take it easy on me and I'll make it easy for you." I placed my hands on their thighs feigning willingness to give them what they wanted. It was something I often said and did in those situations.

"Fuck easy," said Ron. His large powerful hand took a firm grip of my butt cheek.

"Sorry, guys, no grabbing tits and ass outside the VIP Room." I pushed away from them, or tried to. They were big men and didn't let go. Ron's hand squeezed my butt so hard it hurt.

"Don't be a cunt," said Ron holding me tighter.

I ignored the C-word. "I'm dancing next. I'll be back after I finish."

"I bet you got a tight pussy, Alexandra," said Ron, sliding his free hand under the waistband of my daisy dukes to rest on my clit. He fingered my button then pushed inside me. I couldn't believe Security hadn't come to my rescue. It turned out Seale was in Avery's office having a heated discussion about next week's work schedule.

My survival instincts took over. "Oh fuck, yes," I moaned as I closed my eyes, forced my body to relax, and pushed my groin against Ron's fingers.

ON THE POLE

"The cunt likes to be finger fucked," observed Sam as he twisted my nipple.

"We're going to take you outside and fuck you in the ass. You're not going to shit right for a month," said Ron relaxing his grip as he focused on increasing digital penetration.

"I love to be fucked in my ass," I cooed right before I shoved with all my strength and squirmed free.

"Come back after you dance," said Ron laughing.

"Sure," I said. I had no intention of going anywhere near them.

A half hour later, I was on stage when a darkly handsome man found an empty seat at the tip line. He wasn't dressed like a typical customer. He looked preppie in khakis and an oxford blue dress shirt. From old photos, I recalled my father dressed that way when he went to college.

I decided to ignore the strange attire when he pulled out a roll of bills and placed a five on stage edge.

"I haven't seen you here before. What's your name?" I asked, providing a close up view of my gyrating butt.

"Richard," he replied reaching the five toward me.

He didn't say it like we say Richard. The emphasis was on the last syllable. He sounded French Canadian, an accent frequently heard in New England.

"Where are you from, Richard," I asked?

"Montreal."

"And what brings you to New England," I asked?

"A conference on climate change," said Richard.

"Mind if I call you Dick," I asked making the name sound dirty as I scooped up the five.

"No problem," said Richard.

"I'm Alexandra," I said, rubbing the bill over my nipples and between my legs.

"Dick, you're getting me hot like the climate," I said as I tucked the bill between the folds of my pussy.

I danced away from Dick for a while. You have to ration attention to the customers. Too much and they lose interest.

In another ten seconds, the song ended. I slipped out of the chemise and shook my butt at the crowd as the last note sounded. I ducked behind the curtain, waited until my next song started, and then strode back on stage in a pair of platform heels and nothing else.

"Show us some pussy, Alexandra," roared one of the asshole gropers from before. I smiled and waved at their table as I did a back bend, ending in a reverse tabletop. I opened and closed my legs for a pussy wink. They could see inside my recently violated magic tunnel. The third dance is a moneymaker so I focused. I collected singles and fives, did some of my pole routines, and then danced to Dick because he laid a twenty on the stage. I got down on all fours with my ass inches from Dick's face, and went through my cat stretch routine.

I did a tuck and roll and luckily came down into a split right on top of Dick's twenty. It stuck to my pussy. There are sex clubs in Bangkok where girls pick up quarters with their labia. I wouldn't go to the trouble for a quarter—but for a twenty, why not? Dick was impressed enough to peel another twenty off the roll, and place it on the stage.

As I was about to attempt another snatch grab, I heard loud angry voices from the direction of the six assholes. Shit, I thought. Those bastards are going to fuck this up for me.

ON THE POLE

As I started to roll forward, targeting the twenty, the lights went out. Later, Avery told me someone had broken open the electrical panel at the back of the building and tripped the main breaker. The sudden darkness startled me, and I lost control. My legs kicked out wildly and I fell.

My calf struck something I later realized was Dick's arm. I heard a loud bang and felt something hum past my ear. For some reason, I was thinking of the twenty. As I looked for it in the dim emergency lighting, a narrow red beam penetrated the gloom ending at the center of my chest. My eyes followed it back to the pistol Dick was holding.

I was half standing when Seale jumped on the stage between us. He was rushing to help Tice break up the fight. The bullet hit him in the thigh, sending him to the floor, screaming.

Instinctively, I crawled toward the back of the stage. I heard another pop and saw several pieces of dance floor jump in the air, right beside me. Dick climbed on stage heading in my direction. When I reached the curtain, I rolled under it then got to my feet and ran toward the dressing room.

Gunshots panicked the crowded club. Everyone rushed together at the emergency exits. Exit doors alarms added to the confusion.

Arnie wasn't inclined to spend on frivolities, such as emergency lighting, not when it was cheaper to bribe safety inspectors. The hallway was pitch-black, but I'd been down it a thousand times. I shouldn't have run into the water cooler, but I did. Five gallons of water for thirsty dancers gushed onto the floor. I fell, sliding on ice-cold water as Dick fired twice toward the noise. I cowered behind the overturned fountain.

"Who the fuck is shooting out there?" yelled Persephone. "I've got a gun, too, motherfucker. I'll blow your balls off." Persephone demonstrated it wasn't just a threat by firing a round into the ceiling.

I watched the laser sight search the hall. He was less than fifteen feet away. The club had gotten quiet. Persephone's gunshot worried him enough to stay put. While Dick was deciding, I struggled to keep my teeth from chattering, either from fear or lying naked in ice water.

I heard my assassin turn and walk away. I almost started to stand when he stopped. The laser sight moved back down the hall toward me. I held my breath. Then I heard the sound of a siren. That settled it; he ran away through the curtain.

I slowly got to my feet. "Persephone, it's me, Alexandra. Don't shoot. He's gone," I said.

Chapter 32

While I was seated in the dressing room trying to stop shaking, I arrived at the conclusion that I had luckily survived an assassination attempt. My murder had been planned. The fight and the power failure were distractions to allow Richard to blow a hole in my chest.

Once Avery reset the power breaker, I found Sophia being tended by Persephone. Sophia was sitting with the gropers who started the fight.

"How did the fight start," I asked?

"The one named Ron threw a pitcher in the face of Eddie, the fat dude," said Sophia, holding a bag of ice on her bruised ankle.

"Why?"

"Damn if I know. It happened so suddenly. They all seemed to be getting along fine one minute, then all hell broke loose," she said.

"Did they give you a hard time? Feel you up?"

"No, they behaved, just regular guys."

"So there was no reason for a fight?" I asked.

"None that I know of, but hell, you know how guys are. A funny look can be enough. They were pretty shit-faced. The lights went out as I was running away. That's when I fell. Shit, I wonder how long before I can dance?"

"You ought to have it x-rayed. You could have a fracture." There was a swelling above her anklebone, and the flesh was turning blue.

"I think it's just a sprain." Sophia probably didn't have health insurance. Who wants to face the humiliation that ER's reserve for people without it?

I got home at three in the morning. When I went to bed, I couldn't sleep. Every time I closed my eyes, I saw that red dot. If Seale hadn't taken my bullet, I'd be in a drawer in the Kent County morgue.

Maybe it was time to say fuck it and run for my life. I could follow my dad's example and disappear. I could change my name and move to Las Vegas. I'd become an escort. I'd be frugal and save to buy a small business. I'd meet a casino executive and have a job waiting when I decided to get off the pole.

I heard a noise outside and got up to look, but it was only a stray dog working the trash. Totally freaked, I got my Glock out of the safe and put it on the nightstand. I fell asleep an hour before the alarm went off. There was no way I could sit at my desk and program.

I called Doreen's cell and left a voice mail that I'd had a rough night and was taking a personal day. My cell woke me right after eleven a.m.

"Are you all right?" asked Marshall.

He was concerned. Adrenaline of a different sort cut through the haze. "Sure, it's just the beginning of a cold."

"Sorry to wake you. When I saw you were on the list of absentees, I worried," he said.

"No, I'm glad you called. How have you been?"

"Not good, I confronted Soraya about Justin and Judith. I told her I had to see them in person."

"What did she say?"

"She offered to arrange a video conference through the Internet. Can you believe that bullshit? I lost it. I hit her. She told me if I ever hit her again, I'd never see my children."

"Can you still accept the offer of the video feed?" I asked.

"I suppose so," said Marshall taking a few seconds to answer.

"Where would it take place?"

"I have a webcam on my home office PC."

"If I gave you some special software, could you install it without anybody knowing?"

"I think so. What would it do?"

"Track the video message packets back to the source. It would identify the computers involved in the transmission. With luck, we'd know where the video originated."

"That would be something I could act on."

"Act on how?" I was concerned Marshall would do some stupid macho thing.

"Get some of my guys together and get my children back."

"That's a very bad idea; you would be facing well-armed, highly-trained men. They will shoot you down without hesitating."

"How do you know that?"

"You're going to have to trust me on this one," I said.

Given what happened with Soraya, trusting womankind didn't come easy.

"You're not what you appear to be," said Marshall sounding tired like a man who had realized the world was a much worse place than he had thought.

"No, but I am one of the good girls and I care about you. I am going to help you get your children back but I need you to stay calm and focused."

There was another long pause before he spoke. "When can we get together?"

"I have to burn a copy of the program for you. When we meet, I'll teach you how to install it."

"I won't ask where you got a program like that," he said.

"Good, because I won't tell you. I want you to promise me you will be as non-violent as Gandhi. No more physical stuff. Apologize to Soraya for hitting her."

"Why should I?"

"I don't want to see what a bullet would do to that handsome face."

"You think I am handsome?"

"Yes, and as soon as I get off this call, I'm going to get out my vibrator and spend time thinking about you."

"I could stay on for phone sex," said Marshall.

"Promise me you won't do anything crazy."

"I promise. What are you wearing?"

"Pooh Bear flannel pajamas. Bye."

I got up and fixed coffee, then headed to DMS world headquarters.

Chapter 33

"You're not trained in law enforcement or you would be more objective and consider alternative scenarios," said Bradley. He sounded like my father, and he was seriously pissing me off.

We were meeting in the coffee shop of a bookstore near my home. It was mid afternoon and the place was empty.

"Your problem is that you find it impossible to believe the ruling classes are as capable of producing terrorists as a Baghdad slum," I replied.

I'd just given Bradley reasonable proof that Millennium Construction was hosting a terrorist cell, and I was getting more push back than I expected.

I had begun my list of evidence with, "Three years ago, G&E, a subsidiary of Millennium, won a contract to build an offshore oil depot in Malabo, Equatorial Guinea. It was a rush job to boost the country's oil exports."

"In the final year of the project, a terrorist rammed a delivery van into a housing complex for American oil workers. The explosion killed thirty-two Americans and seventeen locals and wounded one hundred seven more."

"I remember that attack," said Bradley.

"An FBI team concluded that a male suicide bomber in his early twenties drove the van. There wasn't enough left for fingerprints and the DNA didn't match any known database. Parts of a remote detonator capable of being set off by a cell phone were found."

I recall that a cell phone call detonated the explosion," said Bradley.

"Now, here is the interesting part, Bradley. When I looked through the project's transactions, I got several hits on Stacia McClain's authorization. She personally authorized the hiring of two truck drivers, Ebrahim Al-Mansourri and Azeem Nor-Azami. A notation in the personnel records read, 'Directed to hire—via Stacia McClain per Marshall Sheffield.'"

"Go on," said Bradley.

"Two weeks after the explosion the two were terminated for Job Abandonment. There was a note from the supervisor stating that both men had not come to work for the last five days. They had been on leave the first week, so they were not considered absent until the second week."

For a change I seemed to be getting through to Bradley so I kept at it.

"Their supervisor visited the building where the two shared an apartment. He made the following entry in their personnel data. 'Owner said they got homesick and returned to their country. Respectful and polite, not boozers and troublemakers like other G&E tenants. Spent much of their time at the mosque.'"

"There were other transactions Stacia authorized. The company had donated over twenty thousand dollars to a local mosque. Shipments of medical supplies and other goods had been transported on Millennium's plane. Over two thousand kilograms of charitable donations, collected by a foundation called World Famine Relief, were distributed to the Al Kasseri mosque. Soraya Sheffield is on the board of directors of World Famine Relief."

"Good work. I'll send your research to the Anti-Terrorism Center and see if they agree," said Bradley.

"And if they don't?" I said.

"Just keep on doing what you're doing. You're doing a great job, Hamo. But you need to be more analytical and dispassionate."

It took every ounce of self-control I had to ignore Bradley's stereotypical assertion that I, a woman, was driven by emotions, as opposed to his cold manly logic. I managed not to tell him to go fuck himself.

"I'll see what else I can find." I spoke in a cold, even tone. "Good, I need to make sure we have an airtight case. If we move too early, and it turns out we're wrong, I'll be chasing bank robbers in Montana and you'll be looking for a new assignment."

"All right," I said. I didn't have any choice. Bradley was paying the bills. All I had to lose by arguing was my job.

"Let's have a dinner meeting next week at my place, and go over everything from top to bottom. Maybe I'm missing something. Are you available Tuesday?"

"Yes." I wondered if Bradley noticed I was billing the hours I spent dining with him.

"By the way, you made an impression on my mother by not staying over. She said you were a woman of character who values her reputation."

"Being a woman of character means you won't get anything more than you got last time. "

"There are more important things," said Bradley, sounding very high minded. If I offered to do him under the table, he would have accepted.

"How long before you hear from the Bureau?"

"A week, maybe two," said Bradley.

"You can't put a rush on it?"

"That's with a rush. It would take six weeks normally. The Bureau has more than our case to process."

"Well, let me get back to work," I said.

"I'll be in touch when I hear anything," said Bradley.

Two weeks would have been acceptable if someone wasn't trying to kill me. My attempted murder might have convinced him that I was on to something, but if I told Bradley about the shooting at the club, my ADS job would be history.

Chapter 34

I met Marshall in Sheepsfold, a huge woodland park near my home. I knew the park well because my dad went there when he wanted to go birding close to home. He took Tommie and me along and let us run wild, while he perched on a large rock and scoured the trees for something rare.

It was mid afternoon on a weekday, so the park was almost empty. I hiked along the railroad tracks for a quarter of a mile. Then I climbed a small hill and climbed on the flat top boulder where my dad used to sit.

I took his field glasses and the dog-eared *Birds of North America* out of my backpack. Once again, I was pretending to be a bird watcher. I had to dream up a new cover. Who bird watches anymore? At the appointed time, I saw Marshall walking along the abandoned railroad tracks.

"Love is the enemy of rational thought," I said aloud as I watched him approach through the binoculars. He was wearing khakis, a blue oxford shirt, and a sweater tied around his neck. He looked like an aging preppie. Still my heart sped, and just looking at him improved my mood. I carefully scanned the area behind and around him; nobody was following.

"I've missed you," he said taking me into his arms. It was a long kiss that included rolling around on the hard uncomfortable surface.

"I've missed you, too" was all I managed when we finally came up for air.

"Are you a bird watcher?" asked Marshall, eying the field glasses and book.

"No, my father was and he took me here when I was a kid. It gives me a reason to being here. I brought your training materials."

"Where do we start?" asked Marshall.

I handed him my notebook computer, the disc, and a typed page. "Just follow instructions."

Marshall wasn't that familiar with computer software, so he read the instructions first then proceeded thru the installation step by step. He made it with a minimum of problems and only a couple of questions. I showed him how to run a test to insure the installation was successful.

"This is impressive. You're impressive," he said. He leaned over to kiss me again after the installation was complete.

"You're a sucker for smart women," I said.

"Smart, beautiful, filthy mouthed women," said Marshall. We lay back on the boulder. I rolled on top.

"The park police patrol for couples engaged in salacious activities," I said. Actually, Sheepsfold had become known as a hookup spot for gays who made their initial contact on Craigslist. One of my neighbors had recently been arrested.

"It's only a misdemeanor," he said, grinning.

"And how would you know?" I asked.

"Chelsea and I were arrested for having sex in public at Crane's Beach, shortly before we were married. We had gone back into the dunes, thinking no one would see us. Just as I was gaining traction, two park rangers popped out of the weeds and arrested us."

"Now, you're telling me I'm kissing a known felon," I said.

"Not a felony just a misdemeanor, we had to pay a fine," said Marshall.

"How long was it before Chelsea spoke to you again?"

"It was her idea; so she couldn't blame me. She blamed the Puritanical government of the Commonwealth," said Marshall.

"Sounds like my kind of woman," I said.

"You do remind me of her but you are unique, and brilliant with computers. Chelsea was anything but technical. She couldn't program a VCR. You're our new star programmer."

"You've been talking to Doreen," I said.

"I must plead guilty of talking to her about you; she is a fan of yours. She thinks you're under employed."

"Don't promote me above my level of competency," I said. We were on our backs next to each other now, on a very uncomfortable surface. Marshall's arm was around me, and I was resting my head on his shoulder. We were quiet for a moment.

"If there were no Justin and Judith, I'd suggest we catch the first plane to Rio and spend the rest of our days on Ipanema beach, looking up at the statute of Christ," said Marshall.

"I'd have to fatten up my butt. Brazilians prefer women with a large round ass," I said.

"How do you know that?"

"Read it somewhere on the Internet. Brazilians like junk in the trunk," I said.

"You have a delightful bottom." Marshall pulled us together and cupped one. I felt something very male and aroused pressing against me through his khakis.

"Remember the park rangers," I said.

"I'll pay your fine if they arrest us," said Marshall.

"I don't have time to be arrested." I gently pushed Marshall away.

"Tempus fugit," he said with a sigh. He looked at his watch. "The video conference is set for six o'clock."

"Just because you know Latin doesn't mean I'll have sex with you," I said, standing up and pulling Marshall to his feet. "You leave first."

"I can't walk you back to your car?" He was so sweet.

"No, we shouldn't be seen together," I said. "Hide the DVD."

I'd told him to bring something with pockets big enough to hold a DVD case. The bulky sweater was it. "I haven't seen someone wearing a sweater like that in a while," I said.

"It worked in my day," he said.

Someone once told me that people who grow up rich don't give a damn how they look. I had a feeling that, in Marshall's case, it was true. As I watched him walk away, I told myself I would dress him cooler. Then I told myself to stop. I was acting like a lovesick idiot.

The video conference started promptly at six. I hadn't told Marshall that the spyware he installed would retransmit everything to one of my computers. I was getting a headache from watching both feeds on the same screen. One window had the video from Marshall's home office. Marshall was in a high backed leather chair with Soraya perched standing behind him like a bird of prey.

The dark paneling and shelving, displayed expensive looking object's d'art, made my own home office look shabby. My furniture was purchased used from a consignment store. If things worked out with Marshall, I'd study interior decorating and develop good taste.

The other window showed Justin and Judith AKA Barbara and Brent seated on a bench in front of a plain white wall. The background told us nothing; they could be anywhere. I was hoping anywhere was McClain Castle.

The kids looked miserable. Marshall's eyes were filled with tears. His efforts to sound positive for the sake of his children weren't working. At the next charity gala I would put a bullet between Soraya's eyes while she was sitting on the john. The Herald would print a shot of her slumped forward with her pantyhose bunched at her ankles.

The lights on my computer's hard drive were flickering, writing the video to disc. There was a small window in the corner of the screen displaying the server addresses forwarding the message. I was ignoring the window for Marshall's computer because I knew where the signal originated. The Internet was designed to survive a nuclear war by endlessly rerouting messages until they eventually reached their destination. If a Soviet H-bomb vaporized the servers at MIT, messages would reroute to UMASS in Amherst, assuming the Communists had no reason to target the home of Emily Dickinson.

I was getting consistent address readings from the children's transmission. They hadn't encrypted it. It was a portal owned by one of the company's whose name was painted on a dish behind McClain Castle.

The conversation between Marshall and his children was painful to watch. Marshall started off asking what they'd been learning from their tutors.

"Arabic," replied Justin, his voice saturated with sarcasm.

"That's good. Millennium has a lot of projects in Arabic speaking countries," said Marshall. "It will be useful when you come to work."

"I'm not working for Millennium," Justin said. "I'm going to be a Marine." Left unsaid was, "And kill every Arab I meet." Justin was a tough little bastard.

"Your grandfather was a soldier in World War Two. He worked in a Navy construction battalion called the Seabees," Marshall said.

"I hate it here. When are you going to come get us?" demanded Justin angrily.

At that point, Marshall's eyes glittered. He tried to keep his voice from breaking. Soraya didn't flinch as he covered his face, massaging his temples. "Soon," he finally said.

"Don't worry, Daddy. We're okay," said Judith playing the consoling daughter.

Marshall tried to regain his self-control, but before the session ended, tears were streaming down his face. He promised to bring them home as soon as he could.

"That's not good enough, Daddy. I want to come home now," said Justin, cutting his father no slack. He was probably more like his mother than his father. He softened as they said goodbye and told Marshall he loved him.

I misted up at the end. Syllabus left my lap in disgust. My father had drummed into us never to cry. Tommie ignored Dad's instructions and cried over everything. She balled over her philandering dentist daily. I only cried when I wanted something and tears were a way to get it. The last time I got stopped on the interstate, I let go a flood of tears as I told the trooper how my bastard husband would slap me around if I got another ticket and our insurance rate increased. He let me off with a warning.

Chapter 35

"It's a satellite feed. That narrows my search, but I need time for further analysis," I said. My cell phone had rung minutes after the videoconference ended. Marshall was in his car.

"How long before you know?" asked Marshall? "You said your software would track the messages back to their source."

"When I said source, I meant the Internet address of the router sending the messages."

"Router, what the hell's that?" asked Marshall.

"It's the computer that routes messages within the local network," I said, realizing I had made a mistake. I'd given him hope that once he knew their location, he could go and get them.

"Why is everything so fucking complicated?"

"Once we confirm the router address, we plan how to get them back."

"I'll call the state police and the FBI. I'm the CEO of a five billion dollar corporation. That should count for something," said Marshall.

"The police can't enter without a warrant," I said. "These are ruthless people with friends in high places. They could delay the police at the front gate while they drop Justin and Judith down a very deep hole."

"You know where they are. You're lying to me," Marshall said. Shit, I had mentioned the place had a gate. The thought of having a man around who I couldn't lie to was scary. My dad always knew when I was lying, not that I lied to him that often. A woman needs a man who'll believe her even when she is not telling the truth.

"I suspect where they are, but I need time to confirm it. You're going to have to promise me not to go Rambo when I tell you."

"Look, Hamo, you're not a parent. You didn't have to look at their faces when Justin asked when his father was coming to get him. It's different when they're your children."

That hurt more than I expected it would. "I know it's difficult. Did you remove the spyware?" I said, trying to move on.

"You don't give a shit. You're just some government agent playing me." He was angry enough that I was glad I wasn't there.

"I'm someone who cares enough to keep you from getting yourself killed. If you go charging into that place, they will kill you. With you dead, Judith and Justin will have no value. They will be sold to some rich Arab pedophile who'll butt fuck them twice a day. Is that what you want? Goddamn you, get control of yourself. I'm trying to keep you alive." I was screaming by the time I finished.

There was a long pause while the both of us worked on what to say next.

"I'm just as anxious to get them back as you are," I said, recovering first. "Now I'm going to analyze the Internet traffic. I have a program to trace the message packets back to their source. I'll call you as soon as I have something, but you have to promise me you'll stay in control."

"OK. I promise," said Marshall.

"Then go back home, and if Soraya is not around, remove the software," I said. "Let's do things right, no loose ends."

I'd lied to Marshall about the need for more time. The video messages had come from a single point. The server's address belonged to one of the two McClain Castle communications providers. The Internet address of the originating message belonged to the McClain Foundation.

Earl's spyware hadn't turned up anything suspicious in the Castle's VSAT based email. Someone was surfing for kiddie porn after midnight, probably a security guard. E-mail was mainly related to art. None of the messages were encrypted, even though some of the discussions of which paintings were scheduled for auction struck me as confidential.

I couldn't tell Bradley about Marshall's children. I didn't have evidence that the kidnapping involved terrorism. Bradley would say it was a custody dispute suitable for a family court. If I told him Marshall and I were working together, he would conclude I was personally involved. Besides being jealous, he would have ADS remove me from the case, thereby getting me fired.

I called Avery at the club, saying that the shooting had rattled my nerves, and I was taking a break from dancing. After I got off the phone with Avery, I made my decision. It was too painful to leave Marshall terrified for his children and uncertain of me.

"They're in McClain Castle," I said as soon as he answered.

"Are you sure? You said it would take hours."

"I lied. I was afraid you'd go there and get yourself killed," I said.

"Damn, why didn't I guess that they were there? I always suspected Stacia knew. She talks to Soraya more than I do. I'd like to wring the bitch's neck."

"Are you all right?" I asked. Guilt was driving his anger.

"As all right as any father would be who handed over his children because they got in the way of his job. Justin and Judith deserved better. Chelsea deserved better. They were her children, too. I've failed them." His anger had been a thin screen over guilt.

"You can beat yourself up later. Right now we need to figure out how to get Justin and Judith safely out of McClain Castle," I said.

"I've had time to scheme about how to get them back. I have a family friend who is a judge on the state supreme court. I could get a court order. I'll hire a professional security agency to back me up. There's one in Boston started by several former Special Ops and SAS guys. We've used them to provide security for some of our projects in high-risk areas. They should be able to handle museum guards," said Marshall.

"These people are more experienced and dangerous than museum guards. They're armed, and the Castle has a state of the art security system. They are religious fanatics who won't blink at martyrdom. Give me forty eight hours," I said. I figured if I couldn't convince the FBI to take the castle down, Marshall's plan was as good as any.

"I've already called Dowling Associates. I'm on my way there now to talk to them," he said.

"What did they say?"

"They said they don't take cases involving parental custody of minors," said Marshall.

"Then why are they meeting with you?"

"Millennium is a big customer, and I told them money was no object."

"They need to download satellite images of the castle grounds," I said, thinking of ways to slow Marshall down.

"Dowling will know how to do that."

"But nothing happens for forty eight hours. Provided they'll agree to help, they'll need time to assemble the right personnel. Make sure every detail is covered," I said.

"I'll get back to you after I talk to Dowling," said Marshall. "Where are you? Can we meet somewhere?"

"Later, I have things to take care of," I said.

"I should hire Dowling to figure out who you really are," he said.

"Go home and get some rest. Tomorrow we can meet and figure out alternatives, if Dowling won't help," I said.

"What possible alternative could there be?"

"Kidnap Soraya and Stacia and trade them for the children," I said.

"Now there is a fucking idea I like. We can cut off their ears and send them with the ransom note?"

"Their nipples, too," I said.

"I'm going to stop and have a drink, then go home and sleep in one of the spare bedrooms," said Marshall.

"Don't you and Soraya normally sleep together?" I asked.

"Yes, but I couldn't stand to look at the bitch tonight."

"Play it smart. Skip the drink, go home, and sleep where you normally would," I said.

"And if she wants sex?"

"Give her a good railing," I said.

"I'm not sure I could get it up," said Marshall.

"Pretend you're screwing me," I said.

We agreed to meet the next morning. If I couldn't find proof enough for Bradley, kidnapping those two might become more than a fantasy.

Chapter 36

"Earl, what's the term for embedding hidden messages in digital images?" I asked as soon as Earl answered.

I'd found nothing in the Millennium data beyond Stacia hiring employees and shipping donations to local charities. That wouldn't make a case compelling enough for cautious Agent Dickerson to authorize a full-scale assault on McClain Castle. Soon, Marshall would lose patience. He would gather some kind of posse and go demand the return of his children. The gate guard would grab his assault rifle, and the shooting would start. The chance of all three Sheffields surviving seemed remote.

I was brain dead from exhaustion; I carried Syllabus to my bed and climbed in. I lay there staring at the ceiling. My situation sucked. There was no way I was going to dance until I was certain no one was waiting to kill me. That ended my main source of income. At least DMS was growing. The two contractors I'd hired were quickly reducing the backlog. Unless I lined up more dancers, they would run out of work.

ADS was dying. I would have to find health insurance. I slept fitfully. Images of McClain Museum art started parading through my dreams like a slide show. All of a sudden I was awake and thinking about something that one of my club regulars had shown me months ago.

It was almost closing and the club was nearly empty. Bathsheba and I were sitting with Artie and Charlie, watching Consuela shake her ass at the only person on the tip line. Artie, a long haul truck driver, showed us things he purchased on a recent visit to the Boy's Town section of Nuevo Laredo. He had taken in a donkey show at a bordello, and made purchases in the gift shop. The thought that a Mexican whore house had a gift shop just like the McClain Museum struck me as hilarious.

"See the hidden picture," Artie said, handing a plastic thingamajig to Bathsheba.

"I can't see shit without my glasses," she said, passing it to me.

"I don't get it," I said holding it toward the light. It was an animation of a woman jogging with a dog.

"Tap the edge against the table," Artie said.

The same woman was now nude, on her hands and knees, having sex with the dog. "Cool," I said. One never disses a customer's porn; no matter how disgusting.

"Move your hand back and forth, like this" said Artie using that as an excuse to hold my hand in his leathery paw. The motion animated the image. He snuck his other hand up my thigh until it rested against my crotch.

"It gets me hot just looking," I said, handing it to Bathsheba. I moved Artie's hand down a couple of inches. Being shown porn went with the job. Men who frequent clubs prefer the hardest of the hardcore. They assume we share their enthusiasm, and in the interests of commerce, we go along.

If a picture of a woman jogging could also be a picture of her doing it doggy style, why couldn't any picture be something else. From somewhere I recalled that you can conceal a message in image files. What better place than in the great art of a museum that could be accessed from any place on the planet.

I called Earl Bowers.

"Hamo, it's two in the fucking morning," said Earl.

"I need some software," I said as soon as he answered. "It's important. After we're done you can jerk off and go back to sleep."

"Can't, wakes up the wife and she raises hell. What do you need?"

"To start, I need to know the name of the technique for embedding messages in digital image files."

"There are several approaches, but it's all called Steganography. You could find that out online."

"I'm in a hurry. If I wanted to know if someone was embedding messages in images, how would I go about it?"

"It's called steganalysis. I've got something MIT developed. I had to modify it to make it work right."

"E-mail it to me."

"Sure, I'll send it tomorrow, first thing."

"No, I need it now, tonight," I said.

"I don't have it here. It's on my computer at work."

"You're lying. You told me you have a copy of every piece of code you ever touched at home."

"Shit, did I say that?" asked Earl.

"I wouldn't ask if it wasn't important."

"All right, but you owe me," said Earl.

A half hour later I'd downloaded and installed Earl's program. I extracted ten Renoirs and ran them through it. My heart fell when the screen displayed zero. I tried ten Monets and got the same result. I was beginning to think I was wrong. I switched to lesser-known artists, selecting at random.

I told myself that if I came up empty handed, I was calling it a night. I clicked Start yet again. Minutes later, I watched as Earl's program painted the screen with a long string of text. Something was embedded in Berthe Morisot's *L'Enfant Au Tablier Rouge*. It wasn't anything a human could read.

"Shit, they encrypted it," I whispered to Syllabus, who was lying across the top of my monitor, absorbing the warmth.

Syllabus gave me a look meaning, "Of course they did, stupid."

Messages were waiting for someone to pick them up, there in the gallery site. Were messages also coming in? I looked at incoming messages from art dealers that contained images. I started with London. The first two dealer's images were empty, but a third had embedded messages. I found more messages from Paris and Rome and, not surprisingly, from a dealer in Abu Dhabi.

I congratulated myself on having cracked the case. Adrenalin pumping, I went to the kitchen and made coffee. I had work to do before I informed Agent Dickerson some very wealthy Arabs were running a terrorist network out of an art museum. I would have everything in order. I'd persuade him to dispatch a hostage rescue team to McClain Castle. A grateful Marshall and I would get married. I would live happily ever after as the loving wife of a rich man.

Chapter 37

"When the president appoints you FBI Director, remember the woman who cracked the case that made your career," I said by way of greeting. It was six a.m., and in spite of a lack of sleep, I was feeling feisty.

"What have you found?" Bradley asked, sounding sleepy but interested.

"Solid, incontrovertible proof that Millennium Construction and the McClain Foundation support a terrorist cell—with members including Soraya Sheffield and Stacia McClain among others. Millennium provides the money, personnel, and logistics, and the McClain Foundation the planning and coordination."

"And what proof is this?" Bradley sounded awake now and very interested.

"You're going to be proud of me, and ashamed of yourself for admiring my tits more than my brain."

"Who said I admire your tits?" asked Bradley.

It was time to end the banter. "The McClain Museum's Web site has concealed messages in downloadable images of their art. The messages are encrypted, but I am sure they are related to coordinating terrorist activities. Employees of art dealers in London, Paris, Rome, and the United Arab Emirates send image files containing embedded messages in emails to the museum. There may be other art dealers involved. I haven't time to go through all the messages. If you don't fuck this up, you'll be able to arrest the entire network."

"How do you hide messages in image files?"

"It's called Steganography. But that's a general term for hiding messages in otherwise innocent documents. In the old days, spies used invisible ink to write between the lines of a letter. Now you post a digital image of a leggy blonde with large beautiful breasts, embed a message in the pixels, and post it on your Web site."

"Let's be serious and can the breast talk." He was interested enough that he didn't want to banter.

"All right, when you look at an image on the computer screen, you are really looking at an ordered pattern of pixels. Right?"

"I know that. Mine's set to 1024 by 768," said Bradley displaying his limited technical knowledge.

"Do you know what a color pallet is?"

"My monitor's color pallet has 512 colors."

"Excellent, with study you could join the geeks. An image, when it is displayed on your computer screen, is converted from a digital code describing the location and color pallet assignment of each pixel. It is possible, using steganographic algorithms, to embed text messages—or for that matter almost any kind of data, even other images—in the pixel code. It doesn't in any way change what you see on the screen."

"The Mona Lisa would still smile?"

"No, she'd still look like she had just seen her first twelve-inch cock."

"How do I read the message?"

"Install software that extracts the embedded text. I did a Web search and found six software packages that will embed and extract files in a digital image. An ADS analyst emailed me a copy of his program, and I've detected a significant amount of Steganography."

"You've worked all night on this?"

"Don't worry. ADS will bill you for my time. The terrorist accesses the McClain Web site, chooses the right paintings, and extracts new messages. Each cell probably has a different set of art. The ones in Pakistan may be Manet and the ones in Iran, Monet. Given more time, I could figure it all out."

"But the messages are encrypted, so we don't know what they are or who they are meant for. How can you be sure they are terrorists?"

"What else could they be?"

"They could be messages to dealers about upcoming art purchases, they could be innocent."

"I've searched their email. There are hundreds of messages about auctions and what a particular painting is likely to sell for. None of them is encrypted."

"You may be right. But I don't want to falsely accuse one of my country's most prestigious cultural institutions of terrorism."

"You must have majored in caution at Yale."

He ignored the barb. "Step one is to decode the messages. I'll forward them to NSA. Where are you now?" asked Bradley.

"I'm home. Where else would I be at six in the morning? I've got to get some sleep. I emailed you twenty-six images from the McClain Web site and fifteen from art dealers."

"All right, I'll get the ball rolling," Bradley said and hung up. I wondered if the NSA would have something in twenty-four hours. Marshall wasn't going to wait.

Chapter 38

After I spoke with Bradley, I went to my bedroom and collapsed. My cell phone woke me mid morning. It was Doreen wanting to know if I was all right. I told her I had a bug and apologized for not calling in sick.

"Marshall came by and asked me if I had heard from you," she said, switching to the voice we women use when we are talking about affairs with married men.

"He's interested in my views on whether Millennium is a fair and friendly workplace for women," I said.

"Well, he picked a good person to ask," said Doreen, not believing me for a minute.

I told her I planned to be at my desk tomorrow. The minute I hung up, Marshall called.

"Are you all right?" he asked.

"Yes, I worked all night. We need to talk. I found something that will help us," I said. "I need to tell you in person. It's what we need to get Justin and Judith back."

"That's terrific. Where do you want to meet?"

"There is a coffee shop on Route One south right past the Walnut Street exit. I'll be there by twelve thirty," I said.

In the shower I lectured myself for acting like a schoolgirl about Marshall. If I didn't get a grip on my emotions, I would be writing, Alexandra Thornton Sheffield over and over again in my notebook.

I did not make my meeting with Marshall. My abduction was a well-crafted operation. I'd just stepped out into blinding New England sun as giddy as my mood, when an SUV pulled up to the curb. My first thought was to get my Glock from my purse and run.

"Please, can you help us?" said the young girl on the passenger side. There was another girl beside her holding a map. They both looked upset. They were damn clever. If the SUV's occupants had been men, I would have sprinted to my car.

"Pardon me, could you please help us?" the girl said again. She sounded desperate. They were dressed identically in long, lavender, ugly dresses—bridesmaids.

"We're lost. We're looking for St. Maria Goretti's church," said the driver.

I'd already noted their Connecticut license plate. Whoever organized my abduction didn't miss any details.

"I'm in a hurry. Try a gas station," I yelled back.

"Please, we're late for our best friend's wedding. Could you just point out where we are on the map?"

Who would say no to that? The driver opened the door and stepped out holding an unfolded map. She'd left the door open, and I could see a large box wrapped in silver wedding bell paper with a white bow.

"It starts in thirty minutes," said the girl, handing me the map. With a little luck, I would be choosing bridesmaids for my wedding next spring. Would Marshall let me invite Bathsheba?

I was studying the street map when I heard a noise behind me. I turned, and Twenty Dollar Dick was there with a black plastic gizmo in his hand. There was a loud pop as he touched it to my shoulder. My brain registered stun gun as my body went rigid. What a fucking awful experience. Stunned is the correct term. I felt myself falling slowly toward the ground. I was paralyzed, couldn't breathe, nothing worked.

"Get the door," he said. I was dumped into the rear seat of the SUV. My laptop and purse hit the floor beside me. I was prostrate on the seat, frantically wanting to move, when I felt my sweater sleeve pushed up my arm.

"Good job, girls. You've earned the bonus," were the last words I heard.

I woke up with a splitting headache. I was naked, tied to a chair in a pitch-black room, and desperate to pee. Relief meant sitting in my own urine. While I was debating bladder options, the door opened and light blinded me.

"I need to use the bathroom," I said to whoever it was.

The door closed and I was in darkness again. Minutes passed giving me a chance to make a few observations. The soles of my feet were resting on a cold concrete floor. The place smelled dank like a basement. The sound of dripping water increased my need to pee.

Finally, the door opened and someone tripped a light switch. The room went from pitch black to bright as an operating room. It was seconds before I could see Stacia McClain and two men. I couldn't be sure, but I suspected they were the same two who chased me down the mountain at McClain Castle. Any doubt that I was in the castle ended when Alisha appeared in the doorway.

Stacia said something in the language I assumed was Arabic. Alisha came over and grabbed my hair, jerking my head up. It must have been Alisha's task to identify me as the trespasser who shot the dogs. She peered into my face, making sure I was the one. I noted serious facial hair on her upper lip, but didn't suggest a visit to my electrologist. She exchanged a few more words of Arabic with Stacia then departed.

The men were a Mutt and Jeff pair. One was tall, thin, and rather handsome in spite of the scar across his cheek. The other was short and unhandsome.

"I need to go to the bathroom," I said calmly. "I'm going to pee right here if you don't take me."

Stacia rattled off in Arabic to the men. Handsome's name was Ebrahim, and Shorty was Hassan. They argued back. Finally, Stacia blurted out in English, "I don't want to smell her stinking piss. Take her, Hassan."

Hassan untied me while Ebrahim watched. A wave of nausea and vertigo hit me when I stood. The men grabbed me under my armpits and held me upright. They marched me to the filthiest restroom imaginable. My legs were almost working by the time I sat.

When I tried to close the door, Hassan blocked it with his foot.

Urinating with an audience was new to me. I've heard there are clubs in Mexico where the dancers charge extra to put a squirt in the customer's beer. Unfortunately I'd never danced there so it took a few seconds of concentration to get started.

"Enjoy," I said to Hassan once my noisy and prolonged urination began.

The sound occasioned some smirking comments from my audience. I didn't think I would get a second trip to the john so I squeezed my bladder dry. I caught a glance of myself in the mirror. I'd looked better.

"Kidnapping is a serious crime," I said to Stacia when I walked back in the room.

"Kidnapping, torture, and murder are even worse," she replied, trumping my remark.

They sat me down in the chair and retied the ropes.

"Stacia, what's this about?" I said flexing my forearm muscles as they tightened the ropes around my wrists. I needed some slack.

"Getting rid of a problem," she said.

The contents of my purse and laptop case were strewn about on a nearby table. My Glock was tantalizing close. As Hassan finished tying me, Ebrahim rolled a two-wheeled dolly beside my chair. Twelve volts and ninety amps were printed on the side of the tomato red box resting on the dolly. I'd seen one before. Every filling station has one. He connected the battery up to an odd looking metal box that had dozens of connections. An electrical switch box was my guess. I hoped I was wrong.

"What's that for?" I asked hoping the answer wasn't what I knew it was.

Stacia spoke in Arabic, and the two men laughed.

"I'm missing all the jokes here. If it's going to be funny, please speak English," I said.

"We are going to find out what you've learned about our operation," said Ebrahim in perfect English.

"That's not funny," I said causing him to smile. "You don't have to torture me. I'll tell you everything,"

"We have to make sure," said Stacia.

"A lie detector test would work just as well," I said.

"Don't concern yourself. Hassan worked for Egyptian intelligence. He is a professional," said Ebrahim.

"Is Hassan a board certified member of the Egyptian Association of Torturers?" I asked.

For some reason, Hassan did not find my remark funny. After he shouted what I assumed were Arabic expletives, he slapped me so hard I tasted blood. Maybe the Egyptians had revoked his certification, and he didn't like to be reminded of it.

Ebrahim and Hassan began attaching wires to my body parts. The way they went about it indicated that mine wasn't their first enhanced interrogation.

They worked from my feet to my head. They separated my toes with rubber wedges cut from a tire. They stripped the insulation off then wrapped the bare wire around the base of my big and little toes. Electrician's tape secured bare wires to the back of my knees. Then matters got personal.

Ebrahim lifted my legs to allow Hassan to insert a metal egg in my vagina. When it wouldn't go in easily, he spit on it; then shoved it inside me. Hygiene is not a big concern for torturers.

More spit and Hassan's fingers forced a similar egg into my anus. Stacia didn't leave all the fun stuff to the men. I screamed when she grabbed the tip of my nipple in the jaws of needle nose pliers and pulled hard, crushing the flesh paper thin. Ebrahim circled the base with several turns of wire.

"Are we having fun yet, Alexandra," asked Stacia transferring the pliers to my other nipple?

I was too busy screaming to answer. The more wires they attached, the more terrified I became. I had once attended a lecture by a woman who had been tortured by paramilitaries in Guatemala. She recounted in graphic detail how she'd been gang raped, beaten unconscious, and repeatedly tortured with electricity over a period of months. She was still in therapy and said that even after five years, she woke up screaming. God how I wish I had missed her lecture. There are times I prefer to be ignorant.

"Good, you are sweating. That makes it hurt more," said Stacia buckling a leather head band around my skull. Copper discs on the inside circled my brain.

Stacia was right I was covered in sweat and my heart was beating so fast I thought it would explode. Terrified, I was prepared to beg. "Stacia, this is totally unnecessary. I will answer all your questions. Honestly, I will. Please don't do this."

My fervently stated willingness to talk did not have the desired effect.

"I saved the best for last, Alexandra," said Stacia applying the pliers to my clitoris. My hoodectomy made that easy to do. She squeezed hard and pulled then let a nasty looking set of alligator clamps snap shut on my most sensitive body part.

The three watched with an amused look on their faces until a lack of breath forced me to stop screaming.

While Ebrahim attached the free end of the wires to the switch box, Hassan fondled my boobs and squeezed them, then spoke in Arabic to Stacia.

"Hassan asked if your breasts are real. I told him they were fakes," said Stacia.

"They're real," I lied.

Ebrahim must not have believed me; because he left the task at hand and stepped in front of me. He leaned down to where his face was inches from mine, hooked two fingers in my nose and pulled. When my mouth opened, he spit in it. That was yucky.

"Only a whore of Satan would change the body God gave her, so men will lust after her and ignore the teachings of the Prophet," snarled Ebrahim.

"Bullshit, I bet all the virgins in paradise have fake tits," I said.

Ebrahim did not ignore my smart-ass retort. A series of bitch slaps left me with a bloody nose and a ringing in my ears. I resolved to be more sensitive to the Muslim religion in the future.

From somewhere, Stacia retrieved a small fire extinguisher. She sat it down by my chair.

"What's that for?" I asked.

"In case your hair catches on fire," she said matter-of-factly.

"Why are you doing this? I will tell you everything," I repeated my offer once more.

"Hassan wants to listen to you scream," said Stacia.

"Surely, you must have better things to do. The malls are advertising fifty percent off lowest marked price," I said.

"My sister said you were amusing," said Stacia.

"Your sister?" There wasn't a sister in the dossier Bradley gave me.

"The woman whose husband you are fucking. Consider this punishment for being an adulterous whore," said Stacia.

That took a moment to process. I wasn't fucking anybody. Who did they think I was fucking? The light finally dawned.

"Soraya is your sister?" I said. "You two don't look anything alike. Well, maybe a little."

"Half sister, we share a father," said Stacia.

"Are you sure Ebrahim and Hassan wouldn't prefer to rape me instead? I give a great blowjob." Keeping the conversation going was the only thing I had left. Given a choice between non consensual sex and electrical torture, I'd pick rape any day.

They ignored my offer. When the other ends of the wires were connected to the switch box and they were ready to start, Stacia rolled a chair close and sat, crossing her fashion model legs. She lit a cigarette and settled comfortably like someone who was planning to enjoy herself.

I thought if they brought snacks this would be jihadist home theatre. My thoughts were interrupted when Hassan made his first attempt to jump-start me. He must have been a boob man because all of a sudden my tits were on fire.

Chapter 39

Describing how it felt to be tortured by electricity is impossible. It hurt worse than anything I can recall. Having a baby is supposed to be the gold standard for pain, but since childbirth wasn't in my resume, I couldn't make the comparison.

They kept switching body parts. One minute I felt my brain was being microwaved. Seconds later, the bones in my legs were being crushed. There was a point when I thought the saline solution in my breasts was boiling.

Stacia made sure they didn't neglect my female parts.

"You won't be able to enjoy a man when we're finished with you," said Stacia anxiously taking over the switch box from Ebrahim. She needed to make it personal.

There followed a series of increasingly short bursts in my groin that made me wish she would kill me.

Stacia asked about my relationship with Marshall. "When was the last time you fucked Marshall?"

Since we'd never done it, I said, "I've never fucked Marshall."

"Lying bitch," said Stacia, turning a dial and toggling a switch.

High voltage passed among my vagina, anus, and clitoris. I thought my button was going to explode. When she repeated the question, I said, "Yesterday, we did it three times."

"He and his fat brother love their whores," said Stacia, satisfied with my answer.

Somehow, they knew I was an ADS plant, and most of their questions concerned what I had told management. What did I put in my last report? When did I last discuss the case with my boss face-to-face?

I have no idea how long they tortured me. They took short breaks to plan the next round. I finally passed out. When I came to, I was alone in the dark, unwired thank god. My throat was raw from screaming. Waking brought on a wave of nausea. I wanted to puke but if I did I would wear it.

I sat there feeling sorry for myself. I noticed my right hand had some freedom of movement. The electricity had contorted my muscles stretching the ropes. I tried to slip my hand under the rough hemp. Oh fuck did it hurt. I took several deep breaths and pulled again. What I was doing to myself was as bad as the electricity. I tried several more times without success. The pain made me dizzy, and all of a sudden my mouth filled with vomit. I froze, trying to decide whether to spit as far as I could or choke it back down. For some reason, I couldn't decide. I started to cry. That part was weird. I just sat there with a mouth full of puke while the tears flowed.

So I sat for God knows how long, crying with bile leaking from the corners of my mouth. At some point, my father appeared to me. Actually, it was a memory that seemed real but my brain was fucked up from the voltage.

I was in high school, and we were playing for the state championship in field hockey. We were down two to one, and I was sitting on the sidelines, nursing a sore ankle and a black eye that was starting to swell shut. Our opponents, Winchester High, had caught me in a vicious mousetrap. Being state field hockey champions may not be like winning the Superbowl, but pit pubescent high school girls against one another, and it gets vicious quickly. Sportsmanship was for the boys.

It was late in the second period, and time was running out. I knew we were going to lose. It had that feel to it. I was sitting on the bench when I heard someone calling my name. When I looked back, there was my dad, standing at the fence waving to me. We weren't supposed to talk to our parents during a game. I waved in acknowledgement and turned back around. Again I heard him calling my name, only louder. When I looked again I saw him gesturing for me to come to him.

What the fuck does he want, I thought as I got up. Coach Wilkins gave me a dirty look, and then relaxed. It was the last game of the season. We were losing. I was a senior.

"I'm not supposed to leave the bench," I said when I got close enough to speak.

"You're losing," said my dad.

"That's what the scoreboard says."

"You need to win."

"I'm injured, in case you haven't noticed. They've got a great team. They're too good for us."

"If you lose today, you'll set a pattern for the rest of your life. Find a way to win."

"It's not our day," I said.

"Spoken like a lifelong loser," said my father giving me his absolute look of paternal disappointment. I called it the "why couldn't you have been a boy" look.

"Dad, this is a team sport. I'm one of eleven players."

He walked away without saying anything. On the walk back to the bench, something in me snapped. And I hated him for talking to me like that. Other girl's fathers were supportive.

They would have told me I was still a winner and losing didn't matter. What the hell kind of parent was he? Telling me I was going to be a loser for the rest of my life if I didn't win some stupid game. Couldn't he see my ankle was bleeding and my eye was half closed? None of the other girls had such a lousy, controlling motherfucker for a dad. My friend Cecilia's dad always told us how great we were.

"I'm ready to get back in the game," I said to Coach Wilkins, when I returned to the bench.

"Sit down, Alex, you're injured," said Coach, not taking her eyes off the field.

"I'm a senior and the team captain. I'm going back in," I said.

"You could really get hurt, and I'd be responsible," said Coach.

"I'm going back in." I said, stepping to the sideline.

"I know this game is important to you, but I can't let that happen," said Coach grabbing my arm.

"Stay the fuck out of my way," I said. I must have looked like I had lost it because she gave up and sat back down.

"Coming out to get the other eye closed, Thornton," said Irene Kendricks, the big defensemen whose elbow had smashed my eye socket while her teammate stomped my Achilles tendon.

There were three minutes to go when I passed to Celia, and she hammered it past the goalkeeper tying the score. Winchester thought they had the game won and were slacking off. They had beaten us in the finals the year before.

There was about fifteen seconds left, and we were all playing like madwomen, determined not to lose. I looked over to the side of the field, and there was my father, standing with his arms folded. He wasn't watching the game, just me.

I never hated anyone so much in my life as I did him at that moment. Celia fed me the ball, and I took off toward the Winchester goal. As I was getting close enough for a shot, I saw Hendricks out of the corner of eye, coming in to flatten me. It was going to be an illegal block, but with five seconds to go who was going to care. She had the angle on me, so I couldn't outrun her.

At the last instant, I leaped in the air and twisted my entire body toward her. My elbow smashed into her front teeth. I heard a loud crack, and my arm went numb. Kendricks went down holding her mouth, spitting blood and incisors on the grass. I stumbled over her body and slammed the ball past the goalkeeper.

"Good game," was my dad's only comment afterwards.

Vision over, I swallowed my vomit in one big gulp. I would either get my hand free or rip it off. I screamed, pulling my right hand from under the ropes. It moved a half-inch, and black tunneled my vision. I screamed again and pulled even harder. The rope was flaying the skin off the top of my hand. Blood dripped from my numb fingers. Blood acted as a lubricant. On the next pull, my right hand slipped free. I could feel a flap of skin on the back of it, flopping back and forth. If I managed to get out of this alive, Doctor Keller had a repair job to do.

I sat there trying to overcome the pain. I may even have passed out for a while. I was startled awake when I heard someone opening the door. I managed to slip most of my hand back under the ropes. The lights switched on, blinding me. Hassan walked over, grabbed a handful of hair, and raised my head up.

"Please, no more," I begged.

"Quiet, I won't hurt you," said Hassan gently, reaching down to feel my breasts. "Would you like some water?"

"Yes." I would have said yes if he'd offered to pee in my mouth. He opened a bottle of water and held it to my lips. I took several long swallows and choked. Cold water spilled down my chest.

"More," I said when he took it away. He let me have several more swallows. He held the bottle with one hand while the other roamed places of interest.

"Thank you," I said, looking up and him and trying to smile. I recognized the look on his face. I'd seen that look a thousand times in strip clubs. I was naked and he was horny. He planned to rape me.

"I won't hurt you," he said again, placing the water bottle on the floor and kneeling to untie my ankle. Apparently, Hassan didn't share Ebrahim's disdain for Satan's whores.

He was armed. A semi-automatic was in a holster fitted under his left side. It was angled so he could draw it with his right hand by reaching across his body. I moved my right foot around to gain back some sensation as he untied the left. As soon as both my legs were free, he lifted them onto the chair arms. My thigh covered the hand I'd worked free.

I was surprised when he knelt down and began to lick my vulva. He unzipped and began stroking himself as he ate my pussy. The good news was that I could feel it. Stacia hadn't succeeded in neutering me.

"Feels so good," I said between moans.

ON THE POLE

After he satisfied his desire for cunnilingus, he stood up, still stroking. It was time for theatre. I licked my lips pretending that I was dying to suck his hairy, uncircumcised cock.

From somewhere above, there was a noise. He glanced at the door, possibly considering abandoning the idea of rape. He waited a few seconds but when the noise wasn't repeated, he requested fellatio.

"Suck me," he said kneeling between my legs.

I would call putting your cock between the teeth of someone you recently tortured a lapse in judgment. Still I didn't intend to bite it off. Nor did I want him to finish in my mouth.

"Fuck me, please fuck me," I whispered after I had him as hard as he was going to get.

Hassan must not have been the brightest terrorist on the planet to assume I meant it. He climbed off the chair, took a second or two to figure out how to penetrate me then lifted my legs high off the chair arms. I did my part, wrapping them around his waist and locking my ankles.

"Put it in my fuck hole, Lover," I said, inching forward to signal my eagerness. As he pounded away, I gasped and moaned like a good whore. "You're so big. You're going so deep." Actually, he was average at best.

When I sensed he was totally focused on blowing his load, it was time to act.

"Now or never," I told myself as my free hand grabbed the back of his head. Smashing my forehead against his almost knocked me out. The head butt momentarily surprised and stunned him. I pulled his pistol from the holster and slammed it against the side of his head. The handgun went flying out of my hand, skittering across the stone floor.

My rapist collapsed to the floor. I got busy untying my left hand. When it was free, I stood up and promptly fell down. My legs were useless. The sensation of blood returning to the muscles was like being electrocuted again. I crawled across the rough concrete floor. I'd almost reached the gun when a hand grabbed my ankle. I looked back to see Hassan lying there with his eyes open. His face was covered in blood and he didn't look pleased at how intercourse turned out.

I lashed out with my other foot and kicked him in the face. My big toe caught his eye. He howled and let me go. I crawled the final two feet in record time, grabbed the pistol and whirled around. My legs were white fire, but starting to work again.

I climbed on top of Hassan, straddling his round belly. His eyes popped open, and maybe for an instant he thought I wanted cowgirl sex. This time I had a good grip on the barrel, and the pistol butt landed with a loud thud in the center of his forehead, making a deep indentation. I sat there breathing heavily while his blood pooled on the floor.

I was using the chair to help me stand when I heard a voice whispering from the side of the room.

"Kill him, Lady. Shoot Hassan," said a child's voice from somewhere.

I turned in the direction of the voice but there was no one there.

"Where the hell are you?" I whispered.

"I'm behind the grate, under the table." Then I recognized the voice of Justin Sheffield AKA Brent.

"Justin," I said.

"Yes."

"Come out."

"I can't. The grate's screwed to the wall. I got all the screws out except one. I got a Phillips head you can use."

I hobbled over to the table. Justin was peering at me through the grate of a heating duct. He handed me the screwdriver, and I removed the remaining screw. Out of the duct crawled twelve-year-old Justin Sheffield. When I looked at the tiny black opening of the duct, I was amazed he fit through it. He must have no fear of claustrophobia.

"What happened to your hand?" said Justin, pointing to the back of my right hand. I'd peeled back a flap of skin almost as wide as my palm. You could see the bones move when I curled my fingers.

"I injured it getting free," I said.

"Put this on it for now," said Justin grabbing a roll of duct tape. He tore off a strip, put the skin in place before I could object, and wrapped it around my hand.

"I need to get dressed and get out of here," I said.

"Take me with you," said Justin.

"Do you know how to get out?"

"I can get us to the cars. You can drive us out."

"Where is your sister?"

"On the second floor."

"How do we get her?"

"We have to go there. She's too fat to use the ducts," said Justin.

Chapter 40

"Let's kill him," said Justin, as he finished tying Hassan's hands and feet while I dressed. Hassan was groaning, smearing the blood pool as he shifted. Duct tape covered his mouth

"We need to get out of here. He's not going to stop us," I said. I was barely mobile. It felt like someone had given me arthritis in every joint from ankles to shoulders. Black spots kept showing up in front of my eyes.

"I'll find something that won't make any noise," said Justin. He picked up a claw hammer off the table and gave it a test swing.

"No, we don't have time." In truth, I wasn't capable of cold-blooded murder. I'm a bad girl, but not an evil one.

"He deserves it." Justin stepped over Hassan with the hammer raised.

"I'm sure he does, but we'll let the police deal with him," I said putting my hand on the hammer handle beside his. Justin had a sweet boyish face, but at the moment, it didn't look sweet. It was pale and twisted, with hard eyes.

"He did things to Judith and me. Like he was doing to you," said Justin.

That caused me almost to reconsider my decision. Pedophiles are on my list of those who should not be allowed to exist. However, I didn't want Marshall's son to be a killer.

"My friends at the FBI will make sure he gets a special cell with some Arab hating rednecks," I said, taking the hammer out of his hand.

Justin surprised me by putting his arms around me and hugging me. He buried his face in my boobs and sniffled. At twelve, he could only carry the tough guy act so far, and it had run out. I hugged him back, not knowing what I should do or say.

"Let's go find Judith and get out of here."

According to Justin's watch it was two thirty in the morning. Everything was quiet. Hassan's semi-automatic was a brand new Sig Sauer Equinox. There were fifteen cartridges in the magazine. My Glock also contained fifteen bullets. If shooting started, I had enough ammunition to make a stand.

Justin reluctantly agreed to carry my purse. I decided to leave my laptop behind. That was a tough decision. It was like another appendage, and it had been expensive. I settled for popping out the hard drive and putting it in my purse.

I put one hand on Justin's shoulder and he led me down the pitch-black hallway. The boy had cat eyes. I couldn't see a thing.

"Stairs," he whispered when we reached the bottom of the stairway from the basement to the main floor. The wooden stairs creaked and groaned as we climbed. I kept expecting someone to wake and sound the alarm, but it stayed quiet. Luckily, the wide stairway to the second floor had marble steps.

"Alisha's room is next to Judith's," whispered Justin. "We need to be very quiet."

"Who's there?" whispered Judith as soon as we opened her door and slipped inside.

"Quiet, it's me," said Justin. "I got someone with me."

"Where have you been? Alisha's been looking for you. Who's with you?"

"The lady who killed Rotan and Smoke, she's going to take us to Dad."

I felt bad, learning the names of the dogs I shot. I didn't need to know that although Syllabus would have approved.

"Get dressed Judith. My name is Alex and I'm a friend of your father's."

"Why didn't he come?"

"I'll explain later. Please get dressed."

"They had Alexandra in the dungeon. She was naked. They did the same thing to her with the battery that they did to the fat man. You should have seen what she did to Hassan. He was fucking her, but she bashed his head in," whispered Justin in a torrent of words.

"Is Hassan dead?" Judith asked.

I skipped informing her that Hassan was still alive. In fact, based on blood loss, maybe he wasn't.

"Get dressed, please," I repeated.

Judith slipped out of bed and started to dress. Would you believe she opened a drawer and began looking through her clothes, selecting something to wear like she had all the time in the world? I closed my eyes and did a slow count to five. I felt like death. No, death felt better. We were at risk of our lives and the little miss was taking her time picking out an outfit.

"If you get dressed quickly, your father will buy you an entirely new wardrobe."

"Where?" asked Judith.

"Any store you want, in any mall in America. Just get dressed now."

She sped up after that. We were about to leave when our luck ran out.

"I hear someone," whispered Justin.

I'd heard noises in the hall, too.

"It's Alisha," said Judith.

"Get in bed. Pretend to be asleep," I said to Judith as I took Justin's hand and headed toward the closet.

We barely made it before Alisha opened the door and stepped inside. I left the closet door cracked so I could see.

"Where is your brother?" demanded Alisha from the doorway.

"I don't know. Probably wondering around somewhere," said Judith.

"Have you seen him tonight?" asked Alisha as she walked over to the bed.

"No, maybe, I'm not sure," said Judith establishing herself in my opinion as an airhead.

Alisha was looking at the bed to make sure Justin wasn't under the covers. Her next move was to look under the bed. Justin was behind me in the small closet, and he must have moved because he made a tiny noise. Alisha's head spun around in our direction.

"You both will be punished tomorrow," she said, starting toward the closet.

ON THE POLE

I looked around for a weapon. I had the Sig Sauer, but one shot would wake the household, and the bad guys probably slept with Kalashnikovs under their pillows. When I glanced down, I saw the handle of a field hockey stick. There was a weapon I had wielded through six years of school, seriously damaging the shins, arms, and faces of opponents.

"Justin, come out of there immediately," demanded Alisha, throwing open the closet door.

She looked genuinely surprised when she saw me standing there ready to put her skull through the goal. The stick made solid contact with the side of her head. She made a cry, but not a loud one.

"Help me, Justin," I cried as I struggled to keep her from falling. We three slowly collapsed to the floor. I thought we'd made enough noise to wake everyone but the castle remained quiet. I lay there listening before I rolled her off me.

We moved silently down the stairs to the first floor. When we reached the kitchen, Justin stopped and quietly opened one of the refrigerators.

"Justin, no," I hissed wondering whether he was dumb enough to think we needed food for our escape. Through the back door window I could see several cars parked in front of the garage. We were so close.

"Apollo and Athena will want something," said Justin.

"They got new dogs," Judith added.

Justin grabbed two handfuls of baloney. I was reaching for the door knob when Justin stopped me.

"It's alarmed," said Justin handing me the baloney.

"How do we get out?"

"I'll show you," said Justin stepping past me. He removed a piece of wire with alligator clips from his pocket, and then climbed on a countertop. He attached the clips to wires running along the top of the doorjamb. I stood there with a stack of baloney in each hand while the future B&E artist worked his magic. Circuit bypassed, he opened the door. No alarm sounded.

"I'm surprised you two haven't escaped before," I whispered to Judith as we followed Justin out the door.

"We did once. They caught us. They punished us so we wouldn't do it again," said Judith.

"Hassan wanted to cut our fingers off, but Ebrahim wouldn't let him," said Justin.

We kept in the shadows, moving toward the garage. I heard the clicking sound of dogs' nails on concrete. From ahead of us, I heard growls. Thank God they weren't barks.

"Apollo, Athena, it's me, Justin," said Justin, moving forward in the direction of the growls, baloney in hand.

Judith and I held hands, pressed against the side of the castle while Justin fed the dogs. I heard the sound of their chomping. That would have been my legs except for Justin.

"He's very good with dogs. I'm a cat person," said Judith. "I had a cat back in Boston but they wouldn't let me bring her."

"I'm a cat person too," I said. "His name's Syllabus."

"Syllabus, that's a funny name for a cat."

"I got him while I was in college," I said, an explanation that I realized meant nothing to Judith.

Justin reappeared out of the dark, interrupting our moment of female bonding. "Come on," he said, taking my wounded hand.

We walked quietly past two very large and evil looking Doberman Pinschers. One of them looked up and growled at us.

"It's all right, Athena girl," cooed Justin. Athena decided her deli snack was tastier than me and continued eating.

There were several cars to choose from.

"That one," I said, pointing toward the Suburban.

It was unlocked, keys lying on the console. With Apollo and Athena on guard, who needed to lock their car or take the keys?

"Put your seat belts on," I told them. I had no idea how we were going to get past the gate. I hoped Justin knew how to solve that problem too.

Just as I started the engine, lights went on in the castle. I shifted into drive and stomped on the accelerator. I'd decided not to use the headlights, believing the black car would be harder to see in the dark. That was rendered moot when the outdoor lights were turned on. Instantly, McClain Castle and grounds looked like Fenway Park during a night game.

I never knew who sounded the alarm. Alisha might have regained consciousness. Someone found Hassan. Who knows?

The drive from the parking area curved alongside the mansion. I wouldn't be able to accelerate until I reached the straight run down to the gate.

Just as I cleared the front of the mansion, someone jumped on the running board. There was Ebrahim, and he had a gun in his hand. He aimed it at me through the window and ordered me to stop. Startled, I swerved onto the lawn, glanced off something and back onto the drive.

Ebrahim barely managed to hold on using both hands. His gun hand was now empty. The handgun must be somewhere on the lawn. He started pounding his forearm on the glass. But safety glass is hard to break.

"Here," said Justin handing me the Glock out of my purse.

"Take the wheel," I said grabbing Justin's hands and placing them on the steering wheel. We were bouncing across the lawn.

I chambered a round and pointed the gun toward Ebrahim who had managed to crack the glass. A few more elbows and he could reach in.

I expected him to let go and drop off when he saw the Glock pointed his way. But he gave me a look of pure malevolence then reared back for another attempt. I shot him in the chest.

The glass shattered. I went deaf from the noise. Ebrahim was no longer on the running board.

We were approaching the gate. It was the final barrier to our escape. When I looked in the rear mirror, I could see a pickup truck coming around the side of the castle. Men with what I assumed were assault rifles were rushing out the front door toward the truck.

"Where's the guard," I asked when we slid to a stop in front of the guard building.

"There's not one at night. I'll open it," said Justin climbing out over Judith.

I watched as Justin raced toward the door, stopping to grab a rock on the way. He used the rock to break a window pane then reached in to open the door. Seconds later, he emerged with a remote in his hand. On the way back, he pointed it at the gate. Ever so slowly, the heavy metal gate began to open.

Another glance in the mirror revealed the pickup with two men in front and one in the bed were careening toward us. The one in back was aiming his weapon in our direction.

I put the Suburban in gear. I felt, not heard the shudder, as it scrapped past the gatepost. As soon as we were through, Justin used the remote control to close the gate. Maybe I was in love with the wrong Sheffield.

I watched in the rear view mirror as the gate stopped then started to close. The driver was either going too fast or thought he could squeeze through. The truck crashed into the partially closed gate, catapulting the man in back high into the air. He tumbled end over end before landing on the ornamental spikes decorating the top. Two of the spikes went all the way through him. The truck was wedged between a stone column and the twisted wreck of the gate. One of the men was lying on the pavement in front of the truck. He'd gone through the window, no seat belts.

Chapter 41

I was driving the speed limit on the Mass Pike when Justin announced that we should call his father. Marshall answered on the first ring.

"Hamo, are you all right? Where have you been," asked Marshall?

"Can you talk?" I asked.

"Yes, Soraya left an hour ago. She got a call, then dressed and left without saying a word. Whatever it was upset her. When I asked where she was going, she told me to fuck off. Are you all right?"

"Yes, just tired and frayed around the edges," I lied. "Soraya got bad news."

"I went to your house when you failed to show up, but no one was home. Then Soraya called to tell me they had you, and if I didn't do exactly what they said, they would kill you and mail me the pieces," said Marshall.

"Well, I'm fine. You and the children need to disappear for a while."

"How do we do that? They're in McClain Castle"

"They're with me. We're driving into Boston on the Mass Pike. They want to say hello," I said, handing the phone to Judith.

Judith's conversation was brief but Justin, the motor mouth, recounted how I was naked, tortured, raped, smashed Hassan's head in, and shot my way out of McClain Castle in one long, breathless monologue.

"Are they all right?" asked Marshall after Justin handed me back the cell.

I decided that it wasn't the time to mention that Hassan had been molesting his children. Marshall might grab a gun and head toward the Castle.

"Yes, our hearing finally came back or I would have called earlier."

"What happened to your hearing?"

"Never fire a handgun inside a car."

"Are you sure you're all right?" asked Marshall, sounding very concerned, which thrilled me down to my toes.

"A couple of bruises, I'm fine," I lied again. I was in shock, or my hand would hurt worse than it did.

"They were in McClain Castle just like you said they were," said Marshall.

"They may come looking for you. You have to really disappear. Go somewhere you've never been. Stay on the move. Drive. Don't fly. Use only cash, no credit cards. Stay in motels you wouldn't consider under other circumstances. They have the resources to follow a paper trail," I said.

"I can't believe you did it," said Marshall. "You could have been killed."

"I didn't exactly do it," I said. "I was kidnapped and taken to the castle. Justin and Judith helped me to escape. It's a long story."

ON THE POLE

"Where can we meet? Same place as last time?" asked Marshall.

"No, somewhere more public, I want a crowd."

Marshall's car wasn't in the lot of the busy fast food eatery. He'd mentioned that he would have to wait until the bank opened to acquire the cash he needed.

"I'm starving. Can we get something to eat," asked Justin.

That reminded me I hadn't eaten in the last twenty four hours; so I drove into the drive through lane.

"What happened to your window," asked the girl handing our order over the smashed glass.

"Road hazard, we're on the way to the dealer," I said.

"This coffee isn't strong enough," announced Justin once we were parked.

"Growing boys should drink milk and juice not coffee," I said taking my first salvo into step motherhood.

"Their food made me want to throw up. They made us eat lamb all the time. I hated it. I plan to be a vegetarian," said Judith.

After we finished breakfast, Judith and I had a dutiful daughter versus predatory older female moment. When I looked in the vanity mirror I realized I looked like a woman who had been tortured. I removed my comb and brush from my purse and went to work on my hair. After my hair looked as good as it was going to, I ran a wet wipe over my face and applied some lipstick.

"May I borrow your comb and brush?" asked Judith, eying me suspiciously.

"Sure," I said, transferring them from my lap.

"Are you and my dad good friends?" she asked, attempting to sound casual as you brushed her hair. Judith was going to be a looker like her mother.

"I work for Millennium Construction. I'm a computer programmer," I said.

"Are you dating?" asked Judith, warming to the cross-examination. Possibly she would have preferred to borrow the Castle's electrical gear to assure herself my answers were honest.

"We've been to dinner twice," I said.

"Alex is dad's girlfriend. They screw a lot," Justin chimed in from the back seat, looking up from the book he'd found on the floor. It was in Arabic, and I had no idea what he was reading. It could have been porn for all I could tell.

Before I could deny being Marshall's girlfriend—and not certain I wanted to deny it—Marshall pulled up, and the pair exploded out of the car to greet their father.

It was an emotional reunion. Marshall cried. Judith cried. Justin did not cry. I almost cried.

"I don't know how I am ever going to thank you," said Marshall, climbing into the Suburban and taking me into his arms.

"See you three together is thanks enough," I said leaving my real list for later.

"What's wrong with your hand?" Marshall was looking at the duct tape.

"I rubbed some skin off it getting untied. It'll be all right. Did you get enough cash?"

"Twenty-five thousand," Marshall said.

"Good, do not use credit cards. They can be traced in seconds," I said, relieved

"I thought only the police could do things like that," said Marshall.

"They may have police on their payroll. Assume they have friends in law enforcement," I said. "Right now, there could be an outstanding warrant against me for kidnapping."

"Jesus, so where do we go?" asked Marshall.

"Go anyplace there are large crowds of tourists—Washington DC, Colonial Williamsburg, anywhere. Just keep moving for a couple of weeks."

"Come with us," said Marshall, squeezing my good hand.

"I have to stay here and take care of things. Besides, you need to focus on Justin and Judith. I'd be a distraction."

"A welcome distraction," said Marshall, repeating the squeeze. I was tempted.

"Both of them have been through very difficult times. Right now, they seem fine. But soon they're going to start thinking about McClain Castle and all the bad things that happened there. Justin witnessed people being tortured. They need your undivided attention."

"What are you going to do?" asked Marshall.

"Get the good guys to arrest the bad guys," I said.

"Will you be safe?"

"Yes. As soon as you leave, I'm going to the FBI," I said.

"I should go with you," said Marshall.

"No, you don't know anything. Disappear for two weeks. By then, all the criminals will be dead or incarcerated. These people are terrorists. The FBI will shoot first and ask questions later."

"I suppose you're right," said Marshall.

"You better get going. Justin is anxious to see the Smithsonian, and I promised Judith you'd buy her the Hope Diamond," I said.

"Only if twenty-five thousand dollars covers it," said Marshall.

I stood watching them drive off in Marshall's Mercedes. I wondered if he was up to the job of being a parent instead of a CEO. He wasn't the first widower to marry because he wanted a full time nanny. He'd allowed Soraya to send them to what he thought was a Swiss boarding school. Boarding schools were places where rich parents warehouses children they couldn't be bothered with. Now I'd sent him off for two weeks of family time. They might be ready to kill each other before they reached the state line.

And what about A. H. Thornton? How did I fit into the Sheffield family picture? Can a pole dancer find happiness with two teenage stepchildren? Or after a month, would I be searching the Web for a Swiss boarding school?

Chapter 42

I should have realized something was wrong when I arrived at the Hargrove estate. The gate was open. There was no awkward leaning out the window to identify myself to the security camera. The main house looked deserted.

I assumed the Hargroves had departed for one of their other residences. New England's rich migrate south when winter approaches. They were probably down in West Palm basking in the sun.

I drove to the carriage house, hurried to the front door, and pushed the doorbell down without letting up. I'd called Bradley after Marshall and the children had left.

"Case solved, I've got the proof," I said as soon as he answered the cell.

"You're certain?" said Bradley.

"Yesterday, I was kidnapped, taken to McClain Castle, and tortured by terrorists using electricity. They knew I was ADS. Someone ratted me out. Stacia McClain was there. I managed to escape." I said.

"Are you all right?"

"A little banged up and dead tired but still functioning," I said.

"Where are you now?"

"I just met Marshall Sheffield and returned his children to him. They were being held at the castle to keep him from blowing the whistle on the terrorist cell."

"When did you find that out?" asked Bradley.

"At the castle," I lied. I was delaying the moment when I had to tell Bradley that Marshall Sheffield and I were more than management and worker.

"Bring them here. I'll arrange for around the clock security," said Bradley.

"Marshall's already left. He's taking Justin and Judith on a road trip. We need to get a tactical team to McClain Castle ASAP. My guess is that the bad guys are half way to Canada."

"I need to debrief you first. Come to my place," said Bradley.

"Shouldn't we do it at your office?" I asked.

"No, my place is closer. It'll save time," said Bradley. "I'll alert the office so the team will be ready," said Bradley.

"We're wasting valuable time," I said.

"All the more reason for you to get your butt here as quickly as possible," said Bradley with an edge to his voice.

I was too tired to argue. I was beginning to regret my decision not to go with Marshall. I could have called Bradley from the car. I would be riding shotgun in place of Judith, teaching her the invaluable life lesson that a large breasted blonde can displace a father's affections.

Bradley opened the door, looking the part of the wealthy man who took a low paying government job to show he's got character.

"You look the worse for wear," was all he said as he stood aside for me to enter. As I passed, he grabbed my purse off my arm and pushed me roughly into the room.

"Take it easy," I said. He took the Sig Sauer from the side pocket. Bradley's own gun was in his other hand, and it was pointed at me.

"Sit over there." He gestured toward the couch.

"What's this all about?" I was having a hard time processing what was happening. Why was the FBI guy who'd been intent on getting into my pants acting like I was on the Ten Most Wanted. Then he yelled something in a language I'd heard enough of lately to recognize. Soraya and Stacia stepped into the room, and it all dawned on stupid me.

"Shoot her," spat Stacia, advancing toward me. "She killed Ebrahim and the others. She deserves to die"

"No, it is better she dies with us," said Soraya. "It will confuse them."

"I'll just die when everyone else dies. I don't want to be an early corpse and hog all the mourners," I said.

My harmless statement caused Stacia, who must suffer from anger management issues, to scream something in Arabic and launch herself across the room at me. But Bradley grabbed her arm and delivered a vicious slap to the side of her face, knocking her off her feet. She lay sobbing, a little bubble of bloody saliva on her lips. I thought she looked awfully good that way.

Bradley spewed more vitriolic sounding Arabic at Stacia and threatened to kick her. The usually composed Bradley Dickerson had transformed into a madman. Soraya rushed over to take Stacia in her arms and comfort her. I stayed put.

"Why?" I asked when he looked at me.

"For the love of one true God and Mohammed his Prophet," said Bradley, looking quite sincere and incredibly handsome.

"Does this mean we're not going to get married and give Bunny a pair of beautiful, intelligent grandchildren to spoil?" I asked, trying to buy time for what I wasn't sure.

"Marry you? I consider you an infidel whore who sells herself for money. I would strangle our children in their crib," said Bradley.

"Sounds harsh, Bradley. I'm also an educated computer professional with my own profitable Web business," I said.

"I've watched you dance. You enjoy exhibiting yourself to men. You incite their lust and cause them to forget Allah," said Bradley.

"I just need the love of a good man, and I would give it up. I'd wear a veil if it makes you happy," I said. "Bunny likes me. She said I had character."

Bradley ignored my remarks, reaching down to help Soraya and Stacia to their feet. He tenderly kissed Stacia and mumbled a few words in Arabic to her. She reduced her rate of sniffling.

Then he kissed Soraya, and the three of them did a group hug. I wondered if they wanted me to join them. However Bradley kept his pistol aimed in my direction.

"I already have two beautiful wives," announced Bradley, when the hug ended.

The three exchanged more kisses. They seemed on some sort of emotional high. I wondered if they had swallowed a handful of Ecstasy.

Finally Bradley ordered me to turn around. He snapped his FBI handcuffs on my wrists. Then the four of us walked to the Audi where Bradley opened the trunk and pushed me in. The last time I was in that car, I rode in the front seat. It's more comfortable there.

Chapter 43

The sunlight blinded me when Bradley opened the trunk. I heard the loud squawking of seagulls circling overhead. My dad, birdwatcher and friend to all those with feathers, made an exception for seagulls. He called them rats with wings.

The ride in the trunk had been an opportunity to worry, and I took it. They were taking the car somewhere to drive it into a lake, leaving me to drown. Drowning is not my preferred way to die, so I moved to a less terrifying scenario. They would drive to a deserted spot in the woods of New Hampshire, shoot me in the back of the head, and then bury me in a shallow grave. Feral cats would dig up and devour my remains.

But Soraya said we were all going to die together. The prospect of group suicide didn't help my morale.

I'd learned nothing of interest during the ride. The Audi had a small hatch between the trunk and the back seat. I managed to quietly open it with my teeth. The three were chanting something in unison. It was Arabic, of course, and they kept repeating the same words over and over again. They were praying.

Bradley lifted me none too gently out of the trunk and let me fall to the pavement. I landed on my forearm so hard it went numb.

"You can kill me without beating me to death," I protested as Bradley grabbed a handful of my hair and pulled me to my feet.

I was in the parking lot of a marina in East Boston. There was a faded sign on the side of the office offering slips to rent. I could see Boston's skyline across the harbor. The marina was deserted and definitely down market.

"What are you going to do with me?" I said as they walked me toward the slips. Nobody answered. Stacia and Soraya were holding beads in their hand as they silently mouthed a prayer. I suppose even for a dedicated jihadist, the prospect of martyrdom is not a joyful occasion.

Out in Boston harbor, there was a flotilla of small sailboats and a few large ones. A huge container ship was visible in the distance.

I decided they were going to take me out in the Atlantic, tie an anchor around my neck, and throw me overboard. I was back to drowning.

At the end of the dock were boathouses. The largest turned out to be our destination. Bradley produced a key to a heavy-duty padlock. We stepped inside the dark boathouse. Soraya took time out from her beads to find a light switch. I'm not sure what I was expecting, but I mouthed a silent wow looking at the sleek, unbelievably gaudy watercraft that filled the boathouse.

From the few brain cells undamaged by electricity, the phrase "cigarette boat" was retrieved. A super-shiny, bright yellow craft with fire engine red flame accents floated in front of me. The powerboat was at least thirty feet long. It was the most garish vessel I'd ever seen. It was the nautical version of a pimpmobile.

ON THE POLE

Revenge IV was painted on the side.

The four of us stepped on board. Bradley produced another key to open a hatch, and I was shoved down a small flight of steps. I landed hard and painfully on my chest.

I was in the main cabin. Once again, my hair proved a convenient handle for Bradley to haul and throw me onto one of the couches lining one side of the wall. I hit the couch and promptly rolled back on the deck.

"Shit," said Bradley, making me wonder how the Quran felt about profanity. He repeated the hair lift, held me standing then smashed his fist into my belly. Every molecule of air left my lungs and I crumpled to my knees, desperate to breathe.

He handed Soraya the keys to my handcuffs as he removed his pistol from its holster and aimed at me. "Cuff her hands around the pole."

There was a brass pole at the end of the couch, right before the entrance to the forward cabin. Soraya unlocked one handcuff, then placed my arms around the pole and relocked it.

"That's too fucking tight," I yelled when the cuff was digging into my wrist bone. She surprised me by backing off a little.

"Watch her," said Bradley, handing Soraya my Sig Sauer as he went forward into the cabin closer to the bow.

I was on one side of the cabin. Soraya and Stacia were seated on the other with Soraya's arm around her sister. Stacia looked scared to death. The confident, fashion model bitch personality had evaporated. I noticed that when Soraya turned to comfort Stacia, she dropped the keys to my cuffs on the couch beside her.

"What's going to happen to me?" I asked.

"We are dying a martyr's death and will be in paradise. Infidel whores such as you are destined for hell," said Soraya.

"Stacia doesn't look too happy about it. Why don't you and Bradley go alone to Paradise? Stacia and I will stay here. We'll do lunch and go shopping. I could use some new tops and Macy's has a sale."

"Bradley said you were amusing," said Soraya, repeating something Stacia had said.

"Bradley's very charming. You and Stacia are lucky to have such a stud for a husband. He's terrific in the sack," I said hoping to distract her, so she'd forget about the keys lying beside her.

"Bradley never slept with you," said Soraya.

Actually, I had come very close to riding Bradley's pony. Only the likelihood of being fired kept me from providing more than a blowjob. "Oh the lies men tell the little women at home. Have you met Natalie?"

"Natalie's nothing to him, a rich whore he met in college before he became a follower of the one true God and his Prophet," said Soraya.

I didn't think I had anything to lose by making his wives angry. "He's been banging her since he was a freshman at Yale," I said. "He was going to arrange for a three-way with the two of us. With you and Stacia around, he's developed a taste for two women at once."

At that moment, Bradley came back, interrupting my efforts to rile Soraya.

"It's armed," said Bradley.

ON THE POLE

Soraya spoke rapidly to him in Arabic. They must have been discussing his alleged infidelity; because after a brief exchange, Bradley slapped me so hard I saw stars.

"What was that for?" I asked, tasking blood.

"For lying," said Bradley.

He wrapped his hand around my neck and squeezed. His face was less than an inch from mine when he spoke. "You left us no choice but to become martyrs. We always knew this day would arrive. That is why we prepared this craft for our final jihad."

"So my discovering your terrorist cell was the will of Allah," I said, hoping a religious argument would defer my entry into the hereafter.

That brought Bradley's hand up to strike me again, but Soraya barked out some Arabic to make him stop. Soraya gestured toward their watch, making me think they had to commit suicide by a certain time or it didn't count.

The two talked for a minute, and then Bradley said something to Stacia. She was still huddled in the corner, scared to death. Then he and Soraya went topside, leaving Stacia and me alone in the cabin.

Stacia and I sat there, looking at one another and not speaking. I could hear noises overhead. When the engine started, we both jumped.

"I don't want to die and neither do you," I said. I spoke in the calm voice I use when consoling Tommie about Harold. "If you uncuff me, we can slip over the side together. I am a very good swimmer. I'll make sure you reach shore." The part about being a good swimmer was a total lie. I am a lousy swimmer. It was survival of the fittest when we hit the water.

Stacia started to say something then thought better of it.

"What's the plan, Stacia? What's the bomb for?" I asked.

"A ship carrying gas," she said.

"Gasoline," I asked, not that it mattered?

"No, not gasoline," said Stacia. She didn't say more, burying her face in her hands.

The Revenge IV picked up speed, the engines sputtering and roaring.

"Release me, and I'll get us out of here. Bradley and Soraya can go to Paradise without us. We'll get there eventually," I said.

Stacia stood up and walked past me into the forward cabin where she leaned against the bulkhead sobbing. She left the door open, and I could see dozens of wooden boxes stacked together connected by wires. The words "US Army Handle with Extreme Caution" along with a part number were stenciled on the sides.

I called several times to Stacia, but she didn't answer or, for that matter, move. The keys to my cuffs were lying on the couch. I could possibly reach them, but Stacia would see what I was doing and stop me.

For the second time in two days, I told myself I was going to die. For some odd reason this calmed me down.

The Revenge IV started to bounce like we were pounding through somebody's wake. I automatically reached up and wrapped my hands around the brass pole to steady myself. A wave of nausea swept over me. I wondered if God was having a lousy day and decided to send me to my grave puking my guts out. That of all things gave me an idea. I used the pole to pull myself to standing then climbed up on the couch with my feet under me

ON THE POLE

"Stacia, I'm sick. Do you have something I can throw up in?" I yelled.

"All right," said Stacia, picking up a plastic yellow bucket and stepping out of the forward cabin. She seemed in a daze.

"Use this," she said, not really looking in my direction.

When she was in range, I gripped the pole hard, sprung up and out, and slammed my feet into her chest and head. One foot landed on her chin, smashing her head against the bulkhead. She collapsed to the deck, out cold. Luckily, the noise was covered by the roar of the engines.

The keys were now my problem. They were on the couch seat across the cabin. I looked around for something I could use to lasso them and drag them over but there was nothing within reach. I kicked off my shoes and tried to reach the edge of the couch cushion with my toes. No luck.

I grabbed the pole in my hands and slowly raised my body off the floor. In the club, it's called waving the flag. The handcuffs kept me from separating my hands to a wide enough stance to easily extend my body. I made an effort, but crashed to the floor. I took a deep breath and exhaled, and then another as I struggled to hang my body off the pole. This time I managed to get my toes around the edge of the cushion before I collapsed. I lay there breathing hard.

"Once more, with everything," I whispered to myself.

I moved the cushion in my direction a couple of inches before I lost it. I shut my mouth and took five deep breaths through my nose. My yoga instructor claimed breathing through your nose built energy. I did five more yoga breaths. The next time, I managed to clamp my toes on the bottom and top of the couch cushion and slowly pull it off the couch.

When it fell to the deck, the keys almost bounced off of the cushion. Allah was with this exotic dancer, and they stayed at the very edge.

I dragged the cushion directly underneath me. I sat back down and hooked my big toe through the key ring. I raised my foot as I bent over to take the keys in my teeth. I had to strain like hell to make that happen. Once I had them in my mouth, I transferred them to my hand. Shortly thereafter I was no longer handcuffed.

I took another look at Stacia. She wasn't moving. Then I saw Hassan's Sig Sauer. Soraya had placed it on a shelf below the stairs. I checked the magazine. There were thirteen cartridges, more than enough to take care of business.

Chapter 44

Up the steps, turn, aim, and shoot, don't think. Do Bradley first. He has a gun. Shoot without a second's hesitation. It's your life or theirs.

I was standing on the bottom step of the stairs giving myself a silent pep talk. I was terrified that at any second I would be incinerated in a ball of fire.

Bradley would be in the captain's chair. On three, I told myself then went on two.

I figured wrong. Soraya was driving. Men are supposed to handle testosterone oozing machines like the Revenge IV. I was facing the wrong direction. Bradley was slightly behind me. I went to Plan B, aiming for Soraya.

I squeezed the trigger just as Bradley grabbed my shoulder. My bullet headed toward south Boston after blowing out a chunk of windscreen. He grabbed the wrist of my gun hand as he reached for his Glock. I grabbed his wrist. We struggled for a few seconds.

Instinctively, I slammed my knee in the Dickerson family jewels. He didn't let go even though he wanted very badly to comfort his injured balls. His grip lessened a little. I jerked free, pointed at his gut, and squeezed the trigger.

I saw the moment of impact in his eyes. They were wide with shock as the bullet ripped into his abdomen. His expression curdled to pure hatred then, and he fought for his turn to kill me. But my bullet had taken away his strength. I pulled the trigger again, and this time the bullet hit bone, blowing him to the back of the boat.

I looked down and screamed when I saw blood covering my arm. For a second I thought he'd shot me. But it was Bradley's gore. Blood was spattered all over the canary yellow upholstery.

I struggled to stand in the fast moving craft. We were crashing across wakes. Soraya was seated in the captain's chair, clutching the steering wheel in both hands.

"Stop the boat," I screamed.

She ignored me, eyes straight ahead, like she saw Paradise and was determined to get there. I smashed the Sig Sauer across the back of her head; she fell forward across the wheel.

When I looked forward, all I could see was the side of a giant ship. I pried Soraya's hands off the steering wheel and shoved her out of the chair onto the deck.

I turned the wheel as far to the right as it would go. I'd never driven a boat, and I assumed a boat's wheel acted the same as a car's. Boats don't turn on a dime.

My turn sent the Revenge into a long skid sideways toward the ship. I didn't know anything else to do, other than hold on as the Revenge IV skidded toward the LNG carrier. I knew it was a liquefied natural gas carrier because the words, El PASO LNG, were written across the side of the ship in letters fifteen feet high. I recalled an article I read in the *Globe* that some experts thought a tanker explosion could level a good chunk of Boston real estate.

I was thrown to the deck as the *Revenge*'s port side slammed into the tanker. I clenched my teeth, waiting for an explosion that didn't come. The detonators must have been designed for a head on collision.

The *Revenge* hesitated a moment, then the propellers caught and it took off again. I looked down for a brake pedal and panicked when I didn't see one. That was when Soraya hit me. I'd been too busy to notice she had gotten to her feet and found something to smash into the back of my head. I was semi-conscious as she pulled me out of the captain's chair. I fell to the deck and rolled to the back of the boat.

I could feel the *Revenge* turning. I struggled to my feet. We were once more headed for the EL PASO LNG. In the distance I could see the Coast Guard speeding toward us, but they were too far away. When I looked down at my feet, I saw Bradley's gun. I picked it up, and then almost dropped it when the boat jumped its wake.

Soraya was muttering something as I stepped up behind her. It sounded like another prayer. "Stop the fucking boat!" I yelled as I put the muzzle against the back of her head.

She stared at me then looked forward and went back to her stupid prayer. The side of the LNG carrier was less than a soccer field away. I pulled the trigger.

Soraya thudded forward with her arms through the steering wheel. The top of her head was missing. I would have gotten sick if I had the time. I couldn't disentangle her. My feet kept slipping in blood. With the strength of panic, I managed to turn the wheel just enough. We missed the stern of the tanker by a couple of yards. We were heading toward an abandoned pier.

I was too weak to move Soraya, and anyway, I had no idea how to drive a cigarette boat. The pier looked too close. I jumped over the side.

I am a nautical dunce and did not realize the water would feel like concrete. I skimmed along like a flat rock before I sank. I came to the surface gasping for air—and got one breath. There was as an enormous explosion that sucked it right back out. Then the concussion wave from the blast slammed into me.

I have a slight memory of being hauled out of the water into one of those rubber boats the Coast Guard uses. Someone opened my eyes and shone a light into them moving it back and forth. I watched in silence as he mouthed, "She's alive."

Of course I was alive. One of the men was running his hands over my arms and legs to see if I was wounded. His hands traveled up my abdomen onto my breasts. I said, "36D," and he immediately jerked his hands away. I read the word "sorry" on his lips.

I was immobilized on a wooden board with my head wrapped in a thick foam cushion. I couldn't see anything that wasn't directly overhead. I took my first helicopter ride.

"Keep her sedated," shouted someone over the noise of the helicopter, and apparently they did, because I woke up two days later in a Navy hospital in Virginia.

Chapter 45

"You have been issued a provisional Top Secret Security Clearance," said Larry Prichard, handing me an official looking document along with an old style fountain pen. "You need to sign the top copy."

Larry headed the FBI's counter terrorism organization and reported to the Director of the FBI. We were in my combination hospital room and prison cell at a Navy base in Norfolk. I had been there ten days. I'd been questioned for eight hours at a stretch and learned how to fool a polygraph. If I hadn't been allowed to work out in the gym, I'd have been in the psych ward by now.

The single page acknowledged I had received the document. It reminded me of a similar catch-22 I'd signed at ADS.

"You have been involved in recent events that are classified top secret. If you inform anyone of these events, you can be tried for espionage and imprisoned," said Larry.

"You're shutting me up." I handed him back the paper with A. H. Thornton scrawled across the bottom.

The media had reported the explosion as a horrific boating accident. The powerful craft had gone out of control, possibly due to mechanical failure, and crashed into a pier. The pier's abandoned, but still half full, fuel tank had exploded, causing windows to shatter a half-mile away. It was bullshit, but the press and the public bought it.

"Precisely," said Larry. "But it's for your own good.

"May I ask why?"

"In the past, terrorists have exhibited a tendency for revenge. You killed several key members of their organization," said Larry.

"That's comforting. How soon can I get back to my life; if I still have one?"

"You still have one. Your boss has been briefed on your situation and is anxious for your return to work. When we're done, you can hitch a ride on my plane back to Washington, and we'll put you on a shuttle to Boston," said Larry.

I'd left my purse in a stolen Suburban at the Hargrove's. "I don't have a dime and without any identification how am I supposed to get on an airplane?"

"I'm sure Frank can work something out," said Larry.

Frank was the other FBI dweeb in the room for my final debriefing. He was Bradley's replacement and technically my new ADS client.

"I'll accompany you on the plane and drive you home," said Frank.

"So, if I'm supposed to take all this to my grave, tell me things I don't know. How did Bradley Dickerson, scion of old Boston money, become a suicidal jihadist?" I asked.

"From what we've been able to piece together, Agent Dickerson became a terrorist while assigned to our Yemen office in Sinaa. After he joined the Bureau, he selected counter terrorism as his specialty. He learned Arabic and immersed himself in Islamic culture."

"He joined a mosque, had a change of heart, and declared jihad on the infidels," I added.

"Yes, we believe it began as part of immersing himself in Islam," said Larry. "Somewhere, somehow, he didn't just become a Muslim and leave it at that. Someone persuaded him he was on the wrong side."

"Trust fund baby finds a purpose for his vacuous life," I said.

"It's happened before. Are you familiar with the story of Kim Philby, Burgess and Maclean, Anthony Blunt, the so-called Cambridge Spies?"

I had no clue. "Sorry."

"Young men from titled families, they attended Cambridge in the nineteen thirties, became converts to Marxism, and joined Britain's intelligence community under orders from their Soviet handlers. They served at the highest levels and did enormous damage before they were discovered."

"Bradley used to say there was no way wealthy Middle Eastern elite could be terrorists. It wasn't in their financial interest," I said.

"He was probably laughing to himself as he said it."

"How did Bradley convinced them he was genuine?"

"That brings up something that has puzzled us for years. We had six agents working in Yemen. Bradley was one of the six. Five of them were killed within a matter of days. Thinking someone had compromised our team, we withdrew Bradley immediately."

"So Bradley offed five co-workers to establish himself with the terrorists," I said.

"Probably, but we've no proof."

"So how did Soraya and Stacia fit into the picture," I asked.

"In their case, we think terrorism is a family pursuit. Their father and even their grandfather practice a strict form of Islam. In Soraya's case, there is reason to believe her immersion in our society and culture was part of a long-range plan. Stacia joined later, after a life of dissipation."

"Soraya's father raised her to be a terrorist. What happened to marrying well and having a couple of grandkids to please Daddy?" I said.

"Unfortunately the people who know for certain are either dead or unavailable to us."

"Sorry about that," I offered. "But it was me or them."

"Stacia ensnared the financially troubled McClain Foundation. The Museum was almost broke due to Branson McClain's poor financial management when Stacia and her father came to his rescue. Once they had his trust, Stacia—aware of Branson's sexual preferences—made videos of him with underage boys. We found them in a safe in McClain Castle. They blackmailed Branson into marriage, and he turned over control of the foundation."

"So while the FBI is watching the local mosque for terrorists, they're in Lenox attending art appreciation classes," I said.

"Who would ever suspect a museum foundation of harboring a terrorist cell," said Larry. "Your deduction about the use of steganography to communicate with other terrorists was brilliant, by the way. Over a dozen suspected terrorists are under arrest in Paris, London, and Rome."

"Why didn't they kill me after I met Marshall's children?" I asked. Not that I was ungrateful, but they could have shot me at any time.

"They didn't recognize you, even when Bradley faxed this picture of you to the castle," said Larry, pulling the charity gala picture of Bradley and me out of a folder.

I could understand why Alisha couldn't recognize me. Mrs. Kabel had trouble believing that photo was her least favorite CSSIP analyst. "And I thought he kept it around to whack off with." Larry smiled but ignored my remark. I was beginning to think not having a sense of humor was required for the top Bureau jobs.

"We also found the recently dug graves of three men on the Castle grounds. One of them is Ebrahim Al-Wahid. We've been looking for him for a long time."

"Did he have a bullet hole right about here?" I said putting my hand right below my heart.

"Your work?" he asked.

"Yes. Any reward?"

"I'll look into that," said Larry making a note. The way he said it, I wouldn't be seeing the money any time soon.

"While the McClain Foundation was useful as a base of operations, Millennium Construction was the crown jewel. Mr. Al-Kuuzaai bankrolled a minor league company into a global giant with contracts all over the world. It was a ready excuse to move people, money, and material at will."

"It was a perfect cover," I added. "How did Bradley and the two women get together?"

"That's something we don't know. Possibly, whoever was in charge saw an opportunity and put the three in touch. Bradley became their mole inside the Bureau. He could head off any investigation of the McClain Foundation or Millennium Construction. We're still evaluating what other information he may have passed on to our enemies."

"Another serious black eye for Hoover's boys, better to declare it top secret and keep quiet about it," I said.

"I hadn't thought of it that way," said Larry, lying through his teeth.

"They killed Marshall's wife so he could marry Soraya," I said. The thought occurred that I had killed Soraya so I could marry Marshall, interesting coincidence.

"Yes, we're almost certain Ebrahim was the truck driver who hit her. You not only rescued Mr. Sheffield's children, you revenged the murder of his first wife," said Larry.

"And Soraya was right there to console the widower," I said.

"Marshall Sheffield met Soraya and her family when he visited Kuwait to partner with her father's construction company on a joint bid. Marshall was intent on building his company into a global operation. His ambition was obvious and they took advantage. "

"Where is Soraya's father?" I asked.

"He is untouchable at the moment. He's in Kuwait, and the royal family won't allow us to interview him, let alone extradite him. He is well connected. The Bureau has received inquiries from Congress, asking why we are harassing this gentleman."

"Marshall admitted to being very taken with Soraya at first and totally in awe of her father," I said. Once again, I pushed aside the possibility Marshall slept with Soraya before Chelsea's death. "Soraya consoles the grieving widower, and her dad offers to fund an acquisition program for his construction company. Millennium becomes a player overnight."

"That's pretty much the way we see it," said Larry.

"After the wedding, they whisked away his children. They told him certain activities within his companies were to be ignored, or they would kill his kids." I said.

"Child prostitution was mentioned," said Larry.

"So how did I get into all this?" I asked.

"Dumb blonde syndrome, a big mistake in your case" said Larry.

"Huh?" spoken like a dumb blonde.

"Eighteen months ago, a CIA asset infiltrated a terrorist cell. He was instructed to accept a job on a construction project belonging to a Millennium subsidiary. He was shown a set of blueprints for a building they had targeted. That building was built by Millennium. The explosives and detonators were scheduled to arrive on a company plane, disguised as a donation to a local mosque. Bradley was directed to investigate."

"What happened to your source?"

"The plot to blow the building was cancelled, and he was sent home. Later our asset was killed."

"Didn't you find that suspicious?" I asked.

"He'd been involved in other situations that could have compromised him. Honestly, we should have asked ourselves more questions."

"And along comes Hamo, dumb blonde extraordinaire," I said.

"Bradley was smart enough to suggest he investigate Millennium, a preemptive move. He decided to go to ADS. His mother knew Mrs. Kabel, giving him an inside track. He made a good case to Washington by pointing out our lack of expertise in the computer field. He convinced everyone the place to look was in the computer department, which was a red herring, by the way."

"So he picked me on purpose."

"Very much on purpose, he compiled an extensive dossier on each of the eight members of your group. He followed you and discovered your other employment. That meant he could control you if needed. Bradley was thorough for someone who seemed otherwise."

"Acting rich and bored was easy for him, he was born that way," I said.

"The other members of the regional counter terrorism coordinating committee argued for a more seasoned investigator. Mrs. Kabel said Bradley was absolutely adamant you be given the assignment. I gather your selection caused quite a disagreement in a meeting held the morning you got the job."

"So that's why there was a delay in letting me enter the conference room."

"Bradley had to trump them with money to win the argument. Since the FBI was paying the bill, the Bureau would choose."

"So where did you find my dossier?"

"We found it at his carriage house on the Hargrove Estate. Bradley constructed a false wall to hide a room where he kept documents and his computers. He was quite a techie, you know."

"He always pretended that his computer skills were nil. So he chose me because he thought his charm would keep me under control."

"I suppose a man with his looks and money was used to charming the opposite sex. He also worked hard to worry you. I understand you have been receiving e-mail from a stalker, one Elizabeth Schuyler?"

"God, that was Bradley?" I was dumbfounded. My mouth dropped open.

"Yes, he felt between nude dancing, your Web business, college debts, and all the other things you had going on in your life, you wouldn't have the time, energy or inclination to investigate. But for some reason, he decided to maintain contact on another level."

"He must have enjoyed screwing with me," I said. Elizabeth Schuyler had taken years off my life.

"From the emails we've found on his system, we know that at first he felt he had you under control but soon, he started to worry."

"And that's why he decided to have me attacked in Nairobi," I said.

"If the attack had been successful, it would have delayed you weeks or even months."

"So why not just kill me?" I asked.

"That would have been a big mistake. Your death would have triggered alarms, but rape and robbery in a dangerous place like Nairobi would have been considered bad luck."

"I spent a lot of time worrying about Alexander Hamilton's wife."

"I'm sorry but I don't follow you," said Larry.

"Alexander Hamilton, our first Secretary of the Treasury, was married to Elizabeth Schuyler. I thought my stalker was so fucking clever calling himself that."

"I guess our researchers missed that little detail," said Larry, looking unhappy as he wrote something on his legal pad.

"When you started bringing up Soraya and then Stacia, he began to panic. He was appalled you overheard Soraya and his phone call. And when you asked him to find out all he could about Stacia, he decided he had to stop you somehow. What put you on to Stacia and Soraya?" asked Larry.

"From a woman's point of view, things just did not look right."

"Give me an example."

"A co-worker told me Soraya and Stacia were very close, and Soraya had gotten Stacia her job as Marshall's assistant. Do you have an Administrative Assistant, Larry?"

"He's not called that, but it's basically the same thing."

"If your second wife were choosing someone to sit right outside your office, would she pick someone as beautiful and immoral as Stacia?"

"Marie would pick my current secretary, since he is male."

"You're muddling my point."

"I understand, go on."

"The fact Stacia was willing to work in that capacity was highly suspect. If my husband had Branson's McClain's money, I wouldn't be getting the boss's coffee. Someone would be getting mine."

"I see what you mean," said Larry.

"Of course none of that meant much, until I searched the MillProMan database and found where Stacia had been entering transactions for Millennium projects. The impacts were small, but there was a pattern," I said.

"Looking back on everything, what are your thoughts?" asked Larry, sounding philosophical.

"Bradley Dickerson made a complete fool out of me for many of the same reasons I fooled him. I saw a rich, good-looking, egotistical man who was playing FBI agent and bought it one hundred percent. Until he took my gun away and pointed his at me, I never suspected a thing."

"Don't be too hard on yourself. He fooled everybody. Members of the Bureau are finding it difficult to believe Bradley Dickerson of the Boston Dickersons was anything other than he appeared to be. His superior has asked to be placed on medical leave."

"I'll get over it," I said.

"I have to be back in Washington tonight, so our time is about done. I think we've covered everything," said Larry. "Frank will see you back home."

"Good, I'm anxious to see my cat."

Epilogue

I took one more look at the envelope sticking out of my purse, just to make sure I hadn't dreamed it. Mrs. Kabel had handed me a fifteen-thousand-dollar bonus check while a photographer took our picture for the company newsletter. Of course that was the gross amount, after deductions I was getting a little over nine thousand dollars. And I had been promoted to Computer Forensics Analysts II with the lofty salary of $62,500. Good things do happen to bad people.

ADS had received a consulting contract from the FBI, and I was given some of the credit. I'm not sure why it was only *some* of the credit, when I was the one who single handedly uncovered the terrorist cell at Millennium Construction. But getting sole credit is un-corporate. It means you're not a team player.

What I had thought would be my economic Waterloo had not happened. Someone from the FBI had visited Arnie, when they were checking my story, and informed him I was in protective custody. To Arnie, being incarcerated was a badge of honor, and it only made him respect me more. I planned to dance this weekend and work a shift as manager trainee.

Solomon had managed to keep DMS operating. I was now almost three weeks behind on adding Web sites. My voice mail and e-mail were filled with "where the hell are you" messages. I was telling everyone that my boyfriend beat me up, and I had been in a hospital. I figured it was something most of them could relate to and they would cut me some slack.

I thought about Marshall, and that brought me automatically to the topic of us as a couple. He appeared to have a thing for me that went beyond the desire to spend time between my legs. He was now a widower, thanks to me, and he had no problem with that. He was almost twice my age, and I had no problem with that.

"You'll be a young widow, a rich young widow," was Tommie's summary, when I told her about Marshall.

"Hey, we're discussing my love life here, not estate planning," I replied testily.

In the brief time I spent with Marshall's children, we seemed to get on. The thought of other human beings calling me Mom or Stepmother terrified me. Telling them to brush their teeth and do their homework seemed beyond my level of competence.

That brought up the secret I had managed to hide from Marshall. He did not know that the woman he professed to love danced in the nude for tips. One option was to quit dancing, keep my mouth shut, and hope we never met anyone who recalled me giving him a lap dance. The other option was to confess my career in the demi-monde, tell Marshall his love had redeemed a fallen woman, and beg his understanding and forgiveness. I was leaning toward option one as I walked into Mom's, excited to share the news of my bonus and promotion.

ON THE POLE

"I got great news," I yelled, kicking my shoes off in the mudroom. Mom had a strict no shoes in the house rule.

"We're in here, Alex," yelled Mom from the kitchen.

I stopped in my tracks when I reached the kitchen doorway. There was my father standing with Tommie and Mom. He was older and grayer, but there wasn't a moment of not recognizing him.

"Your father's come back," said Mom, beaming like an idiot.

"Can you believe it?" said Tommie, a similar happy grin on her face. The fact that he disappeared, leaving us penniless almost a decade ago didn't seem to make a difference to them.

"Hello Alex, you look so different," said my father, stepping toward me with his arms open. When he left, I was a flat-chested brunette with a bump on her nose.

"I don't believe this," I said, holding up my arm like a traffic cop. If he thought it was time for family hugs he was mistaken.

"I know my coming back is going to take some getting used to. But with God's help we can become a family again. I want to be part of your lives."

"No fucking way," I replied.

"I see your language has grown more colorful since I left. That's something we'll have to work on."

"If you come near me or ever speak to me again, I'll shoot you," I said before I turned around and walked out.

Made in the USA
Lexington, KY
20 December 2010